MW01037048

MARINES

CRIMSON WORLDS I

Jay Allan

system 7
publishing

Crimson Worlds Series

Marines (Crimson Worlds I)

The Cost of Victory (Crimson Worlds II)

A Little Rebellion (Crimson Worlds III)
(December 2012)

The First Imperium (Crimson Worlds IV)
(March 2013)

www.crimsonworlds.com

MARINES

Marines is a work of fiction. All names, characters, incidents, and locations are ficticious. Any resemblance to
actual persons, living or dead, events or places is entirely
coincidental.

Copyright © 2012 Jay Allan Books

All rights reserved.

ISBN: 978-0615694917

Casualties many; Percentage of dead not known; Combat efficiency; we are winning.

- Colonel David M. Shoup, USMC

Chapter One

Landing Bay 3
AS Guadalcanal
In orbit above Epsilon Eridani IV

"Ninety seconds to launch. Activating final lockdown procedures now." The mechanical voice of the assault computer was deafening as it reverberated in my helmet. Almost as loud was the metal on metal sound as the locking bolt on my armor clicked firmly into the steel frame of the landing craft. I was now securely held in place – between the bolt and the sheer weight of my armor, I couldn't have moved a centimeter if my life depended on it.

I've always been claustrophobic, and standing there held rigidly in place was starting to get to me. It was more than just the closed in feeling; to tell the truth I was scared to death. It was cold enough in the launch bay to make the metal of my armor uncomfortable against my skin, but I could still feel a thin sheen of sweat on my forehead. I kept trying to concentrate on the launch procedure and put everything else out of my mind. That's what they teach you in training, but I can tell you it's pretty damn difficult when you're bolted into a landing ship waiting to get blasted out into the upper atmosphere of an enemy planet. Especially the first time.

I guess everybody feels pretty much the same right before his first assault. You're waiting for the launch you know is coming. You've done it a dozen times in training, but this is for real. A few thousand kilometers down there are real enemies waiting to kill you. Ok, got to get that out of my mind right now, got to concentrate on the launch. It's a job, and I'm a trained professional.

Actually, that's not really true. You don't have to concentrate on the launch. It would be a lot easier if you had something to do to keep busy, but the truth is everything is pretty much controlled by the ship's computer until you hit ground. Nothing to do but stand here and count off the seconds. And think about what was waiting down there.

"Sixty seconds to launch. Activating armor power circuits." There was a loud whine as the nuclear power plant on my back kicked in and fed juice into the circuits of my armor. I could see the green indicator light on the display above my visor indicating that all systems were fully powered and functional. Of course the indicator was of minimal importance – the relevant flow of information was from the microprocessors in my suit to the ship's assault computer.

It didn't make much difference anyway, not a minute before launch. All of the suits go through a full diagnostic check right before an assault, and any that don't pass 100% are red-flagged. No malfunction can slip through this failsafe procedure, at least theoretically. In actual practice it does happen occasionally, and when it does it usually means serious trouble. Any problem discovered this late was just that much tough luck for the wearer. There was no way to get you out of the harness in a malfunctioning suit of armor. Not in 60 seconds. And you can be damn sure they weren't going to postpone an assault because one grunt's armor was on the fritz. So the best you could do is stand there motionless and reflect on the greatly increased odds of your turning up KIA on this mission.

With the suit power activated there was at least some relief from the crushing claustrophobia. I still couldn't move, but the unrelenting feeling of more than two metric tons of dead weight around me was gone. The neural impulse sensors of the suit are tied into the servo-mechanical systems that move the armor just like a human body. Once on the ground and unlatched from the landing craft, you just move like normal. Walk, run, jump, whatever – you just move and the suit goes along. Of course the armor is a lot stronger and faster than you are, and it takes some getting used to before you are comfortable running 80 kph and jumping 10 meters straight up. You can lift at least 500 kilos in your arms and you can crush an unarmored person like so much overripe fruit. If you're not careful you can kill yourself walking across the room.

I was pressed hard against the front of my suit as the Guadalcanal's braking thrusters fired. Sub-orbital insertions can make for a pretty rough ride, as the ship executes a series of abrupt maneuvers to position itself for the launch. After about ten seconds of rapid deceleration we went into free fall. I had undergone intense conditioning during training and had been given the normal drugs and the standard 36 hours of intravenous nutrition prior to launch. I knew that it was almost physically impossible for me to get sick at this point, but that didn't stop the bile from rising at the back of my throat as we plunged toward the launch point.

When the dull roar of the ship's engines died down there was an almost eerie quiet in the launch bay. There was a very faint buzz; I think it was coming from the lighting track on the ceiling. A couple of guys were talking softly to themselves. I thought I could make out a few words of a familiar prayer.

There was a red tint to everything from the battlestations lamps in the launch bay. The naval personnel had all left about 5 minutes prior to launch and we were alone - 2nd Platoon, A Company, 1st Battalion, 3rd Regiment, 1st U.S. Marine Division – and ready to go.

The launch bay was sealed off from the rest of the ship, but there was still a heavy smell of burnt machinery in the air. The Guadalcanal had taken at least one hit on its approach. The sailors didn't seem to be concerned, so the damage must not have been too bad. Stunk up the place, though.

"Thirty seconds to launch. Transferring life support function to marine armor." My visor clicked down automatically and there was a whooshing sound as my suit replaced the Earth-normal air of the Guadalcanal with the oxygen rich mixture designed to maximize alertness and physical endurance during combat operations. My armor was now 100% operational and could keep me alive, even in deep space.

With my suit sealed and the blast shield down over my visor I couldn't see or hear anything going on in the bay. But I knew from training that exactly 5 seconds after my visor clamped down, the bay of the Guadalcanal was depressurized to match the atmospheric density of the launch point. Five seconds after depressurization our suits were pressure coated with a special foam designed to absorb the intense heat of the atmospheric entry. Then the hatches would open.

The TX-11 Gordon atmospheric assault craft is designed to accept modular armor plating panels that effectively make it an enclosed ship rather than an open landing sled. However, the panels severely reduce its speed and maneuverability. The armor was effective against small arms fire, but was useless against the SAMs and other ground to air armaments that were the biggest threat during an assault landing. These weapons were best countered with the enhanced maneuver capabilities of the light, unarmored ship.

"Ten seconds to launch. Good luck marines!" The skipper's voice had replaced the coldly mechanical tone of the assault computer. By tradition the ship's captain delivered the final pre-launch announcement and wished the assault team luck.

I counted down in my head, five, four, three - I gritted my teeth and braced myself for the shock of launch – two, one…

I felt the jarring in every bone in my body as the catapult accelerated the assault lander down the launch track and out into the upper atmosphere of Epsilon Eridani IV, commonly known as Carson's World. By the time the assault ship cleared the hatch and fired its own thrusters, our velocity was 1,200 kph. The G forces caused by the launch would have killed an unprotected man, but with my fighting suit on I only lost my breath for a few seconds.

With the blast shield down I still couldn't see anything outside, but the monitors in my helmet activated automatically, feeding me all sorts of information – altitude, velocity, armor skin temperature, heart rate, and a dozen other informational tidbits of questionable usefulness. I pressed the small button under my left forefinger and the deployment display was projected on the inside of my faceplate. I could see 50 tiny green dots in ten groups – the entire platoon in ten landing craft. It looked like our formation was perfect (though as the junior private in the squad my only real concern was my location and that of my fire team leader). I knew the 1st and 3rd platoons were scheduled to launch 20 and 40 seconds after we did, with the company command and heavy weapon sections right after them. I had no reason to believe that they hadn't launched as planned, but their assigned position was considerably outside the range of my deployment display, so I didn't know for sure. I didn't need to know.

The Gordon is a five-man disposable sub-orbital insertion vehicle designed to rapidly land attacking forces onto a hostile planet. Actually, "vehicle" is a strong word – it's really just an open steel frame with a large triangular heat shield in the front. The entire thing looks a little like something you could build out of a child's erector set. With 5 armored marines bolted to it.

The ride down started to get pretty rough as we entered the denser levels of the atmosphere, and the lander's thrusters fired to lessen the angle of descent. Despite this and the protection of the forward heat shield, the status display indicated that the external temperature of my suit was rising as the protective foam coating burned off. The readings were well within the expected mission parameters, so I felt pretty confident that I wouldn't be incinerated during the landing. Unless we were hit, of course.

The comlink crackled to life. "Altitude ten kilometers, retract blast shields and prepare for landing." The lieutenant's voice was calm and steady – I doubt mine would have been so reassuring. Fortunately, no one was waiting for instructions from me.

I depressed the small lever under my left thumb to retract the blast shield and with a loud click the steel plate slid up over my helmet, and I could see. Mostly I could see the back of Will Thompson's helmet. As the squad's junior member (and only new recruit), I occupied the last position on the assistant squad leader's lander. Will was the senior private in the squad – traditionally the one given the task of babysitting new guys – and he was positioned right in front of me.

I was still locked in place on the lander and couldn't even turn my head to look around. It was just about dawn over the landing site, and even if I could have taken a look, the visibility in the early morning light was pretty limited.

I did have a peripheral view of the lander's top-mounted point-defense laser turret (there was a bottom mounted one as well) as it whipped around and fired at something off to the right. I didn't see any explosion, but we weren't hit by anything either, so the laser must have been on target.

Fleetcom had told us to expect minimal ground-based fire during landing. There had been a few orbital platforms hastily positioned by the enemy, but the navy had blasted those long before we stepped into the launch bay. We had total local-space superiority, a prerequisite to any landing that wasn't going to be a bloodbath.

According to Fleet, there were no ground-based installations whatsoever, so any surface to air fire would be from hand-held rocket launchers and maybe a light vehicle or two – nothing the Gordon's onboard point defense couldn't handle. Of course, no one from Fleet was bolted into a lander right now, so I suspect all of us were a little more concerned than they were. I certainly was.

The top laser turret whipped around to the left and fired twice within two or three seconds. Only the onboard tactical computer knew whether there were two incoming targets, or the first shot was a miss.

I rolled my eyes up to check the status monitors. Our altitude was just under 6 kilometers, a bit high to be taking this much fire from hand-held rocket launchers. According to the training manual, most hand held surface to air weapons had a generally effective range against a point defense equipped target of 3 km, though the theoretical maximum ranges were far greater. Most likely there was some kind of vehicle mounted SAM down there. Not a huge danger if there weren't too many of them – the Gordon's point defense was state of the art. Besides, the SAM couldn't fire too many times without moving. The Guadalcanal was still monitoring the landing area and would provide suppressive fire if the launcher gave up its position.

The lander's thrusters fired again, and we banked sharply to the left. I couldn't see any of the other ships, but a quick click of my finger brought up the deployment display again, and we were still in perfect formation. Our altitude was 3.5 km and descending rapidly.

The comlink crackled to life again. "Four minutes until touchdown. Landing proceeding according to projection. The tactical plan is unchanged....I repeat, the tactical plan is unchanged."

Every specific aspect of a planetary assault is thoroughly planned before a single marine enters the launch bay, but with so many variables it is crucial that modifications can be made at any time. If any of our landers were off course, or if the resistance on the ground was substantially stronger than expected, the battle plan could be altered in response to the change in conditions. Our platoon commander remains in constant contact with the company CO, who himself is tied in directly with tactical support services on the Guadalcanal. If changes are required, he would revise the plan, and the new instructions would be downloaded into the squad leaders' personal AIs. After a briefing by the platoon commander, the squad leaders would then be responsible for transmitting revised orders to their own troops.

With the landing going as expected, the mission was to proceed as planned. The entire population of Carson's World lived in a cluster of small mining towns in the southwestern section of the single major continent. The Central Asian Combine had sent in an invasion force about three months before and had taken control of the developed areas. With no regulars stationed on the planet to support them, the local militia had been unable to hold the towns against the CAC assault troops.

Intelligence reports indicated that the militia, rugged miners all, had hurt the CAC regulars badly and had withdrawn into the hills with much of their strength intact. Based on these reports, Fleetcom had decided to launch an immediate counter-invasion with a single battalion rather than wait for more units to arrive.

"Two minutes until touchdown. Power-up weapons systems." I clicked the levers under my right middle and forefingers. There was a series of loud clicks as the autoloader fed five grenades from the magazine on my back into the launcher on my left arm. My AI could have done that for me, but I felt better feeling the switches under my fingers.

"Squad two, weapons check. Report status." The voice on the comlink had changed. It was Sergeant Harris, our squad leader. One by one the members of the squad sounded off. "Jenkins operational. Kleiner operational…."

I glanced up at the status monitor. The two green weapons control lights indicated that my battle computer had successfully completed a full diagnostic test of armaments. My grenade launcher and auto-rifle were loaded, charged, and ready. As the only raw member of the squad I had not been outfitted with any other weapons, though my armor could have carried and powered at least two additional systems.

"Thompson operational." The rest of the squad had sounded off; it was my turn. My throat had gone dry, but I managed to croak out the required report. "Cain operational."

The second squad was ready. Although I couldn't hear it on my comlink, I knew the squad leader was reporting this status to the lieutenant over the command circuit. Weapons power-up was our last procedure prior to landing. I couldn't speak for the other three squads or the command group but our two fire teams were ready.

The lieutenant's voice came over the comlink again. "Touchdown in one minute. Squad leaders initiate tactical plan upon landing. Good luck, marines!"

Even from my closed in position I could see the ground now. We were landing in an area of rugged, sparsely wooded hills, about 10 km west of the nearest settlement. We were to establish contact with and rally the local militia units believed to be dug-in up in these hills. Once we linked up with the locals, we were to evaluate the situation, and if command gave the go-ahead, drive toward the built-up areas. The assault was to be coordinated with the attacks of the rest of company A, who would be moving in our direction from their landing points along an arc stretching 20 km northeast of our position. Company B and the heavy weapon section would move toward us from 50 km south. If all went according to plan, the CAC troops would be caught between us and penned in. If the plan went awry Company C was still in reserve, buttoned up on their ship and ready to launch.

I was slammed against the front of my armor as the lander's braking thrusters fired causing us to decelerate rapidly as we neared the ground. The forward pressure ended abruptly as we came to a virtual stop 30 meters up. The landing jets mounted on the underside of the assault ship activated and eased us slowly down. We hit ground with a gentle thud. There was a metallic scraping sound as the locking bolt retracted, releasing me from the lander.

"Fire team B, disembark. Come on, let's move it!" The gravelly voice on the comlink belonged to Corporal Gessler, my immediate superior. Gessler commanded fire team B, my half of the squad, consisting of the five occupants of this particular lander.

I scrambled out of the harness and onto the rough, rocky ground. The dirt of Carson's World was a reddish gravel, a sign of extremely high mineral content, particularly iron. There were some tufts of bristly weeds, but most of the ground was nothing but bare dirt.

I glanced up at the tactical display and confirmed that there were no enemy contacts within 2 km. An experienced marine would have done this before disembarking, but I was lucky this time – the LZ was well outside of the enemy's defensive perimeter, and our landing was unopposed.

I was still scared out of my mind, but I managed to remember what I was supposed to do. The entire squad was forming a skirmish line at 100 meter intervals and heading northeast toward the last reported location of militia activity. If they had landed in the right spot (and if I'd thought to check out the status monitor I could have confirmed that they had) the 1st squad would be deploying to extend this line to the northwest of our position. The 3rd squad was to deploy in reserve about a klick behind our line.

I headed out toward my designated position at a slow trot. The rest of the squad was doing the same except for Kleiner, who was retrieving the squad heavy weapon from the Gordon's cargo hatch. She was just strapping the massive M-411 rocket launcher over her shoulder as I trotted by. An unarmored person couldn't even have lifted the 300 kg weapon, but it was no trouble at all for an armored marine.

The lander itself was in pretty rough shape. It was a disposable vehicle designed for a one-way trip to the surface. The heat shield was three-quarters gone, and the remaining portion was pitted and blackened. The frame, though bent and twisted in a few spots, was essentially intact. Although they appeared to be in decent condition, I knew from training that the Gordon's thrusters pretty much burned themselves out during the landing. The ship would stay here, with its upper point defense laser remaining operational and providing the immediate area with some protection against missile attack.

If all went well we would never see the lander again, but if the mission went seriously awry, the Gordon, with its anti-missile defense and emergency ammunition and supplies, was our designated rally point. Of course if the rally command came it would probably mean a lot of us were already dead.

I continued toward my assigned position at the trot, and I could see Will Thompson jogging off to my right. My position was second to last in line with Will positioned on the right flank of the squad. His blackened armor was speckled with a few remaining chunks of partially charred, heat-resistant foam. For all its equipment and capabilities, the Model 7 fighting suit was remarkably trim. The wearer looked like a slightly bulkier version of a medieval knight.

I glanced up at the mission clock – it read 00:21:05. To avoid any confusion, all aspects of an assault were scheduled according to mission time, measured from the moment the first lander launched. This avoided any confusion, since ships were run on Earth Greenwich standard time, and every planet had its own timekeeping system. Mission time was consistent for all troops in an op, whether a single platoon or an entire army.

I glanced up at the area display. I was about half a klick from my assigned position, jogging slowly. I was almost a minute ahead of schedule. I forgot the amplification factor of the power armor, and my slow jog was moving me at about 40 kph as I bounced along. It had just occurred to me that I should keep lower when Corporal Gessler's voice barked over the comlink. "Cain, get your god-damned head down before you get it blown off!"

"Yessir!" I hoped I sounded confident, but I was pretty sure my voice cracked a little. I slowed my gait and concentrated on keeping low. Actually, there were no enemies showing on my display, but if there's one thing they tried to beat into us in training, it was that carelessness gets marines killed. I was ahead of schedule and there was no reason for me to rush, not when those big, exaggerated strides bounded me high enough to be a perfect target for any enemy within 1,000 meters.

I had drawn a pretty good mission for a first assault. Because we were trying to contact and rally the locals, we landed much further from the enemy than we would in typical assault. That gave us plenty of time to form up before we were likely to see any action. And because we were attacking an enemy who had recently seized the planet themselves, we didn't have to face entrenched defenses. At least nothing serious.

I reached my assigned position, approximately 2 kilometers northeast of the landing point about 45 seconds ahead of schedule. I took a quick look down the line, and it looked like most of the squad had reached the assembly point. The terrain was fairly rugged but relatively open for most of the way. Ahead of us the ground was rocky with scattered patches of the yellow-green fungus that seemed to be Carson's World's equivalent of grass. Our intel had advised that there was a militia group positioned somewhere in the area ahead and we were here to establish contact.

"Second squad, slow advance. Crank up to magnification level three. Report any signs of militia presence." It was Sergeant Harris, the squad leader, on the comlink.

A slow advance was a very moderate pace, about 5 kph. I headed northeast, taking care to move very cautiously. I depressed my right thumb three times, activating my visual magnification system and toggling it up to level three. My vision was now sharpened and enhanced. Level three is just enough to double the range at which you can pick out a man-sized object. In theory the price for amplification was a loss of detail, but the suit's computer worked constantly to sharpen the images, so usually you couldn't detect any change in focus at less than mag 10.

As we advanced, we moved into an area with scattered stands of scrubby, grayish brown trees. There were tangled clusters of the thorny weeds around them. After about fifteen minutes of moving through the sparse woodlands, we came upon a section that was burned out. The ground was blackened, and the few remaining trees were charred and splintered. It was obvious that there had been some pretty heavy fighting here, and I knew I needed to report this to Corporal Gessler and the squad leader. I was still processing all of this when Will Thompson beat me to it.

"Thompson reporting. Signs of some kind of action at coordinates 45.05 by 11. The area's all burned out....looks like there was some pretty heavy fire here, some kind of incendiary strike, maybe. Scanning...stand by for results." There was a brief pause before he continued. "Temperature normal, spectral analysis negative...looks like whatever happened here was at least a day ago."

Will's report had been broadcast over the squad frequency, so the entire unit was aware of the situation. Nevertheless, after a brief pause (during which he'd probably reported to the lieutenant), Sergeant Harris addressed the squad. "Alright second squad, we know there was some kind of fight over near our right flank. Keep your eyes open and report any contact immediately."

Over the next 20 minutes there were no additional contacts in our sector, but there were three other burned out areas in the first squad's zone. It appeared that the enemy had been conducting search and destroy ops in this area, trying to hunt down the locals who were operating out of these hills. There was no sign of casualties at any of the sites.

I was just thinking that the CAC troopers didn't seem to be doing too well when I crested a small hill and saw what looked like six or eight bodies in the center of a blackened section of grasslands at the extreme edge of my visibility.

This time I didn't hesitate. "Cain reporting. I see some bodies up ahead." My voice was shrill with excitement. I could feel the droplets of sweat running down the back of my neck.

The sergeant snapped back quickly. "OK, Cain. Get a grip, and give me a full report. Now!"

I swallowed hard and said, "Estimate six to eight bodies, range 1000 meters. Area burned out. No energy readings, no enemy contacts." After a second I added, "Should I move up and check it out, sarge?"

This was our most important sighting so far, and I wouldn't have been surprised if the sergeant had told Will to check it out. But that's not the way the Corps works. I may be the new guy, and this may be my first assault mission, but I was a marine and I was expected to be able to perform as one. As far as my field commander was concerned I wouldn't have been assigned to an assault unit unless my instructors, combat veterans all, considered me ready.

"Squad, halt. Cain, move forward and reconnoiter the area. Thompson, move in and provide cover."

I started forward slowly, checking my display for any signs of artificial energy output that could indicate a hidden enemy. Negative. No power output. I glanced over and could see Will moving in on my right. He maintained a distance of about 40 meters, to the right of and slightly behind my position.

Temperature readings were all normal as I approached the bodies. Whatever had happened here, it had been at least a day ago. The area had clearly been subjected to some type of incendiary or high explosive fire – the grass was completely burnt and a small stand of trees nearby had been blown into matchsticks. I reported as I advanced, doing my best to sound calm despite the fact that I was so nervous I could hardly take a breath.

The bodies were clustered on a small rise. There were seven of them in total, three wearing the uniform of the planetary militia, the others in civilian miner's dress. All of them were clad in heavy protective vests and metal helmets. Their faces wore horrid expressions, their features twisted in agonizing contortions. Their mouths and nostrils were caked with dried blood.

As my mind reached its conclusion, a warning light on my tactical display confirmed my deduction. Gas. "Cain reporting…seven bodies total. They appear to be victims of a gas attack. My sensors confirm the presence of…." I looked up at the tactical display for the answer. "…trace quantities of Kirax-3 nerve gas. Current concentration .032 parts per million…within the danger zone but below immediately lethal levels."

So they were using gas to hunt down the locals. The militia's little guerilla war must have been doing some pretty serious damage for the CAC forces to resort to these tactics. Nerve gas is a nasty weapon, usually used against second line troops lacking effective counter-measures, and then in only the most desperate situations. By custom, those who employ gas can expect no quarter if the battle turns against them. Why would they take such steps in a fight over a relatively unimportant hunk of ground like Carson's World? I would get an answer to that question, but not until years later.

There were several moments of silence – the squad leader conferring with higher authority, no doubt – then the comlink crackled. "Alright second squad, continue advance. Full chemical warfare procedures in effect."

That last command didn't really change anything. We still had our suits fully sealed, although the atmosphere of Carson's World was well within the acceptable range. Normal operating procedures would have called for us to switch to filtered external air after twelve hours, leaving a full day of atmospheric capacity in reserve. Standard chemical warfare procedures dictated that we would remain on our internal air supply/regeneration capacity until we were down to a four hour reserve. As with many of our procedures, there was a certain element of overkill. The atmospheric purification systems in our suits were perfectly capable of filtering out most known bacteriological and chemical agents, including Kirax-3 nerve gas. Still, better to be overly cautious than to see a whole company wiped out by some new or unexpected weapon.

It took us ninety minutes to cover the next two klicks. There were still no enemy contacts, but further up the line they found two more groups of bodies. The first was had four corpses, definitely gas victims.

The second group consisted of eleven bodies, but these were spread out over a much wider area. They were all wearing protective breathing gear and had been killed by rifle and grenade fire. Though we found no enemy bodies in the area, there were enough bits and pieces of CAC armor lying around for us to conclude that the enemy had in fact suffered casualties in this firefight.

A full analysis indicated that this action had occurred within the past eighteen hours. From the look of the tracks leaving the location, the enemy had withdrawn back toward the settled area. Whether they had been repulsed or had simply completed their mission and retired was unclear.

We continued our advance, but about fifteen minutes after leaving the site of the last skirmish, we were ordered to halt. The first squad had made contact with the locals.

The militia had been advised of the basic tactical plan through scrambled pulse communications from Fleet, but they were not provided with specific schedules or locations for fear that the enemy would intercept the transmission. Their instructions were to be ready for action on short notice, and apparently they had listened.

We held our position for almost an hour, and if there is one thing I learned quickly in the corps, nothing makes a sergeant crazier than watching his men relax with nothing to do. Fortunately, Sergeant Harris managed to come up with lots of ways for us to use the down time. We checked and re-checked our weapons, ran a system diagnostic on our armor and did a full analysis of the surrounding area – atmosphere, energy readings, chemical residue.

Finally the orders came. Our squad was to advance due east toward the settlement of Warrenville and take the position. Our attack would be supported by one fire team of the third squad. Warrenville was the smallest of the dozen or so towns that made up the entirety of the inhabited area of Carson's World.

According to the locals, the town was lightly garrisoned and we could expect minimal resistance. Most of the guerilla activity had been to the north and the enemy had deployed its strongest forces to that sector.

Our attack was essentially a diversion. We were to go in first, take the objective, and hold it against any counterattack (It was the "any" part that worried me the most). After the enemy had moved troops south to deal with us, the rest of our platoon would link up with the first platoon and a large group of militia for the main attack against the northern defenses. The third platoon was to cover the eastern and southern perimeter to intercept the enemy retreat.

We covered the first eight klicks in about two hours. The sergeant halted us just short of a small rise and sent Wilson, the platoon's scout, to report on visibility from the top of the rise. I watched him scramble up the gentle slope and crouch down just below the crest. His recon armor had a different look to it... sleeker, lighter.

"Wilson reporting. Good visibility to target, estimate distance to nearest structure 1,800 meters. Twenty to twenty-five buildings, look like modular plasti-steel structures. The terrain's completely open between here and the town, no cover at all. Looks like there's some kind of trench dug along the perimeter. No enemy sightings."

No cover. Shit. That meant we'd be advancing almost two kilometers over open ground, probably under enemy fire.

"Alright marines, form up at 30 meter intervals behind the crest. We're gonna advance leapfrog fashion – first even numbers, then odd. Fifty meter intervals, grab some dirt between moves. Stationary troops, I want heavy covering fire. Assault to commence in 90 seconds."

We were really going in. I'd been nervous about this for weeks and flat out scared to death since we stepped into the landing bay, but for some reason knowing we were heading into battle right now actually calmed me down. Maybe it was the training or some kind of silent resignation to my fate. Or the massive dose of adrenaline surging through my veins (some natural, some courtesy of the performance drugs my armor was pumping into me). Whatever it was, I suddenly had a clarity of thought I hadn't felt in weeks now. I had been trained for this, and I was ready.

I was the ninth one in line so I was supposed to provide covering fire while the evens went forward. I was pressed against the ground behind the hill - my head was maybe half a meter below the crest.

"Covering fire, now!"

I threw my arms up over the crest and rested my auto rifle on the ground in front of me. I had it set for burst fire and when I pulled the trigger it began to spit out 12 rounds a second in micro-bursts of four. The fire left a faintly glowing trail of plasma as the hyper-sonic bullets ionized the air.

The M-36 auto-rifle is a state of the art projectile-firing weapon. Specially designed for use with powered armor, the gun uses electromagnetic force to propel the projectiles at tremendous velocities. Without the need to carry their own propellant, the bullets are extremely small, and a single magazine holds 500 rounds. Despite their tiny size, the hardness and speed of the osmium/iridium darts makes them extremely effective, even against armored enemies.

Two klicks was well within the range of our rifles and the entire western edge of the town was raked by our fire. I still couldn't see any enemy soldiers through the dust and shattered rocks we were kicking up, but the main purpose of our fire was to keep their heads down. Any hits at this point would be just dumb luck.

"Alright evens, move it out! Odds, continue covering fire."

Half of the squad leapt over the crest and ran forward. I kept up my fire, stopping only to grab another clip off my waist and reload. The guys who were advancing came under fire from the trench, but our covering fire was hampering the enemy response. Their shooting was sporadic and poorly aimed.

"Evens, stop and hit the ground! Covering fire!"

The advancing troops dove forward onto the ground and began spraying the enemy positions with fire.

"Odds, move out! Seventy-five meters."

I stopped firing and climbed up over the hill. Although we were to advance in 50 meter intervals, our first move was an extra 25 meters so that our positions would be staggered with that of the evens. It took less than 20 seconds to cover the distance, but it seemed like we'd been running for an hour when the comlink crackled again. When I flopped down on the ground I let out a deep breath. I couldn't believe I wasn't hit.

"Odds, down and fire! Evens, forward 50 meters!"

We continued in this fashion until we had covered almost half the distance to the trench. We still had no one down.

The evens had just hit the ground, and the order came for us to advance. I scrambled up and headed forward. Before I had covered 10 meters, something else opened fire from the enemy trench. The volume of fire increased dramatically and I saw two of our guys go down within seconds of each other.

"Odds, hit the dirt! Cease all movement! All units fire!"

I dove to the ground, bringing my rifle up to bear as I went down. Damn! They had a heavy weapon in there. I remembered something from my ordnance training – the Shadeng-7 heavy auto gun, primary infantry support weapon of the CAC assault forces. I couldn't recall all the details, but I was pretty sure the thing had a rate of fire of better than 3,000 rounds per minute.

The sergeant spoke again. "Ferguson, report your condition." He didn't ask about anyone else, though I was sure that I'd seen two casualties. I found out later that the other was Jenkins, and the sergeant's monitors had already confirmed he was dead.

The reply was quick but a little shaky, "Took one in the leg, Sarge. I'll be OK. Don't think I can walk, though."

The armor was designed to minimize the effects of a wound – the longer a wounded marine can survive, the greater the chance he will be recovered and given real medical treatment.

The injury control mechanism automatically injects drugs to treat shock, minimize pain, and slow the metabolism to reduce blood loss. Additionally, there is a kit attached to the exterior of the armor containing bandages and other items that the marine himself can use if he is able, though there isn't much you can do when suited up.

"Stay put, Ferguson, keep your head down. We'll be back for you."

In a larger operation we'd probably have an imbedded medic with us. But with a single company spread over 100 square kilometers there was no workable way to provide supporting services. The wounded would just have to depend upon their suits' trauma control and hope that we go on to win the battle.

"Second squad, maintain positions." The lieutenant's voice. "Evens, continue fire. Odds, grenade attack. Target the section of trench in front of those storage tanks, three rounds each. Reserve team, I want you to flank that heavy weapon – advance 500 meters to the right of the second squad."

My rangefinder confirmed my estimate that I was about 1100 meters from the target area. I clicked the small button under my left thumb to lock the range into the firing system and, pointing my arm in the direction of the target, loosed three grenades in rapid succession.

A few seconds later the ground all along the target area erupted as nine 100 milliton high explosive grenades exploded within a 5 second period.

The automatic fire from the trench stopped, at least momentarily. We had no way of knowing if the gun had been hit or if the crew had merely been stunned or knocked to the ground.

"Odds, covering rifle fire. Evens advance 50 meters."

We had leapfrogged another 200 meters with only sporadic enemy fire when we got our answer, as the big gun opened up again, pinning us down about 800 meters short of the trench. This time we weren't surprised, and no one was hit as far as I could tell.

By this time the flanking force was in position on a small hill to the right and opened up on the trench. If there had been a few more enemy troops, they could have engaged the flanking force and held the entire position firmly. As it was, however, the flank force was only challenged by a single enemy trooper firing from behind one of the small buildings on the edge of the settlement. About thirty seconds after he opened fire a lucky shot landed a frag grenade about a meter behind him. Five or six pieces of osmium-iridium shrapnel slammed into him, one tearing his head clean off his body, eliminating the only effective opposition to the flank attack.

With no other protection from the enfilade fire, the enemy had to fall back from the trench leaving three casualties and the auto gun behind. A few seconds later, with the other half of the squad providing covering fire, my team took possession of the trench.

The flank force had pursued the three retreating enemy troopers, picking one off as they ran for the cover of the nearest building. The two survivors sought refuge in a small, concrete structure that looked like some kind of warehouse.

Sergeant Harris' voice barked over the comlink. "All troops, cease firing. Kleiner, take that building out."

With no fire coming from the broken CAC forces the rest was child's play. Kleiner moved down the trench about 10 meters to get a clean line of sight to the building. Once in place she braced herself against the walls of the trench and selected a high explosive, short range rocket (we were way too close to use the normal charge, and an armor piercing round would blast right through a small building). She yelled, "Clear!" and pulled the trigger. Behind her there was a meter long blast of fire from the rocket's backwash. Less than half a second later the area of the building was engulfed in fire, smoke, and shattered concrete.

A couple seconds later the sergeant said, "Flanking force, advance north. Fire team A, advance east. Leapfrog house to house with at least two men covering each move. Fire team B, stand by in reserve in the trench."

The sergeant's orders may have seemed a little overly cautious, but they were strictly by the book. I think we all agreed that there were no more live enemies in the town, but there was no percentage in betting anyone's life on that assumption.

It took about half an hour to complete the house to house searches. As expected, the town was deserted. Intel had reported that the locals had all been removed to a central holding area and, from what we could see, that info seemed accurate.

From their insignia we determined that the six CAC troopers killed in our attack were the remnants of a single squad. If so, they had already suffered losses of 50%+ in the campaign (CAC squads have 13 men). It looked like the militia had put up one helluva fight.

We spent the next four hours fortifying the eastern and northern approaches to the town. Our armor made each of us a miniature backhoe, and in a few short hours of work we had extended the trench along the entire northern and eastern perimeters of the town.

We moved the CAC auto gun and set up a real strongpoint at the corner of the northern and eastern sections of trench. We had plenty of ammo for the gun – one of the buildings held crates full of extra ordnance.

By nightfall we were ready for any attack. We had detection devices positioned out about five klicks; they wouldn't take us by surprise. We even managed to grab a few hours of sleep in shifts. We were ready for the counterattack. But it never came.

Later I managed to piece together what had happened. Apparently the plan was working perfectly. The enemy had sent an entire platoon supported by two light support vehicles to deal with us and retake the town. That would have put us knee deep in it, but would also have fatally weakened the northern perimeter where the main attack was coming.

Our attacking forces were supposed to wait until dark to give the enemy time to divert his forces. Unfortunately, one of the planetary militia units ran into an enemy patrol, and the local commander panicked and sent his men in five hours early.

Without the coordinating attacks along their flanks, the militia was in big trouble from the start. The regulars could either hold back and watch the militia get chewed to pieces, or attack now, hours ahead of schedule. The captain had no choice.

Realizing that a major attack was developing in the north before the force heading south toward us was engaged, the enemy commander recalled these troops to strengthen the main defensive line. He left a small force to delay any thrust we might make out of the town, but the rest of the diverted forces were recalled in time.

With no way of knowing that the forces we expected to attack us had withdrawn, we remained in our defensive positions all night. By the time we got the order to advance it was just about over.

The firefight had raged throughout the night, but just about an hour before dawn the enemy lines were broken in two places. After that it was just a question of mopping up.

On our way north we ran into a few enemy troops who tried to surrender. They must have known what to expect since they'd used gas on the locals, but they tried anyway. They were more fortunate, at least, then the ones who fell into the hands of the militia. That is if the stories I heard later were true...and I have no doubt they were.

The reconquest of Carson's World was complete. The tactical plan had been excellent and would have worked perfectly except for the failure of one militia officer to follow orders. But such is the friction of war, and few battle plans survive the start of combat unmodified.

After the battle the captain made some noise about bringing the responsible officer up on charges, but it didn't get very far. I suspect if the battle had been lost instead of won, there would have been more of an appetite for an investigation, but with the planet back in our hands, the attitude seemed to be that no harm was done.

We felt differently, of course. The company lost almost 20% of its strength, and most of the casualties occurred in the heavy fighting on the northern perimeter. How many of those losses were caused by the foul up? No way to tell.

Our squad had one killed and one wounded. Ferguson's wound turned out to be a single clean shot through the left leg. He'd be back in the line before our next assault.

The rest of the squad – the entire company, actually – remained on the planet as garrison for six weeks. This kind of duty is usually pretty slow, but not this time. We were busy as hell the entire time. We rebuilt and expanded the ground fortifications, digging trenches and building bunkers everywhere. We provided the strong backs for the engineer platoon that arrived a week later with a freighter full of ground-to-air defense systems. These were emplaced not only around the developed area, but also near what looked like an entrance to a large mine, where we built a veritable fortress.

By the time the relieving force arrived, every one of us was exhausted, and we were in line and ready the morning the shuttles from the Guadalcanal landed. While waiting for the order to board, I watched the new garrison troops unloading and forming up. They were marines, not assault troops, but marines nonetheless. And there were a lot of them. From where I was I couldn't see all of them, but they landed in at least a dozen ships and there were a good 300 already formed up in the center of the landing area. I guessed there must have been seven or eight hundred in all.

Extensive prepared defenses and a reinforced battalion as a garrison? It seemed like a lot of effort to defend a small, relatively insignificant mining colony. Of course, that was up to the high command and they didn't ask my opinion. If I'd known then what I know now, I would have understood, but at the time I had no idea. One thing was certain – if the CAC wanted to take this planet again they were going to need one hell of a bigger force than they sent the first time.

A few minutes later we boarded the three transport shuttles and headed back to the Guadalcanal in a considerably more comfortable and leisurely fashion than we'd departed six weeks before. The ships were designed to evac a full platoon plus wounded, medical personnel, and equipment, so there was plenty of room for the 28 of us.

After docking we had to hang around the landing bay until we got checked out by the doc. There were two other newbies in the company. We'd actually landed with five, but one was killed and the other evac'ed with a partially severed spine. The three of us were last, so I had about three hours to kill. We'd been in the field for six weeks, so the captain gave us a break and cut back on the discipline. We were pretty much had the time to ourselves. I played a game of chess with Vergren, the platoon's sniper, but he was really good, and I lost pretty quickly.

A lot of the guys had been pretty standoffish since I joined the unit, but now people who had barely said two words to me in the past four months were coming up and asking me how I was and congratulating me on the mission. A few of the privates from the first squad invited me to play poker while we waited. I won about 15 creds.

After my examination I headed down to my billet. It was about midnight, ship time, but there was a message waiting. I was to report to the landing bay in full dress uniform immediately.

My mind raced. What had I done? I figured I must be in trouble. My heart was racing as I threw on my dress blues and hurried down to the bay.

I was in the corridor outside the bay when the lights went out. I felt at least two pairs of hands grab me from behind and someone threw a sack over my head. They dragged me into the bay and threw me down to the deck. Someone pulled the sack off my head and then the lights snapped on.

The entire platoon was standing in a circle. Sergeant Harris was standing over me holding a small container. No one said a word. He leaned over and poured a few drops of the contents on my forehead. At first I didn't know what it was, but then I realized it was blood. I figured it was animal blood of some kind. I was wrong, but I didn't find that out until much later. Everyone in the bay started cheering.

The sergeant reached out his hand and helped me to my feet. The blood ran down my face as I got up. I nearly retched when a few drops trickled down to my lips, but I held back the impulse. I was beginning to understand. This ceremony had meaning - it was a baptism. I had proved my worth to them in battle. I was one of them. After so many years on my own, I had finally found a home.

Chapter Two

Manhattan Protected Zone
New York City, USA
Western Alliance

The Marine Corps saved me.

I was born Erik Daniel Cain in 2232 AD in Lenox Hill-Fargus hospital. My father, John Cain, was a project manager for Metadyne Systems Corporation, and we lived in a company-owned apartment block in the Midtown Protected Zone of Manhattan. My family wasn't rich, but we weren't poor either, and we lived better than most people in 23rd century America.

New York was the third largest city in the country, with over a million residents, though you could tell that this was a small fraction of the number that had once lived there. North of the Protected Zone, outside of the 77th Street gate was the semi-abandoned northern sector, and beyond that the badlands of the Bronx, a wasted area filled with centuries-old factories still producing basic goods and decrepit ancient apartments occupied by the lowest strata of workers. The whole area was ruled at night (and day) by the Gangs, who owned the illegal narcotics trade and terrorized and preyed upon the outcasts living beyond the armed bastions of the Protected Zone.

Below the 10th Street gate was a forbidden buffer area and 500 meters further south, the Crater, the still radioactive pit remaining from the worst terrorist attack in human history.

Between these two urban no-man's lands was a clean and well-ordered cityscape where law and order reigned. The Protected Zone was the home of the educated workers who ran a modern, high tech society, and if there were some murmurs that past generations had enjoyed far higher living standards and much greater personal freedom, these were never more than hushed whispers. Certainly such things were never taught in school, where we studied how modern America and the whole Western Alliance was the highest pinnacle yet reached in the development of the human condition. If anyone had any doubts, all they had to do was take a look outside the gates of the Zone to appreciate what they had. And keep their mouths shut.

Manhattan was crowded, but there was enough food, more or less, and there were plenty of diversions to keep people busy in their free time. Twenty-third century bread and circuses, though I never thought of it that way back then. If laws were strict, the mail monitored, and people conditioned to accept the wisdom of their leaders without question, in return they were fed (well enough), entertained, and protected from the harsher realities facing those unfortunate enough to live outside the walls of the Zone.

The northeast corner of the Zone was called Sector A, and it was the home of the Political Class and their Corporate Magnate allies. Most of the residents of Manhattan never set foot inside the inner walls that separated Sector A from the rest of the Zone. I did, but that was years later under circumstances I could never have imagined as a child, and I can tell you that no one in America lives like the politicians and their corporate cronies.

My parents managed something extremely rare for anyone outside the Political Class – they had three children. Reproduction rates were strictly controlled everywhere in the USA, but they were especially restricted in crowded Manhattan where the legal limit was two – and that only for the most skilled workers.

My parents got around the limitations in a pragmatic way. Three years after I was born my mother gave birth to twin girls, Beth and Jill. A compulsory abortion would have been standard procedure, but in a bizarre turn of events the technician did not identify the second fetus at the single pre-natal exam my mother's health care ration allowed. So my sisters, both born alive and healthy, were something of a surprise.

With my father in a responsible position for a major government contractor, he was able to obtain a waiver legitimizing the births. We were lucky – a post-natal termination would have been mandatory for a less educated and affluent family.

My childhood was a pretty normal one for the middle class. My father worked long hours, but his position allotted us almost 70 square meters of living space within the safety and comfort of the Protected Zone. We were happy and content, and my early memories are pleasant ones of family and childhood. That happiness came to an abrupt end shortly after my eighth birthday.

When they were four years old, my sisters became infected with the G-11 super-virus. Developed as a bacteriological weapon during the Unification Wars, the virus caused a deadly disease that was commonly called the Plague, though it was far deadlier and more difficult to treat than its historical namesake. Although the frequency of infection had declined dramatically in the decades since the virus had last been employed in war, it was still a serious health problem throughout the world. Advances in medical technology and treatment had resulted in a reduction in the mortality rate from 100% to approximately 50%, but no outright cure had ever been developed. In many cases the survivors suffered serious damage to vital organs and other bodily systems.

My sisters were young and strong, and they both survived the disease itself. Unfortunately, though Beth recovered fully, the virus had virtually destroyed Jill's liver. Her only hope of survival was a transplant or regeneration. While organ regeneration had been perfected in the previous century and offered a virtually 100% success rate, it was extraordinarily expensive, and my family's health care ration was nowhere close to allowing the procedure. In fact my sister's medical priority rating was extremely low, so even a transplant was out of the question. In the government's analysis my sister's life simply wasn't worth the resources required to save it, particularly since my parents would still have two other children.

My parents didn't give up though. Black market organs and cut rate transplants were readily available outside the Protected Zone. Though illegal and dangerous, it was the only way to save Jill's life, and my father and mother didn't even think twice.

A black market transplant was still expensive, and my parents sold everything we owned and borrowed every credit they could. My mother even tried to go back to work. She had been an assistant chef at the Plaza Hotel before she married my father, but with more than 50% of the population unemployed the government allowed very few two income families. When my parents were married my mother lost her work permit.

My mother and father did what any parents would do – they scraped together the money. My father requested additional work assignments, usually almost impossible to get, but thanks to a huge contract for the guidance system in the new Gettysburg class battleship, he was able to get an extra four paid hours a day. With her experience at the Plaza, my mother was able to get some unauthorized and illegal jobs catering for various functions. Somehow, and I was never quite sure how they managed it, they put together enough money to fund the transplant, which in true black market fashion had to be paid in full upfront.

The operation was performed secretly, in a storage room instead of in a hospital, but in spite of the less than ideal conditions the transplant was successful. Extensive drug therapy was required to force acceptance of the poorly matched organ, and the high dosages caused permanent damage to her immune system. But she was alive, and with proper medication, which would also come from the black market, she could live something approaching a normal life.

Just when it seemed that everything would work out our world fell apart. I never knew exactly what happened, but the authorities found out about the illegal operation, my mother's freelancing...everything.

We were in the closing years of the Second Frontier War and the government was looking everywhere for revenue. So my parents were offered the chance to pay a large fine and escape further punishment. Having just spent every mil they had on the surgery, it was impossible for them to come up with the demanded funds.

I vaguely remember the inquisitor visiting us. My father told me to stay in the room I shared with my sisters and not to come out until he came back for me. It didn't matter that the entire situation was the result of parents desperately trying to save the life of their child. They had broken the laws, and that was all the inquisitor cared about.

After he had left my father came in and told me to go to bed. I wasn't even nine, but I could tell he was scared. It was the first time I'd ever seen my father afraid of anything. I knew something terrible was happening, but I didn't say anything – I just said goodnight to my father and got into bed. He whispered, "Goodnight," and turned off the light on the way out. Laying there in the dark I could hear my mother crying in the next room. All night I could hear my parents talking, the sounds of them walking around the apartment, and most of all, my mother's sobs.

The next day six armed government marshals summarily seized all of my parents' property including their occupancy rights to the apartment. My father was terminated from his employment (his job was excellent and could easily be sold to another qualified candidate), and our residency permit was revoked.

We were forced to leave the Midtown Protected Zone, and I will never forget the image of the five of us huddled together as the 77th Street gate slowly slid open. I remember taking a last look behind me before my father wrapped his arm around my shoulder and led me out over the cracked pavement north of the gate.

Northern Manhattan had once been densely populated, but now it was mostly abandoned. The two kilometers immediately north of the wall had been completely razed during the Disruptions to prevent rioters and gangs from sneaking up on the Protected Zone. It was an eerie landscape of ancient, crumbling roadways and scattered pillars of broken masonry - the remnants of demolished buildings that had once housed thousands. There were deep trenches in several places where the ground had collapsed on abandoned underground rail lines. Partially filled with putrid brown water, they looked like nightmarish canals making their way northward.

Slicing through the terrain to the northwest was a clear plastic tube raised 30 meters above the ground on massive steel pillars. The magtrain connected the MPZ to Fort Tyron Transit Center in the northwest corner of Manhattan Island. Fort Tyron was the terminus for bullet trains from other major cities as well as a major freight handling center, and the magtrain brought passengers and supplies into the city 24 hours a day.

But we were heading northeast. My father's friends had helped him get a contact for a job in a basic materials factory in the South Bronx, located in a neighborhood informally known as The Devil's Playground.

There was no mass transit operating north of the Zone other than the magtrain, so we had to walk three or four miles to the bridge over the Harlem River and then into the Bronx. There were a few clusters of occupied buildings along the way, like small villages on the outskirts of the MPZ, but mostly there was just debris from buildings that had been demolished or simply collapsed. The bridge itself was old but sturdy-looking, and the Manhattan side was protected by a gate and a small guard tower occupied by a squad of police rather more heavily armed than those who patrolled inside the Zone. My father showed the guards our papers, and after a cursory inspection we were ushered across.

The Bronx side was unprotected, and while the immediate area around the bridge was cleared, about a hundred meters from the river we started to walk past ancient, but occupied, apartment buildings scattered among burnt-out shells and rubble-strewn vacant lots.

It was early afternoon, and there were some people moving about their business, though it was very sparse and nothing like the crowded bustle of the MPZ. Along one broad avenue there were a number of businesses, mostly stores carrying various supplies, but also a small medical clinic with a long line snaking out the door and 30 meters down the street.

Everything was old and dirty, and the streets were pock-marked with deep ruts and holes. There was a faint reek in the air, no doubt from old leaking sewer lines among other things.

We moved into a fourth floor apartment in a decrepit 300

year old building five blocks from the ruins of Yankee Stadium. There was a small lobby with a single light fixture hanging from a wire and the wreckage of an elevator that looked as if it hadn't functioned in a century. There was a single staircase, old and rickety, but still standing as far as the third floor. From the third floor landing there was a wooden ladder used to access the fourth and fifth levels. My parents tried to be strong for us, but my mother started sobbing when she saw our new home. My father was silent. He helped my mother up the ladder and then carried my sisters up one at a time. I climbed up myself before he came back for me, but he reached over and helped me up onto the landing.

My father was ludicrously over-educated for his new job managing the outdated technology systems of the plasti-steel plant, but he was lucky to have any employment at all. As violators of multiple statutes, my parents were not eligible for any form of government assistance, so without a job we would go hungry. I don't recall hearing my father complain about working 12-hour shifts for sustenance wages, but I don't remember ever seeing him smile again either.

The neighborhood was a nightmare, totally overrun by warring drug gangs. It had been eighty years since the police department had withdrawn from regular coverage of the areas outside the Protected Zone, and the gangs completely owned the place. My parents quickly learned that residents paid the local gang leader for protection if they wanted to survive, and if two gangs were fighting over the turf they paid both just to be safe.

Long before the police departed, most other city services had already been suspended. There was no operating mass transit, no real hospitals, and no outside lighting. The streets had deteriorated to the point that they were impassible to vehicles, and in many places even walking was a challenge. There was an electrical grid of sorts, and we usually had about 4 hours of power each day, though there were times we went a week or more without. We had battery-powered heaters, so if the electric stayed off for a couple days in winter and we couldn't recharge them, we just bundled up against the cold. The water service was usually working, though we only had hot water if the heaters were functioning. It was brackish, untreated water, but filtering it helped considerably, leaving just a mildly oily taste.

Most of the residents of the neighborhood were Cogs, uneducated workers born there who worked at menial and dangerous, jobs and who had a life expectancy less than half that of Zone dwellers. But there were Outcasts as well, skilled workers like my father who had been expelled from the MPZ for one infraction or another and who now survived however they could in a world for which they were wholly unprepared.

Then there were the Gangs. There wasn't a lot of hope in the neighborhood, and to many the Gangs offered the promise a better existence...or at least the chance to be one of the bullies instead of the bullied. The truth was that life in the Gangs was violent and usually short, and Gang members caught by the authorities were typically summarily executed. Still, there was no shortage of recruits.

The Gangs fought each other also, and two of them warred over our neighborhood - the Reds and the Wolfpack. The Reds were bigger, but the Wolfpack seemed smarter and better led, and there was a stalemate between the two, neither able to gain an advantage. The constant warfare was hard on the locals, who not only bore the extortion from both sides, but were also stuck in the crossfire.

For three years my family lived in this new reality, and as people usually do when confronted with a previously unimaginable situation, we adapted. The lost luxuries of life in the Zone were slowly forgotten, and we began to learn how to make life bearable in our new home.

My mother never really accepted things, and she withdrew more and more into herself until she barely spoke at all. But my father tried tirelessly to make our lives more comfortable. The work, the regret, the resentment...I know it devoured him, but he never really let us see that, and he never quite gave up.

My father was an educated man, and I think what got to him the most was the fact that, with no schooling available outside the Zone, my sisters and I would have no real hope of a better life. Despite the hours he worked, he made time to tutor the three of us every day. Somehow he even scraped up enough to buy me a small solar-powered infopad, and I'd sneak up to the roof and connect to the Net whenever I could. For three years, that was our life, and as much as possible it had become normal to me.

I was up on the roof with my 'pad late one day. My mind wandered into a daydream, and I wasn't really paying attention to what I was reading. I was gazing absent-mindedly across the sea of battered, half-standing buildings that stretched as far north and west as I could see, and then I heard it. A quick shout, then a crashing sound, and after that, a blood-curdling scream.

I jumped up and ran to the hatch that led back into the building and, grabbing the rope handle, I yanked it open. Gunshots, then more screams. I climbed over the edge onto the ladder, listening to my raspy breathing and feeling my hands go numb from panic. More shots. No more screams, just scuffling sounds and a door slamming. In my rush I put my foot down too hard on a half rotten rung, and it snapped in half. I tumbled off the ladder about halfway down to the top floor landing. My 'pad slipped out of my hand and shattered when it hit the floor.

I was stunned for a minute, then when I tried to get up I realized I'd twisted my ankle. The fall probably saved my life. By the time I managed to get downstairs, it was over.

I managed to get up, favoring my injured ankle, and climbed down the ladder to the fourth floor. A sharp pain ran up my leg with each step, but between fear and adrenalin I wasn't troubled by it. I could hear the thunderclap of my heart in my ears as I hopped off the ladder onto my good foot and stumbled to our apartment. Our door had been kicked open and was hanging loosely at an angle, still connected by one hinge like a child's tooth almost ready to come out. Inside, the apartment was a nightmare.

There was blood all over the floor and walls. The furniture was knocked over and scattered around, and the tattered rug was covered with the shards of what looked like every breakable item in the place.

My mother was in the kitchen, lying on the floor next to the counter. There was blood all around her, and though I could tell she was dead, I couldn't see exactly where she'd be shot. I couldn't bring myself to touch her or even look, and I forced myself to turn away. That was the last glimpse I had of my mother.

I stumbled back out into the main room and saw my father. I'd missed him when I had first run into the apartment. He was lying next to an overturned desk, looking straight up at me, lifeless eyes wide open and two bullet holes in his head.

The whole thing is a blur to me now, and I really don't know how long I was in the apartment. It could have been just a few minutes, or it could have been much longer. To this day I really can't remember.

I frantically looked for my sisters, and I found them in our sleeping room, lying under the remnants of the mattress where they'd been shot at least ten times as they tried to hide. There were bloody pink bits of foam everywhere.

After 30 seconds, five minutes, an hour - I really don't remember - I stumbled out of the apartment. I didn't take anything with me; I didn't even look to see if we'd been robbed of our meager possessions. I just hobbled out into the hall, down the ladder and stairs, and out into the street. It was a sunny day and I recoiled from the brightness that assaulted my eyes. In a daze I ran around to the back of the building into the dark comfort of the shade, and I fell roughly to my knees and bent over as my stomach emptied.

I must have wandered around for days - or weeks - stumbling through the streets, scavenging something, anything, to eat, and at night hiding in whatever spot I could find. I never went back to the apartment, or even near the building.

At first I was sure I was going to die, and truth be told, I didn't really care. More than once I thought to myself, just lie down and stay there until it's over. Or climb up to the roof of one of the buildings and end it in an instant. But something kept me going, pushing me forward. It's not like I really had any hope or any real reason to live.

As time went by, though, I became better at living in the streets. I found relatively secure places to stay...there was an endless labyrinth of abandoned tunnels and chambers under the city. I learned to steal too, first for survival, but in time I just began victimizing the Cogs for no reason other than I was angry and I could.

Eventually I hooked up with the Wolfpack, and over the next five years I committed every manner of crime and outrage imaginable. The less said about those years the better, so we'll just say I was angry at the world and felt I owed it and its inhabitants nothing but retribution. They were there for me to use and exploit, like a crop in the fields, and that's how I lived for a very long time.

Life in the gang brought with it a crude sort of luxury. It was nothing like the clean and orderly environment in the MPZ, but we took over the buildings we liked, and stole whatever we wanted to fill them. If anybody complained, we killed them. Simple.

I also got back into the MPZ several times, making drug deliveries and, on one occasion, conducting a robbery. We used the vast underground city to get past security and into Midtown. The ancient tunnels, power conduits, rail lines, sewers, and other infrastructure, much of it abandoned, weaved a tangled web under the entire city, and we had a number of routes mapped out.

We owned the underground mazes, but trips into the MPZ were still dangerous missions, and it was on one of these narcotics delivery runs that I was caught. We made our way through underground rail tunnels to an abandoned station that was situated below a large apartment building. There was a rough cut passageway from the station to the sub-basement of the building.

The exit from the passage was hidden behind some machinery, but someone must have found it, because as soon as we squeezed out, the doors opened and cops in riot gear poured into the room. We opened fire simultaneously, but they had body armor and better guns. It was over in less than a minute.

There were seven of us, and four were wounded. The rest of us were hit by stun rods, and by the time we woke up we were shackled and leaning against one of the walls.

There was a neat row of four bodies along one of the walls, each one with a single hole in the forehead in addition to whatever original wound they had. Gang members had a zero health care priority, so the police didn't even bother bringing in the wounded. However, they did try to arrest the occasional live prisoner to dispel the image, largely accurate, that they just went out and shot anyone they felt like.

They dragged me outside and into a waiting transport and shoved me through the rear hatch. The inside was a large open area with no seating. There was a long metal pole running along each side, and my wrist shackles were fastened to the one on the right. My two companions were chained to the pole on the other side.

The transport drove to another location where four more prisoners were loaded and then down to the main detention area. The detainee processing center was a large building with about 100 floors, located in the Government District on 34th Street. There were no windows in the transport, so I couldn't see the building, but I'd walked past it once before when I came down to the Government District with my father to renew one of his licenses.

We were dragged roughly from the transport and down a corridor to the pre-trial waiting area. The hallway was gleaming white plasti-steel, and ended at a large processing room. There were ten corridors from the processing area, all leading to blocks of cells.

The holding cells were packed with so many detainees that there wasn't room to even sit on the floor, and the place was so reeking I could barely keep myself from retching. The cell was filled with all sorts of people. Some looked like me, gang members or other serious criminals. But most of them looked like normal citizens who were probably arrested for some petty offense or another. The hardcore types looked angry and defiant, but the others were in a state of shock. Some of them were crying; others were almost catatonic.

The regular citizens, the minor offenders, were victimized by the real criminals, of course, and though I'd done my share of horrific things, it really turned me off. I'd abused my share of the Cogs during my gang days, but in that cell I didn't like watching it, and I certainly didn't want to participate. There was one woman in particular, who was really being harassed by two of the hardcores. They'd given her a pretty harsh beating and stripped her down, making her sit in the cell naked while they tormented her. Finally they both raped her against the wall, and when they were done they offered her to a bunch of the others. She screamed piteously for the guards, but they ignored it for a while, and finally when one did walk past the cell he just laughed and told her to stop making so much noise.

She looked like a normal MPZ resident to me, probably some type of office worker. Certainly no one who was likely to have committed any serious crime. Why the hell did they put people like that in here with animals like us?

That was a passing thought at the time, driven by my anger, and probably some unrecognized shame for not helping her. I figured it out much later, though. Being in that cell was her punishment for whatever she had done, and it was something she would remember with more pain and fear than any administrative penalty the Court might give her.

The jailers, the Court, everyone in that building - it wasn't about justice; it was about obedience, about maintaining order. Fear accomplished that with far greater effectiveness than due process and measured punishments. My memories of daily life in Manhattan were those of a child, but when I thought about it I could recall how tense my parents were whenever they dealt with any government official. I remembered how people would hurry to get out of the way of police officers and, of course, I remembered the terror in my mother's eyes when the inquisitor visited the apartment.

I was in that cell for four days with nothing more than a trough along the one wall for voiding bodily wastes and a single faucet that dispensed a trickle of cloudy, stinking water.

When they finally came to get me they took me to a small tiled room with a drain, stripped me naked, and washed me with a high-powered hose. I was given a clean set of yellow overalls to wear and escorted to my court appearance.

The courtroom was small and utilitarian, with just a raised platform holding the judge's bench, and a single row of hard plastic chairs. Two armed guards stood rigidly against the wall on either side of the judge. I was brought in and seated in the middle chair. The officer who had brought me in stood directly behind me.

I had no attorney, no witnesses, no time to try to defend myself. They just sat me down while the prosecutor read the charges. The one time I tried to speak the court officer hit me in the back of the neck with a rubber club and told me to shut up.

After the prosecutor finished the judge spoke almost immediately. "Guilty. Sentence, death by gas. To be carried out immediately."

I jumped up and started to protest, and then everything went black as I felt the officer's club impact the back of my head. I don't know how long I was unconscious, but when I started to come to I was strapped to a cold metal chair in a small white chamber. There was a glass window of sorts, with what looked like a steel door closed over it. There were large vents on the otherwise featureless steel walls at both the ceiling and floor levels.

My wrists and legs were held fast by worn fabric straps. I started to panic and began yelling as loud as I could, but the room looked pretty soundproof. I pulled as hard as I could against the straps, but I couldn't budge. I could feel the sweat beading up on my brow and trickling down my face as I wildly struggled.

After a few minutes of that the door made a soft hissing sound and opened. A tall man dressed in a spotless gray and black uniform stepped through and stood quietly for a few seconds, looking at me intently, as if he was trying to read my mind.

Finally he said, "Hello, Erik. I'd ask how you were doing, but I think I have a pretty good idea. My name is Captain John

Irving. You can call me Jack. I was wondering if you had any interest in discussing an alternative to staying here and choking to death on poison gas."

After five years on the street and in the gang, after sitting in that cell of horrors, after that mockery of a trial...I had just about had it with police and anything with a resemblance to police.

"Go get fucked, scumbag. Just gas me so I don't need to look at any more pus-sucking cops."

He looked at me with an amused grin for a moment, and then let out a short but hearty laugh. "I'm not a cop, Erik. I'm a marine. And I'd like to make you a marine too."

Chapter Three

Marine Orientation and Deployment Center
Brooklyn, New York, USA
Western Alliance

Training was nothing like I expected. Actually it started pretty much exactly as I anticipated, but it wasn't long before things veered sharply from the familiar.

I decided I'd call my new friend Captain Jack, which seemed sufficiently disrespectful without being outright provocative. I'd given Captain Jack a few more minutes of nasty expletives, but I couldn't get a rise out of him. And going with him seemed like a better option than snorting toxic gas, so of course I accepted his mysterious invitation. I'd be damned if I would fight for this miserable excuse for a country, but my options were somewhat limited, so I played along.

He called in the guard and told him to un-strap me. The cop looked like he tasted something bad, but when he paused slightly Captain Jack gave him a quick look, and he scrambled over and unhooked the straps and backed away. I watched the whole thing with surprised amusement. These cops were used to being bullies, but this guy was scared shitless of Captain Jack. I enjoyed watching that more than anything I'd seen in a long time.

I'd been shackled and locked up and generally treated like a grave threat to anyone around me for the last four days, so it surprised me when Captain Jack turned around and just said, "Follow me."

"How do you know I won't just jump you and take off the minute we're out of here?"

He didn't turn, but I could hear the amusement in his voice when he said, "I'll just have to take that chance."

I didn't realize it then, of course, but Captain Jack could have killed me in an instant. I thought I was pretty tough, but after years of marine training I have a good idea of how many different ways he could have dropped me without working up a sweat.

We walked through the building, took the elevator down to the lobby, and stepped out onto the street. Captain Jack had an anti-grav waiting right outside. It was a sleek gray vehicle with the U.S. Marine Corps logo on the side. We stepped through the open door and sat down in the spartan, but comfortable, seats. Captain Jack barked out a quick command to the driver and with a whoosh the door closed and we took off.

I'd never been in an anti-grav copter, and I was plastered to the small window, watching as we climbed high over the Manhattan streets. We banked right and headed downtown, and in just a minute or two we were passing over the South Wall.

To the right I could see the rubble-strewn edge of the Crater. It had been almost 150 years since half a million New Yorkers were killed by history's worst terrorist attack, but you could still get a bad dose of radiation just standing next to the edge.

The semi-abandoned areas south of the Protected Zone were similar to those in the north, except for the old financial district, where the buildings were much taller. A few of them had collapsed, but the rest still stood defiantly, abandoned relics of a past time. The whole area still had an unhealthy level of radioactivity, but there were still a few people who eked out an existence among the crumbling cityscape. There were jagged, water-filled trenches everywhere - apparently there had been more underground train lines down here than in the north.

We banked left and I suddenly got a view of the Protected Zone, its kilometer-high towers gleaming in the sun. It was beautiful, and it seemed the very image of prosperity and vigor rather than the dying relic it truly was. It was the last time I would see it for a long time, and when I finally did visit again I would be utterly and irrevocably changed, and New York wouldn't be my home anymore.

The copter streaked across the sky, passing swiftly over the streets of Brooklyn. I looked down on row after row of old, poorly maintained buildings. Brooklyn appeared to be a moderately nicer version of the Bronx, with things not in quite the same desperate condition. There were more people milling

around in the streets, and I could make out a few trolleys running down the main thoroughfares, so it looked like Brooklyn
still had some level of city services. Nothing like the MPZ of
course.

We were heading for a huge structure built in the middle of
a large cleared area. The outer perimeter was surrounded by a
large plas-crete wall with several guarded entrances. The building itself was trapezoidal, kind of like a pyramid with the top
third sheared off.

We landed on the roof and took an elevator down several
levels. Finally, Captain Jack broke the silence and said, "You've
got to be tired. Orientation starts tomorrow at 0500, so let's get
you someplace you can get some rest."

He took me to a small windowless room with drab gray walls
and a bunk. The door closed behind him as he left, and I couldn't
see any kind of controls to open it from inside. Another cell,
but far more comfortable than the last one I'd been in.

I was exhausted, but also wired. My body was a jumbled
combination of adrenaline, fatigue, and wild emotions. Anger,
fear, confusion. I'd been minutes from death, only to be whisked
away at the last instant. It was surreal and hard to get my head
around. I had no idea what to expect, and while I was well aware
I'd be dead by now if it hadn't been for Captain Jack, I certainly
didn't plan to whip myself up into a patriotic frenzy for the old
Western Alliance. Fatigue won out in the end, and I fell asleep
pretty quickly and didn't stir until they woke me up to start whatever it was I was starting.

Basic training was everything you'd expect it to be, and then
some. But before I even got to camp, I experienced some of the
busiest and most hectic days of my life.

It started with a comprehensive medical exam, and I do
mean an extensive one. I was poked, probed, and prodded in
every spot and orifice on my body. They took samples and then
more samples. Blood, DNA, spinal fluid, urine, stool, skin,
saliva, semen, blood marrow, and just about every variety of tis-
sue in my body. They put me through every manner of imaging
and scanning device, and when they were through they plugged

a bunch of monitors into me and put me through the most vig-
orous exercise I had ever experienced.

But they were after more than my body, and the physical tests
were followed up by a series of mental and emotional exams. I
sat at a terminal for hours taking one test after another. Some
seemed to evaluate my logical responses, others just my store
of knowledge. Still others were completely baffling in purpose,
asking odd questions like, "If mankind could possess only one,
what is more valuable, an inexhaustible energy source or a drug
that cures all disease?"

Then came the batteries of psych testing, and some of this
was really bizarre. It started with normal interviews, questions
about my childhood, my beliefs, my thoughts on all sorts of
things. I got a little uncomfortable talking about my years with
the gang, as I had done some really bad things. But they didn't
seem to care about that. I guess being a teenage killer was good
prep for a marine career.

They did a series of tests under a variety of stimuli. I was
drugged and questioned very aggressively about a wide and
seemingly random variety of things. I was stripped naked and
strapped to a chair in a freezing cold room and interrogated for
two hours about everything from my thoughts on the government to why I don't like sweet potatoes. I couldn't even remember the last time I'd seen a sweet potato, but they managed to get
me to confess to an aversion for the things.

They finished up by sending in an officer to inform me that
my testing indicated I was not suitable for marine service and
that I was to be taken immediately to the Justice Center for my
capital sentence to be carried out. He then got up and walked
out without a word while they monitored my reactions for 20
minutes before telling me it was only a test.

Sore, exhausted, and disoriented, I was finally taken back to
my room and told I could sleep, which I did for the next 20
hours. I woke up ravenously hungry, and I had just gotten up
and started toward the door with the intention of banging on
it until someone let me out, when it slid open and Captain Jack
walked in.

"You look well rested," he said with an obnoxious little smile on his face. I think he could see that I was trying to come up with something nasty to say, because before I could open my mouth he went on. "Relax, Erik, we all got the same treatment you did...and we've all been through everything you're going to be dealing with."

I didn't catch the half mocking, half sympathetic tone at the time, but looking back it was definitely there. Of course every marine starts the same way. Every one of us goes through the same recruiting and training, and if we get through it, we all make our first assault as privates. It was no different for me than for anyone else.

The whole thing struck me as odd when it was first explained to me. I didn't have any military history education at the time, but if I'd thought about it at all I would have assumed that the senior officers were members of the political classes or some other privileged elite. The terrestrial armed forces were set up that way, but that's not how the off-world military worked. I'd learn a lot more about all of that much later on, but at the time I had no idea what to expect.

"So are you going to tell me what's next? Hopefully breakfast." Honestly, food was all I could really think about. I hadn't eaten anything in days.

He smiled and let out a small laugh. "Training is going to be the biggest challenge you've ever faced, but one thing we're not going to do is starve you to death. Let's go." He motioned toward the door. "You're shipping out to camp tonight, and you've got a right to do it on a full stomach."

I followed him through the door and down the same brightly lit corridor I barely remembered stumbling down the day before. The walls were spotless, the floor was polished to a glossy shine. One thing about the marines - everything was immaculate. Much cleaner than the public areas of the Protected Zone, not to mention the filth of the outer sectors.

We walked past about a dozen doors just like the one leading to my room - no doubt more little cubbies filled with new recruits sleeping off various medical abuses and other wear and tear. After a short walk we came to a large dining hall, filled with maybe 30 big tables that could each seat 10-12. It was at most one-quarter full, and though my just awakened brain had focused on breakfast, we were actually catching the tail end of lunch.

Captain Jack wasn't kidding about the full stomach either. Twenty-third century America was a land where virtually everything was rationed to some extent or another. Things were better in the Protected Zone, of course, but food, clothes, and medicine were still subject to various controls and shortages. So now, as a condemned criminal press-ganged into the military as my only escape from execution, I found myself for the first time in my life able to eat as much as I wanted without question.

While I sat and doggedly attacked the slightly obscene pile of food in front of me, Captain Jack grazed on a salad of some sort and tried to keep enough of my attention to let me know what was ahead of me.

"So, after we eat we'll go down to the quartermaster, and you'll be issued your uniform and kit. Then there are a couple of orientation sessions, and after those you can see how much damage you can do to the dinner menu before your transport leaves for New Houston."

So I ate as much as I could, on general principle once my hunger was sated, and then we went down to the quartermaster. A few minutes later I walked out wearing my first uniform, a set of gray training fatigues that looked nothing like Captain Jack's crisp attire. It was the only thing I would wear for a year.

I was given three sets of fatigues, socks, boots, a grooming kit, a bedroll, towel, and a duffel bag to carry it all. I was also given a personal data unit, but it was restricted, and the only things I could access were regulations and selected military history.

The orientation sessions were harmless but boring, and I'm pretty sure I dozed off once or twice during the video presentations. The one thing I did note from the sessions, and this was something no one had mentioned to me up until then, was that the training regimen was six years. Six years!

Training for the Earthbound army was only three months. Sure, it made sense that fighting in space required more skills, but six years? What could possibly take that long?

So I'd be 23 years old before I even started to serve my active duty time, and 33 before I could get my discharge. At 17 that seemed like an eternity. Not that I had a choice. Other than a bullet in the head. Or more accurately, a lungful of poison gas.

After the orientation we went back to the dining hall, with about an hour to go before I had to be on the train. I made a reasonable effort but didn't match my lunchtime performance. I think Captain Jack was a little disappointed.

We stowed our trays, and I got 5 minutes for a quick bathroom break before we walked down to an assembly hall where I finally said my goodbyes to Captain Jack. Watching him walk away I started to feel really alone. I'd only known him for a few days, but he'd been the one thing I could latch on to. Everything around me was unfamiliar, and things were happening quickly. I really had no idea what to expect. A few days ago I was in the Bronx, a member of the Wolfpack who lived by terrorizing a bunch of poor workers. Now, after a close brush with death I was on my way to becoming a marine? To fighting in space? I couldn't get my mind to focus on anything. I was in a state of shock.

The mag-train ride to New Houston was comfortable and quick. Once we cleared the city the train accelerated to 500 kph, so we reached New Houston in less than five hours.

The train car I was in was full of other recruits, all dressed in the same gray fatigues I was wearing. They looked like a pretty motley bunch, but of course I looked that way too. They were mostly men, but about 20% of them were women. We all pretty much kept to ourselves, and there was very little conversation. I don't know how they all ended up here, but most of them looked about as stunned as I was.

It was dark for most of the trip, which was disappointing. I'd never been out of New York, and I would have loved to see some of the scenery. With nothing much to do I slept through most of the ride, and I woke up to the announcement that we would be arriving in fifteen minutes. The trained slowed, and we passed through a large plasti-crete wall and past two security towers before stopping at a long, open platform.

"Alright boys and girls, up! Let's get moving. Now!"

I hadn't even noticed the sergeant enter the car, but there he was, standing in the doorway barking at us in a voice that seemed to be half hostility and half amusement. People started getting up and moving toward the front of the car. I reached up to grab my duffel, as about half the others were doing.

"Don't forget your bags, kiddies! The porters are all busy elsewhere, I'm afraid! Now move your asses. I want everyone out on that platform in three minutes!"

We stumbled out of the crowded car and out onto the platform, milling around aimlessly until the sergeant came over and yelled at us again until we managed to get into a fairly neat line. We marched into one of the buildings where we went through a check in and orientation process that took several hours after which we were led into a large auditorium.

We'd only been sitting a minute when a man walked out onto the stage. He was tall and muscular, with thick black hair speckled gray. He wasn't dressed in the same gray fatigues as we and everyone else we'd seen were wearing. He wore a spotless dark blue coat with polished silver buttons and one platinum star on each shoulder. His neatly creased white pants were tucked into shiny black boots, and a short sword with an intricately carved hilt hung from his waist.

"Hello, and welcome to Camp Puller. My name is Brigadier General Wesley Strummer. As you can see, I've worn my dress blues in honor of your arrival. Take a good look, because you probably won't see another uniform like this unless you graduate. And less than half of you are going to make it that far."

He paused for a few minutes to let that sink in, then continued. "If you don't graduate then you will go back where you came from, and for most of you that wasn't a very pleasant place. Unless of course you die in training. Which will happen to some of you. Maybe a lot of you."

Again, he stopped and let us consider his words. His voice

was calm, almost gentle, but without so much as raising his voice he had everyone's complete attention. You could have heard a pin drop in the room.

"Those of you who do graduate will join the most elite combat formation in the history of the world. You will serve wherever you are needed, anywhere in explored space, and you will perform that service with valor and distinction. And after you make your first assault, all of your past crimes and offenses will be wiped clean."

That was the first hopeful thing he'd said. A bit of carrot to go with the stick.

"But first you have to complete training. The regimen is unlike anything soldiers have experienced before, and when you have completed it you will be the deadliest human killing machines that have ever existed.

"But before you even begin your training proper, you are all going to the infirmary. You have had varying health care priority levels, most of them pretty low, so you haven't had much medical care. Well now you are going to have every treatable deficiency corrected. Plus, we're going to make some improvements to the original design. When we're done you will all see and hear better than any civilian, and you will have enhanced reflexes.

"After you are released from medical, you're going to do six months of basic field training. Trust me, whatever you think you've been through before, field training is going to teach you the true meaning of physical fitness. You'll probably all survive the medical procedures, but some of you will die during field training. So take it seriously."

That was the second time he mentioned dying in training. I figured it wouldn't be the last.

"After we get you in decent physical shape you're all going to go through a customized remedial education program. Honestly, you're all ignorant and uneducated - totally unqualified to serve in my marine corps. But we're going to fix that. A marine private has the equivalent of a six-year post primary education, and you're going to get it in less than a third of the time it takes lazy civilians.

"Then, we're going to teach you to kill. I know your backgrounds, and a lot of you think you already know how, but take my word for it, you are all amateurs. We are going to make you professionals. Stone cold death machines that strike terror into the hearts of our enemies.

"You think you're tough because you abused or murdered a few helpless workers? Or even another tough guy gang member?" He laughed derisively for a few seconds, the first sound that came out of his mouth that wasn't flawlessly polite. "I've personally killed at least 75 men and women, and troops under my command have killed over 50,000. And all of them were shooting back. So if I were you, I'd pay very close attention to your training, because all of your instructors are combat veterans who have been where you are going and came back to tell about it.

"Of course, you need to get through your training first before you have to worry about surviving combat, and it's going to take everything you've got to get to graduation. And if you wash out, remember - you go back to wherever we found you. For almost half of you that's death row; for most of the rest it's some miserable cesspool where your life expectancy ranges from a few weeks to a few years.

"We offer all of you a chance at redemption, but our price is high. Your mind, body, soul, and every last measure of effort you can muster. If you fail we will leave you dead and bloody on the training field. Or I will personally sign the order to haul your sorry ass back to whatever hangman we snatched you from."

He stopped for a few seconds and methodically scanned the room. Every eye in the place was trained on him. It wasn't just what he said; it was the way he said it. I'd never seen anyone with such a commanding presence and serene confidence. He hadn't raised his voice or spoken an angry word, yet he'd been as ominous and threatening as anything I'd ever encountered.

I'd been living in a world of angry confrontation. In the gangs, a dispute over a nutrition bar could get loud and ugly, and likely violent as well. General Strummer spoke softly and politely enough to be sitting at a dinner party. Yet I had no doubt he'd sign an order sending a lazy recruit back to the gas chamber without a second thought.

"Ok, I think I've made my point. I hope you enjoyed my dress blues, because it's the last free show of respect you're going to get. From now on you earn everything. Do your best, listen to your instructors, and one day I will see you again on the graduation field."

He turned, and walked off the stage, the sound of his boots on the floor echoing loudly in the otherwise silent room. As soon as he'd cleared the stage a captain came out and gave us instructions on getting our billet assignments and meeting with our provisional platoon leaders. Then we were dismissed.

I made my way through the line to get my bunk assignment, but I was lost in thought the entire time. The general had made quite an impression on me. I'd never encountered anyone like him before. I loved my father, but he had been a gentle sort of man, and I'd seen what the world did to people like him.

When I was with the gang I'd seen the other side of humanity too, the vicious, animalistic, malicious side. I'd lived that as well, and in my years with the gang I did some terrible things. But I never really felt like one of them. I never understood the needless brutality, the wasteful violence that went beyond the opportunistic.

The authority figures I'd met were mostly corrupt, vindictive bullies. Certainly none of them commanded any respect. The closest they came to respect was fear, and that they extracted with threats and force.

But Strummer was different. He left me wanting to know more, to understand his way of things. I had no doubt he could act just as summarily, just as harshly, but I somehow felt his actions would be fair, or as close to that as things got. I didn't realize it at the time, never having really experienced it before, but these thoughts and feelings were the beginnings of respect for another human being.

Training was an unbelievable experience, and I learned more things than I could have imagined. We started with the medical review. They had all our test results from exams we'd been given on induction, but they still did a lot more checking. Apparently the Corps likes its marines healthy, and we were going to meet that standard no matter what it took.

I didn't have too many problems. As a child my family had a relatively low health care priority rating, but I'd still seen a doctor three or four times. Of course, once we left the Protected Zone there was no real access to medical care. I was generally very healthy, so I finished the battery of treatments in less than ten days, while some of my classmates were in the infirmary for three weeks or longer.

I'd broken my ankle while I was with the gang, and it never healed quite right, so they re-broke it surgically and fused it perfectly. Other than that, they addressed a few minor deficiencies caused by years of poor diet and malnutrition, and they corrected a few small genetic abnormalities.

The improvements were far more noticeable. The retinal enhancements not only increased my vision over long distances, but I found I could see in very dim light as well. My hearing was more acute, and I felt much more active and energetic. Certainly my reflexes were the best they'd ever been, and I could run faster and jump higher than before. A couple weeks later, when I cut myself during basic training exercises, I realized that I also healed faster. Actually, about twice as quickly as before.

Speaking of basic training, the general wasn't kidding when he said it would be the hardest physical exertion we'd ever experienced. It was about getting us into great shape, certainly, but it was also about testing us, pushing us to the limits of our endurance.

Camp Puller was just outside New Houston, not far from the edge of the quarantined zone around the ruins of the old city. For the record, southeastern Texas is hot as hell. And humid. And the worst of our training was thoughtfully scheduled during the height of summer.

A lot of people couldn't take it and washed out, even though the consequences of dismissal were grave for most of us. But the torment was more than just a weeding out process. The rest of us began developing a confidence we hadn't had before as we survived challenges we couldn't have imagined overcoming.

I almost lost my new found confidence when we started the classroom portion of training. Everyone needed some level of remedial work, but I hadn't seen a classroom since I was 8 years old, so I needed a lot. After the initial adjustment, I took to it pretty well, and by the time we wrapped up course work I had an education roughly equivalent to the one my father had, though mine was a bit more generalized.

I hadn't had time to think about anything while they were beating us into the ground in basic, but about halfway through the classroom training it started occurring to me that my life and attitudes had begun to change. I wasn't a gung ho marine yet by any stretch of the imagination. But up until that point I had been living day-to-day, and to the extent I thought about it, I figured I was there because I had no real choice.

Now I started to look ahead, to think about what it would be like to get to graduation and beyond. I knew I would be leaving Earth and everything familiar to me, possibly forever. That I would fight on strange worlds and quite possibly die on one of them. Yet I started to look to the future in a way I never had before.

My performance improved as time went by. I barely made it through the first year of course work without getting washed out, but by the end of the second I finished tenth in the class.

Then it was on to combat training. We learned hand-to-hand fighting and military history. But most of all we learned unit tactics. We started with lectures and demonstrations, but soon we were doing non-stop war games, tramping all over the hot, flat terrain killing each other in various simulated ways.

We took turns acting as squad leaders, but the higher positions were played by actual sergeants and officers. We were learning to be troopers, not commanders, and part of that meant experiencing what it would be like to fight under experienced leaders.

Once we'd mastered small unit tactics we started learning how to fight in armor. Our fighting suits are the most sophisticated and complex weapons ever constructed, and using one well - and not killing yourself with it - took extensive training. The armor is powered by a miniaturized nuclear reactor, which is built onto the back of the suit and looks a little bit like a large backpack. This is what really makes the armor such a powerful weapon. The energy created by the mobile plant is sufficient not only to operate the very heavy armor itself but also to power some very potent weapon systems. The Mark V powered infantry suit, the one in current usage, can accept four modular weapons systems, so a marine's arsenal can be tailored to the specific mission.

The primary infantry weapon for normal fighting is the GD-211 electromagnetic rifle, which fires a tiny projectile at extremely high velocity. Because of the high speed of the dart, the energy transference to the target is extreme, making it a very hard-hitting weapon with a very long effective range.

For fighting in vacuum or near-vacuum we have a variety of lasers and other energy weapons that are extremely effective in such conditions but subject to diffusion in higher atmospheric densities.

We also have grenade launchers, flame throwers, and a wide variety of highly specialized systems. Then, of course, we have the big boys - the nukes. Our armor can support several nuclear weapon delivery systems, delivering warheads of up to 20 kt.

Of course you can kill almost anyone just by punching them. The fighting suit vastly increases the strength of the user, allowing us to literally run through walls and jump 20 meters straight up. A skilled marine can deliver fire from mid-jump, reaching target locations that are blocked from the ground.

We were all anxious to start blasting the countryside with our new weapons, but the first month of training was spent learning how to walk. We'd had a few casualties during our war games and maneuvers, but these were mostly the results of scattered accidents. It was during suit training that the general's prediction that many of us wouldn't survive really came back to haunt us.

We lost 5 on the first day we actually wore the suits, mostly because they didn't listen to the instructors and tried to do too much, too fast. I started suit training with a healthy respect for the danger, and this only increased when I saw the bloody results of recruits who tried to run or jump without the right training.

Jumping wasn't difficult, but landing was another matter, at least landing safely. The suits provided a lot of protection, but you could still mess yourself up falling hard from 15 meters. It took a lot of practice to learn to land safely and even more to do it without losing a beat. After all, when we were in the show we'd be doing this under enemy fire. If you managed not to hurt yourself jumping, but you stumbled and faltered on the battlefield you could end up very dead, very quickly.

Once we were proficient with our suits we redid all the war games, fully armored this time. The final event was a full scale simulated assault against an entrenched defender. Half of us were attackers and half defenders. When we finished, we switched sides and did it all again. Projected casualties for the attacking forces were over 50%. I hoped we'd do better than that when we hit dirt somewhere for real. I knew from my studies that the average assault force in the Second Frontier War lost 18.2% killed and wounded, which was bad enough, but it was a hell of a lot better than 50%+.

At the end of our fourth year we left Camp Puller and boarded a transport for the orbital transfer facility. There we were loaded onto a ship called the Olympia and we headed out toward Sol Warp Gate #2, bound for Van Maanen's Star and the base located on the second planet of the system.

We were ready to start assault landing exercises and begin training for fighting in space. The Sol system was demilitarized by the Treaty of Paris, so all of our bases conducting anything but maintenance and refueling had to be located in other systems.

The trip was hard on a lot of our class. None of us had ever been in space, and the zero gravity and acceleration periods were rough on the digestive system. Cleaning up partially digested rations in a zero gravity environment might have been my least favorite part of training. We did have a number of methods though, and we got quite good at it.

I'd read an account of a sailor from the old wet navy who said that recruits got used to the waves and that their seasickness passed in a couple weeks. Well, I can tell you that it takes longer than two weeks in space, but the principal still holds. By the time we made our third jump and entered the Van Maanen's Star system, most of us had adapted to normal space travel. We'd get another chance to acclimate to the wild maneuvers preceding an orbital insertion, but that pleasure was still a few months away.

The next two years were filled with training similar to what we'd had already, but in increasing difficult and dangerous circumstances. We practiced on Van Maanan's 2, but we also did maneuvers on the sun-baked first planet and on a moon of the seventh planet where the temperature hovered a balmy 40 degrees above absolute zero.

We let loose with all of our weapons, and in year six we trained with the "specials." Unleashing nuclear warheads was dangerous business, and you certainly didn't want to undershoot with one.

We didn't have any washouts after we left Earth - they'd weeded out all the losers long before. But we did have casualties. Those last two years cost us 102 dead, and my class ultimately graduated 382 out of 1,011 who started.

We got a trip back to Earth for graduation. When we got there they gave us two weeks of leave and transport anywhere in the Alliance. I didn't have anyone to visit or any real desire to see New York again, so I just went to New Houston. That's what most of the class did. The marines seemed to seek recruits with no real ties or family.

Graduation was held on the parade ground at Camp Puller. General Strummer had been true to his word. We not only saw lots of blue full dress uniforms - we got our own. Strummer wasn't there, though. There had been a lot of skirmishes along the frontier, and the general had been transferred to a sector command.

There was a lot of satisfaction in having finished six years of hard training. My life before joining up felt like some bizarre dream, and I could hardly form clear memories of that time. This was my life now.

My class had been together for a long time, and I think we would have liked to serve with some familiar faces, but new recruits were generally assigned in small numbers to existing commands. We got parceled out to units all over Alliance space, and I was the only one sent to my new company.

A week after graduation I boarded a transport, and two months later I got bolted into a lander and blasted out into the upper atmosphere of Carson's World. It was the beginning of a long journey.

Chapter Four

Tau Ceti III
During Operation Achilles

"Cain, pull your troops back to the refinery. Fast. The whole company's falling back." Sergeant Barrick's voice. Great. That meant that all the officers were down.

I snapped out a series of orders to my acting fire team leaders, telling them to retreat in hundred yard intervals, one team covering the other while they fell back. Between the smoke and the confusion I couldn't be certain, but my best guess was the company had already lost about half its strength.

We were in the middle of Operation Achilles, the invasion of Tau Ceti III. That may have been its official name, but to us it was a fucked up mess, colloquially known as the Slaughter Pen.

It was my seventh mission since the Carson's World assault and I'd made the last three as assistant squad leader. A few days earlier an enemy frag grenade had made me acting squad leader. Sergeant Thompson wasn't dead, but with both legs blown off he wouldn't be leading the squad anymore either.

By this time the undeclared war we'd been fighting for fifteen months had become official. The Third Frontier War had begun in earnest, and we'd been pretty roughly handled so far. We'd lost two major land battles and a half-dozen mining colonies, and the navy had suffered a pretty serious defeat at the Algol warp gate. With the fleet on the run there were several dozen colonies cut off without support or resupply.

The war had been tough on my squad too. Wilson killed in the raid on Altair V. Kleiner dead on some miserable asteroid in the 61 Cygnus system – she was only hit in the leg, but decompression and cold killed her before we could do anything. Gessler, Andrews, Worton, and Stanson wounded and in the hospital. Will Thompson and I were the only ones remaining in the squad from the Carson's World mission to hit the dirt of Tau

Ceti III, and now there was only me.

The Tau Ceti III mission was supposed to be a big start toward regaining our momentum and turning the tide. Instead, it almost lost us the war.

The planet was the Caliphate's largest and most important colony. Operation Achilles was the most ambitious planetary attack ever attempted. The initial landing by four full assault battalions was supported by a division of regular marines, British special forces, planetary militias drafted from nearby systems, a couple units of allied Russian commandos – almost 25,000 troops in all. Achilles took every ship Fleetcom could muster plus three dozen civilian craft commandeered for the operation.

Everything went wrong from the start.

The huge concentration of Fleet units managed to take out the orbital and ground-based installations, albeit at a heavy cost. Then, it was our turn – over 2,000 assault troops in the first wave.

About five minutes after we launched we realized that the bombardment had been a lot less effective than the reports had indicated. The enemy had a prepared network of strongpoints connected by deep tunnels, and it turned out these were mostly untouched.

First came salvo after salvo of surface to air missiles, launched from super-hardened underground silos that had survived the orbital attack. Our launch procedure was designed for an assault against heavy resistance, and the sky was filled with debris, decoys, and every manner of ECM device. They still managed to shoot down about 15% of our landing ships.

The initial plan called for us to secure a perimeter and set up a makeshift landing area for the heavy forces. As soon as we hit ground the word came down – we had to take out some of those missile sites first, assaulting the bunkers one by one.

The logic was sound – if they'd managed to shoot down 15% of our agile 5-man landers the heavy troopships and tank carriers would get blown away. But it still meant launching a series of search and destroy missions against very long odds. Infantry, even powered infantry, going up against an enemy armed with tanks and artillery can expect to take it hard. And we did. Very hard.

To make matters worse, while our troops were hitting the missile sites the enemy was hitting us, trying to snuff out our foothold before we could bring in reinforcements. The fighting went on for three days without a break. It was a damn close race, but we just managed to knock out enough of their missile capacity that the General decided to launch the phase two landing. By that time most of our units on the ground were down to 50% strength.

Air cover was critical during these early days. We had established total air superiority over the entire planet on the first day. Atmospheric fighters launched from our orbiting fleet carriers conducted continuous sorties throughout those first three days, providing crucial support to our efforts on the ground and annihilating the enemy air forces.

The high command had been certain about our control of the sky, but the enemy had another surprise ready when the first wave of heavy landing ships came in. They had maintained a large reserve of aircraft in a hidden underground base, and these were launched in a single massive strike against the inadequately escorted landers. They were mostly antiquated cargo planes reconfigured to carry batteries of close range air-to-air sprint missiles. Against fighters they would have been annihilated, but as launch platforms targeting landers armed only with point defense lasers the result was disaster – less than half of the first wave made it to the surface. In addition to the loss of almost 3,000 troops and 80 tanks, the attack resulted in the destruction of a large percentage of our available landing craft, retarding our ability to get the rest of the force down to the surface.

Fleetcom responded quickly, and Admiral Scheer scrambled every atmospheric fighter we had. They didn't arrive in time to save the landers, but they did manage to intercept the enemy aircraft as they were returning to base. Outgunned, outclassed, and low on fuel, the enemy planes were wiped out.

While the air battle was raging, the enemy launched another full scale attack all along our perimeter. We had to fight desperately to hold on while feeding in reinforcements from the surviving landing craft. We came very close to being overrun, but just as our lines were caving in at all points a wave of our refueled and rearmed aircraft halted the enemy attack. I have to commend the pilots. They flew mission after mission, utterly disregarding the devastating AA fire, and they saved our asses.

By planetary nightfall, the enemy was pulling back to their starting positions. Our casualties were high, not least among the fighters, who lost a third of their number in six hours of sustained combat, on top of 50% casualties they had suffered previously in the campaign. Only one in three were still flying.

My company had been assigned to landing facility construction and defense, so we had suffered comparatively few losses to this point. We hadn't seen any combat until that afternoon when the enemy almost penetrated to the landing areas. Even then we were defending prepared positions, and my squad suffered only two casualties – both wounded. But one of these was Will Thompson, and when he went down I inherited the squad.

With many of the heavily engaged units down to 25% of their initial strength, our company was rotated into the front lines the next morning. We marched through a hellish scene of destruction, and the ground was so cratered and full of debris it was difficult to make progress, even in armor. But we picked our way methodically through the wreckage and the ravaged landscape, and we reached our assigned position right on schedule.

My squad took over a section of the jagged trench line about 200 meters long from the two survivors of the original defending unit. I positioned the Squad Auto Weapon in the center of our line and the rocket launcher in reserve, ready to deploy as needed. Then we watched and waited.

There had been heavy action here, and looking around you could see where the area had been shelled pretty heavily. The trench itself was partly collapsed in several spots, where hasty repairs had been made, but no materials for bracing were available. You could dig like a backhoe in armor, but you still couldn't stop dirt from caving in, especially when it is getting pounded by artillery.

All of our dead and wounded seemed to have been evac'd, but looking out across the plain in front of the position at amp factor three I could see at least 20 enemy bodies, or parts of bodies, scattered around.

It seems to me that the smart call would have been to cancel the mission and begin the withdrawal. I realize that I'm looking back with perfect hindsight now, and it's a dead certainty that no one in the high command asked for my opinion. But we'd already lost almost 30% of the ground forces and two-thirds of the atmospheric fighters, and all we had to show for it was a sixteen kilometer radius foothold.

But like I said, the high command didn't consult me...or anyone else on the ground, I'd wager. So we spent two days manning a trenchline on the outskirts of the LZ while our sadly depleted flotilla of landing craft brought down the rest of the invasion force. During this period things were very quiet. The enemy, just as badly battered as we were and having failed to stop the landings, used the time to regroup their own scattered and exhausted units. We'd exchanged only sporadic fire and had no new casualties.

I was probably one of the only unit commanders to have more troops than he started with, though of course I didn't start as a unit commander at all. Our company still hadn't suffered too badly at this point, but the losses we had taken had fallen disproportionately on the non-coms, so Captain Fletcher reorganized the company. I'm pretty sure she wanted a veteran noncom running every squad, and there were some that would have been under a senior private if she didn't move things around. I ended up with 3 four man fire teams instead of two with five men each, so there were thirteen of us including me.

I did my best to make sure my three teams had someone experienced in charge, but I only had one other corporal, so two of them ended up with senior privates in command. Team two was under Harris, who was up for a bump to corporal anyway, so I stuck close to team three since it was under the most junior leader.

Our section of trench overlooked the ruins of a small city,

really an industrial complex with an attached residential area. It had been bombarded from space, and we'd hit it a number of times with land-based ordnance too, so the place was in pretty rough shape. Of course Fleet could have flattened it completely, but we actually wanted to take it, not destroy it, so the barrage had been limited.

I knew the complex was going to be our objective, and I didn't like what I saw. We were about three kilometers out, and the approach was mostly flat and open. Our position was slightly uphill from the town, but there were no intervening ridges or cover. The ground, which was originally covered with scrubby grass that looked like some type of Earth transplant, was churned up and pockmarked from the shelling.

"Display unit status reports." My non-com armor had enhanced AI with voice-activated control - a nice improvement over the buttons and levers in a private's suit.

"Displaying requested data now." The AI's voice was calm and somewhat mechanical sounding. It had some type of minor accent I couldn't quite place. No doubt some task force spent a long time figuring the ideal combination of cost-effectiveness and psychology. Or something like that.

The default projection area was just above eye level, so the data didn't obscure the ability to see through the visor. But rolling my eyes upward always gave me a headache, so I'd reconfigured the system to project information below, so I could look down rather than up.

I scanned the blue holographic symbols as my AI cycled through reports of each member of my expanded squad. Everybody looked good. Two had minor damage to their armor, but nothing serious and, just as relevant, there was nothing we could do anything about anyway. One trooper was running a slight fever, but if it got any worse his suit would automatically medicate. All weapons checked out and were loaded and fully functional.

I knew things would get started soon when other units began moving up and taking position around us. It looked like the whole battalion, or what was left of it, was forming up. My AI

gave me very limited information outside of my own unit, but
the best I could figure there were about 300 troops supported by
6 light tanks to attack along a ten kilometer front.

Just before dark on our second day manning the trenchline I got my answers when Captain Junius, who was running
the whole battalion at this point, came through the comlink.
"Squad leaders, prepare to assault the objective."

He paused for a minute - probably interrupted by his own
message from higher up - and then continued. "We're going
to hit the place with a fast, hard bombardment, and then we
advance. I want the lead units - Cain, Warren, Stanton, that's
your squads - to move fast. Use the torn up ground for cover,
but get your asses up there ASAP! You'll have supporting units
right behind you, so if you get bogged down you'll stall the
attack, and we'll get bunched up."

He went on for about ten minutes, giving instructions to
each squad leader and reminding us at least five times that speed
was the key to taking the objective. After he was done, I spent
a few minutes staring out at the terrain for the thousandth time,
punching up my visor to amp 10 to compensate for the failing
light, and then gave orders to my team leaders.

About an hour later the barrage began. We were too close to
the enemy for orbital bombardment, but we had several ground-
based artillery batteries as well as the company mortar teams,
and they all unloaded at once.

The night sky was instantly illuminated as rounds impacted
all along the front edge of the objective. We knew the enemy
was there in some force, and it was a good bet they had some
ordnance of their own, but they didn't return any fire.

After about five minutes of conventional fire the batteries
switched over to incendiary and smoke, and as soon as they did
we got the order to advance.

The field ahead of us was a maelstrom of fire and dense
clouds of smoke. The night and smoke obscured visibility,
while the incendiary rounds interfered with heat and infrared
guided fire.

"Let's go!" I snapped out the command, surprised at how

cool and calm I sounded, and jumped over the edge of the trench. "All teams advance 500 meters and grab some cover. Remember, zigzag approach - no straight lines! And move it, but keep low."

After I finished issuing commands, I focused on getting myself up 500 meters. I ran an irregular pattern, trying to move as quickly as possible while staying crouched. The ground was a little more rugged than it looked, but it was no big deal in armor, and it took us less than two minutes to reach the first position.

There was heavy fire, but it was random and not aimed. The bombardment was doing its job, at least for the moment. Still, a quick glance at the unit status display showed I had two troopers down. The data showed both as flatline, though that didn't mean they were necessarily dead. Maybe their armor was just damaged and not transmitting life scans. Maybe.

As I moved forward I spotted a good-sized crater and headed for it, diving in as an enemy mortar round exploded way too close for comfort. The crater was about ten feet deep, and the high water table meant it was half full of watery muck.

"Teams one and three, move forward 500 meters and take cover. Team two, hold 90 seconds and advance 500 meters." I still sounded like a rock. It's amazing how much of command really boils down to some type of bullshit.

We continued to advance, and we started firing once we were within 1,500 meters. Our fire was as blind as theirs, and they had the cover of the town besides, but we wanted them to have as much to worry about as possible.

They had dug a shallow trench just outside the built up area, but our artillery had really hit it hard, and when we reached it there were only two defenders left standing, and two of my teams tore them to pieces with fire.

With all my troopers in the trench I did another quick check and was stunned to see we hadn't lost anyone else. I took a few seconds to look into the complex. Stanton's squad was advancing on my right, moving toward a cluster of small buildings that looked like some type of storage. I couldn't tell for sure, but it looked like they'd taken more losses on the advance than us.

There was a forest of piping and tubes in front of my squad - some type of refinery or something. Visibility was poor. The scattered fires provided some light, but interfered with infrared scanners. My suit's AI combined the infrared and visual data to give me a computer-generated enhanced image. It wasn't great, but it was a hell of a lot better than anything my eyes could have produced.

I couldn't see any enemy positions, but that didn't mean there weren't any. There was a small metal shed that looked like some sort of control building about 200 meters in, and I sent team one to take it. The rest of the squad stood fast, providing covering fire and scanning for any enemy movement.

They moved up out of the trench and started toward the building. There was some scattered fire, but nothing heavy, and within two minutes they reported back that the building was empty.

"Team two, advance to the storage tank to the left of team one. Team three, on me!" I knew there were units right on our heels, so I leapt out of the trench and ran toward a dense collection of vertical pipes that would offer decent cover and a vantage point to get a look deeper into the complex. The fire was very light, and I couldn't see any enemy troopers until I was almost up to my objective. I saw him half a second before he saw me. He was running across my field of fire, clearly separated from his withdrawing unit. I whipped around my mag rifle and fired on full auto, hitting him with at least ten projectiles just as he was launching a spread of grenades in my direction.

My shots ripped through his bronze colored armor and tore the top half of him to shreds, but not before the first two grenades were loosed. I paused for an instant to see my shots hit the target instead of diving for cover, and I felt myself flying through the air as the grenades hit just off to my left.

I could hear the fragments impacting on my armor, making a dull clanging sound . My training took over and even before I hit the ground I was watching the electric blue numerals of the damage display projected in front of my eyes. Good...nothing penetrated my armor. I was unhurt and everything seemed to be fully operational. Damn lucky. Stupid, but lucky. If I'd hit the deck sooner, rather than waiting to see my shots hit I'd have dodged the impact entirely.

I ended up face down about three meters from where I was, lying pretty much out in the open. There was a small crater about six feet away that would make a decent foxhole. I twisted my body and rolled into my makeshift cover, and then I scanned 360 degrees to get my bearings.

The grenades had ripped up the piping where I had been standing, and one torn off section was billowing a vast cloud of something that looked like sickly green steam, blocking my view of the rest of the team.

"Team three, sound off! Condition and location!"

One by one all four of them responded. They were all unhurt and in position. That's good at least. Apparently I was the only idiot to walk into enemy fire. I ordered team three to hold fast while I checked on the rest of the squad.

"Team two, report!"

The second team ran into a few defenders at the storage tank. They'd taken them all out, but Anderson had taken a hit. She wasn't badly wounded, but her suit took a lot of damage, and she probably wasn't going to be able to keep up when we advanced. I prompted my AI to display the diagnostic. No, no way she was going to be able to keep fighting. Not without major repairs to her armor.

"Anderson, fall back toward the aid station. Stay low until you get back to the trench. The fire's pretty light, but don't get careless on me now."

She paused just a second, and I knew she wanted to argue with me that she could stay with us. But if there is one thing they beat into your head it's that you don't argue with your commander in the middle of a battle.

"Yes, Corporal Cain." Her tone was dejected but firm. "On my way."

Team one's report was straightforward. They were deployed around the control building and were taking sporadic and ineffective enemy fire from a ridge outside of the complex, just within small arms range.

We were spread out in a semi-circular arc running about 120 meters from the storage tank, past the control building, to the section of pipes behind me. I was ten meters ahead of the line in a makeshift foxhole in the middle of what had once been a street.

The refinery had taken a lot of damage, and up ahead of us there were a number of tanks that had been ruptured, and one that was burning fiercely, pouring a dense black smoke into the air.

There were some structures that would provide moderate cover, but the approach to the ridgeline was completely exposed for the last 1,000 meters at least. If they were going to defend that at all - and it was the best spot to put up a fight if they weren't going to just turn tail and run - they could give us a tough time.

Team 3 had the SHW, but I had given team 2 the SAW. I had a good view of their position from my foxhole. There was a walkway around the top of the tank that was high enough to provide a great firing position against the ridge.

"Jax, get Himmer up on that catwalk with the auto-gun. You see that spot on the northeast end? There's some type of heavy equipment right there that should make pretty good cover. On my command I want that ridge hosed down with fire. Put one other trooper up there too, and you position yourself on the far side. Find yourself a decent spot, and make sure to keep an eye on the position of squad 3 over there. We don't have time to sweep this place carefully, and I don't want any surprises on either flank. I'm covering the right and you've got the left."

"Understood, sir," came the crisp, clear reply. No hesitation from Jax. He was a good soldier, probably better than me. He'd joined the squad right after my first mission, and he was a natural from the beginning. I had the seniority, so I ended up taking over when the sergeant got hit, but if I went down I knew Jax could handle the squad every bit as well as I could.

I had team one advance from the control building toward

the edge of town. They had a row of low structures providing good cover, and it was only 90 seconds or so before they were in position. I was leaving team two in place to provide supporting fire from the top of the storage tank. Once we advanced on the ridge they would follow and form a reserve to plug any holes.

I scrambled up out of my foxhole and dashed across the open street area to the cover of a large building that looked like some type of storage shed or garage. Once in place I ordered team three to follow me, and we made our way cautiously down the street in ten meter intervals, hugging the buildings on our left for cover. The structures were ugly as hell, dull gray plasti-steel mostly - drab, industrial, and half wrecked besides. The entire place was utilitarian and shoddy, and now it was a burning wreck as well.

I was a little nervous because we really didn't have the time to properly sweep the complex. We'd scanned the whole area, of course, but between the fires and the leaking chemicals we couldn't be sure we hadn't missed anything. I didn't relish the thought of being ambushed from behind just as we assaulted that ridge.

"Jax, I'm a little worried about what might be hiding out in these buildings. I'm going to keep your team back for an extra 15 minutes. If anything we don't know about shows itself, it's your responsibility."

"Sir!" Damn, Jax always sounded so cool and under control. I wondered for a minute if he'd ever thought that about me, and if Jax's calm were as fake as my own.

I had 8 troopers lined up along the edge of the complex and another 3 positioned to provide supporting fire. I coordinated with the squad leaders on each of my flanks, and we synchronized our actions. We each had our heavy auto-guns positioned to put the ridge under fire, and we'd give the order to open fire 30 seconds before we jumped off with the assaulting troops.

I counted the last few seconds and gave Jax the order to commence firing. I could hear the distant high pitched whine of the auto-gun and see the stream of fire as it raked all along the ridge line. The auto-gun projectiles became superheated by the atmosphere and glowed a reddish yellow. I knew the fire was a stream of tiny iridium and depleted uranium darts fired at enormous velocity, but it looked like some sort of death ray from a space opera vid, especially in the darkness.

My AI gave me a five second warning and I braced myself. Four, three, two, one. "Squad...attack!" We all leapt to the top of the trench and ran toward the ridgeline as quickly as we could without jumping too high and offering the enemy a tempting target.

I could hear the auto-gun fire as it passed over my head moving to the right. I resisted the urge to scrunch my head down away from the deadly stream of projectiles. But I needn't have been worried. Our unit was well trained, and the gun operator knew perfectly well we were advancing below his field of fire. Still, it's an unpleasant feeling.

But the support fire was doing us a world of good. With three auto-guns firing full out, whatever enemy troops were on that ridgeline were more worried about grabbing cover than shooting at us. My troops made it almost to the top before we took a casualty, and I think the other squads had similar luck.

That luck changed just as soon as we reached the top. The enemy fire was still sporadic, but I had one trooper wounded. Wells. Her armor was holed and she had a pretty serious leg wound, but the suit had patched her up enough to stabilize things. She wasn't going to walk out of here, though, so I told her to find cover and wait for evac.

Then the command coms went crazy. First it was Major Greene, who had taken charge of the entire assault brigade. Her voice was calm and firm, but I could hear the exhaustion in it. "Enemy activity south of the complex. Infantry with armor support advancing. Cain, Warren, Stanton - I'm commandeering your support elements in the town."

Great. So I'd lost Jax's team and my fire support. I had seven troops left, including myself.

Next on the com was Lieutenant Gianni, who was now in command of our company. "Activity on the right. Large numbers of infantry advancing from the wooded areas."

I looked over, and at first I couldn't see anything. But then I could make out the figures moving forward in the darkness. I cranked up my visor to amp 20 and told my AI to clean up the blurry image as much as possible.

It was infantry, all right. Not powered infantry, just troops wearing simple body armor. Probably militia. Hundreds of them. Charging the ridgeline off to the right of my position.

And dying. Dying in huge swaths as our troops raked their lines with fire. Their armor, weight constrained by the need to carry the load under their own power, was no match for the high velocity fire of our nuclear-powered mag-rifles. Our shots tore them to pieces. I even saw a couple who virtually disintegrated as they walked into multiple fields of fire.

They returned fire, of course, but their guns didn't have the atomic power source ours did, and they needed pretty much a perfect shot to penetrate our armor. Still, I suspected some of their shots were finding their mark.

I had my six troopers deployed to receive an attack, and we were just waiting for the enemy to reach our fire zone when I got the fallback order from Sergeant Barrick. So whatever damage the enemy had managed to do, they must have taken out Lieutenant Gianni.

"Alright, let's move. We're pulling out. Odds fall back 500 meters, evens cover." I was the second in line, so I stood fast and took some very long range potshots at the approaching militia while the odds followed my order and scrambled down the ridge.

"Ok, evens. Let's go. One thousand meters. Now!" The other two evens and I raced down the ridge, stopping when we reached the edge of the town and turning to give cover to the odds.

I wanted us back in the town as quickly as possible, so we wouldn't be withdrawing under serious fire from the militia. But the squads on each flank were lagging us, so once I got everyone back to the edge of the complex I formed a firing line so we could provide support as they pulled back.

The squad on our left made it back just after we did, but it was clear that the troops on our right had been heavily engaged along the ridgeline and were having a tough time breaking off. I was just about the request permission to move back up and try to flank the militia attacking them when the recall signal came.

It was code white recall, which was a directive to withdraw immediately to the extraction area. I knew what to do from training, but I'd never actually experienced a code white command. It wasn't a rout. Not quite. But it was close enough.

"Alright troops, we've got a priority withdrawal order. Code white. We're going to move back through the town, using those buildings as cover just like we did on the way up."

We snaked our way through the town, single file at ten meter intervals. We lost Tonnelle, who got hit by an enemy sniper just as we passed the main section of the refinery. My readouts said he was dead, but I sent the rest of the troops on ahead and crawled back to check. Yeah. Dead.

I knew that sniper was still active, so I stayed low and hugged the buildings as I worked my way back to the outskirts of the town and into the trench line we'd assaulted just a few hours before. Jax was there along with one of his men, Russell. The two of them were the only ones who made it back from team two, and they'd had to abandon the auto-gun.

The battle computers running command and control continually adjusted the communications echelons to account for casualties and automatically routed messages accordingly. Apparently we'd lost enough officers to bump me onto the main command channel.

"Attention all command personnel, this is Colonel Wight provisionally commanding Strike Force Achilles. This is a priority one evacuation. We have hostile naval forces inbound from the Vesta warp gate. The fleet is bugging out before it can be engaged by superior enemy forces. You have 30, that's three zero, minutes to get your troops back to the staging area. Command control will download specific location to your AIs. Get your troops there on time, because in 60 minutes the last shuttle is launching, and anyone left here is SOL."

Colonel Wight? She must have been six places down on

the command chart. Seven, my AI reminded me without my asking. So things hadn't been any easier on the high command than they'd been on the rest of us. Actually, I found out later it was mostly communications failures that put her in temporary command. General Everest was killed, and Brigadier Simonsen was wounded, but most of the rest of the top echelons made it through.

The colonel's voice continued, firm but strained. "Reports indicate that the enemy is putting pressure on us at all points. It looks like the hostile ground forces knew the relief was coming. We hurt them pretty badly, and it doesn't look like they have a lot of strength left, but it's probably going to be a fighting with-drawal for us. If we left rear guards they'd never make it back in time to evac, so we're just going to fall back as quickly as we can, fighting the whole way. Do the best you can, and let's get home."

As soon as she finished, my AI chimed in and advised that I'd received our specific rally coordinates. They automatically popped up on my holo display. Hmmm, not far from where we set out a couple days ago. I got my little band up and out of the trench and across the field we'd advanced over a few hours before. We were lucky again, and we didn't see much enemy fire. The troops on our right - well, actually our left I guess, since our front had changed 180 degrees - seemed to be taking the brunt of the attack.

I kept checking my chronometer and the distance to the extraction point. We were OK, barely, but we didn't have any time to waste, so I didn't even pause at the original trench line. We just hopped over and headed back the way we'd advanced to the front.

The ground was torn up even worse than it had been a couple days before, and even in armor we lost time as we scrambled in and out of craters filled with neck-deep water and muck. The strength amplification of the armor let you power your way through the mud, but it didn't stop you from sinking in with every step.

Twice I had to halt the group so we could turn and engage

enemy militia who had caught up to firing range. Both times we hosed them down with heavy fire and they broke and ran. It didn't cost us much time, but every minute counted. I knew those deadlines were real. If the fleet was really in danger they weren't going to risk it to pick up the shattered remnants of a strikeforce. It was brutal mathematics - marines were cheaper and easier to replace than battleships. They'd stay as long as they could...and not a minute longer.

I was surprised that we'd managed to retreat back to the staging area without losing anyone. I'd been waiting for the enemy to hit us hard. If they'd have launched a major attack while we were all retreating, none of us would have gotten off-planet. But the truth is we had just about won the land battle when the recall orders came. The enemy wasn't hitting us while we retreated because they didn't have anything left to hit us with. For all the missteps and enormously heavy casualties, Achilles was failing because we couldn't hold the space above the planet, not because we couldn't take the ground.

The rally area was a confused mess, with units straggling in from all directions and being loaded on whatever ship was available. Our group got hustled onto a tank landing shuttle that launched a few minutes after the hatches slammed shut behind us.

It was a rough ride to orbit. The ship wasn't built to hold infantry, and we were just hanging on however we could. The hold was silent. We all knew what a disaster the operation had been, and while none of us knew exactly how this affected the overall war, we had a pretty good idea it was bad.

We were right. It was bad. But I don't think any of us realized just how bad.

Chapter Five

AS Gettysburg
En route to Eta Cassiopeiae system

I was one of the 14.72% of the ground troops in Operation Achilles to return unwounded.

Technically speaking, I didn't exactly return because the Guadalcanal wasn't as lucky as I was. She'd taken a hit to her power plant during the initial approach, and she was still undergoing emergency repairs when the withdraw order was issued. There was no way she could outrun the enemy fleet on partial power, so she offloaded all non-essential personnel and formed part of the delaying force, holding off the attackers long enough to evacuate most of the surviving ground forces.

The way I heard it, the old girl wrote quite a final chapter for herself, taking out two enemy cruisers and damaging a third before she got caught in converging salvoes and was blown apart by a dozen missile hits.

I'd been on the Guadalcanal for three years, and it was surreal to think that she was gone. Captain Beck, Flight Chief Johnson, even that short little tech who used to play cards with us...I can't even remember his name. All dead.

But those losses seemed distant, theoretical, not quite real. We had plenty of empty places right in our own family. My battalion had landed with 532 effectives. There were 74 of us now.

The major was dead. Lieutenant Calvin was the only officer still fit for duty, so he took command of the battalion, a promotion tempered by the fact that he commanded only 24 more troops than he did when he'd led his platoon down to the surface just over a week before.

Captain Fletcher was wounded. I'd been bumped to sergeant the day after we embarked, and I was in temporary command of the company...all 18 of us. Getting missed has always been a good way to advance through the ranks.

We were loaded onto the Gettysburg with various remnants

of a dozen other units. It was a different world. The Guadalcanal had been a fast assault ship designed to carry a company of ground troops and their supplies. She'd carried about 60 naval personnel in addition to the 140 or so ground troops.

Gettysburg was a heavy invasion ship, carrying a full battalion along with a flight of atmospheric fighters, combat vehicles, and enough supplies for a sustained campaign. At least when fully loaded she did. Over a kilometer long, she was ten times the tonnage of the Guadalcanal.

But now she was carrying 198 troops, the remnants of 3 full assault battalions, along with a vastly depleted store of supplies and two surviving fighters - one hers and one from another carrier.

The fleet managed to escape with serious but not crippling losses, and once we were through the warp gate the massive assemblage started to break up, as assets were redeployed to meet various crises in different sectors.

And there were plenty of threats to deal with. We were on the run, and the enemy knew it. We'd stripped everything bare to mount Achilles, and now the enemy was trying to exploit our weakness.

It was obvious things were pretty bad, but we really knew the situation was desperate when we were rushed to the Eta Cassiopeiae system without any rest or even resupply. Eta Cassiopeiae was vital to us, a nexus with 5 warp gates, three leading to other crucial Alliance systems. Columbia, the second planet, was a key colony and base, and the moons of the fifth and sixth worlds were mineralogical treasure troves.

If they were rushing exhausted fragments of units there without refit, they were expecting the enemy to attack. Soon. So the troops got 48 hours to recover from the Slaughter Pen, while the 2 lieutenants and 6 sergeants available to command them worked out a provisional table of organization and discussed the best training regimen to get them fit for combat again in short order.

I ended up with 23 troops plus myself, divided into four normal fire teams and one three man group with a portable missile launcher, normally a company-level heavy weapon.

The ship was less than half full, so there was plenty of room in the gym and training facilities. We put everyone on double workout sessions, which caused a lot of grumbling. But it also kept everyone busy, without too much time to think - either about where we had been or where we were going.

Just like the Guadalcanal, the Gettysburg's training areas were near the exterior of the ship where the artificial gravity was close to Earth-normal. The deep interior of the vessel, which was close to a zero gravity environment, was dedicated to storage and vital systems.

A spaceship is far from roomy, even with half the normal number of troops present, so it was just as well to keep everyone busy whenever possible. Our expedited itinerary meant lots of extra time strapped into our acceleration couches with nothing to do but think and try to breath while you were being slowly crushed. So, when the troops were out of the couches, I was just as happy to have them working up a sweat as crawling off somewhere to brood on defeat.

Eta Cassiopeiae was three transits from Tau Ceti, and it took us about 6 weeks of maneuvering between warp gates before we emerged at our destination and another ten days to reach the inner system and enter orbit around Columbia.

Since we were reinforcing a world we already held, and not mounting an attack, we were spared the rough ride of a planetary assault. It was a good thing too, because there wasn't a single Gordon lander left on the Gettysburg. We ferried down in the two available shuttles, about 50 men at a time, landing at the spaceport just outside the capital city of Weston.

Columbia was a beautiful planet, mostly covered by one giant ocean and dotted with numerous small archipelagos. The single major continent, where 95% of the population lived, was a small oval chunk of ground just 500 kilometers north to south and less than 300 east to west. Situated in the temperate northern polar zone, its climate was almost perfect.

The small island chains, mostly located closer to the equatorial zone, were sparsely inhabited by a hardy breed of colonists who braved the intense heat to produce a variety of valuable products from the Columbian sea, including several useful drugs obtained from the native fish.

It was good to get off of a spaceship and have my feet touch the ground without someone shooting at me, a pleasure that was tempered by the knowledge that while we weren't attacking, we were almost certainly a target.

All my battles to date had been offensive. We were an assault battalion - that's what we were trained for, and that's what we did. But circumstances had put us on the defensive, and now we would get a chance to dig in and fire missiles at the enemy landers - all those things that looked so good when we were attacking. But now we had a different perspective and sitting as a target and waiting for the enemy to hit us, when and where he chose, didn't seem so appealing either. We were used to having the initiative, and I'm not sure trading it for a foxhole or two was such a good deal.

We'd also be alone, totally cut off on this planet to hold it or die. When we attacked we always controlled local space, and if the battle went against us we could retreat back to the ships. Operation Achilles had been a disaster, but it still ended with almost half of the troops evac'd, even if two-thirds of those were wounded.

But the Gettysburg was heading out as soon as the landing was complete. The navy simply couldn't mount a credible defense of the system. Not now. So the strategy was to dump as much force as possible on the planet and try to hold out until a relief force could arrive.

We were milling about the field, wearing our armor because that was the easiest way to transport it down, but with visors up and weapons systems powered down. Whatever else an attack might be, it wouldn't be a surprise. The warp point probes and the spy satellites in planetary orbit would give us plenty of warning when the enemy was inbound.

I knew from the briefing we'd received on the Gettysburg that the garrison commander was Colonel Elias Holm, a veteran marine who was now fighting his second war. He'd already added two new decorations to the glittering array of medals he'd been awarded during the Second Frontier War. It occurred to me that there was a good chance we'd be helping him win his third. Holm was a high-powered commander for this posting, but he was just what was needed to take a bunch of broken, demoralized units and forge them into an iron defense.

One of the heroes of the Corps, Colonel Holm was the subject of a number of legends and rumors, and we all expected some two and a half meter giant who breathed fire and walked on water. But the man striding our way from the command building could have been any one of us. A bit older, yes, with a head of close-cropped, thinning brown hair, sprinkled with gray. He was a touch under two meters tall, with a lean, muscular build. There was a faint scar running from his hairline all the way down the right side of his otherwise pleasant but careworn face.

Any sense of disappointment that Hercules himself did not step forward to greet us vanished when he stopped walking and started to speak. Everything I learned about truly being a leader started that day. His voice was warm and friendly, but also firm and commanding. "Welcome to Columbia." The man exuded confidence with every word, and just listening to him was inspiring. "I know all of you were in Operation Achilles, and you all deserve a long stretch of R & R after that clusterfuck. But the fortunes of war are not often what we would like them to be, and as marines we do what we must. Always."

He paused and looked us over. He wasn't wearing armor, just a standard gray and black field uniform, which was clean and neatly pressed, adorned with nothing but a simple Colonel's eagle on each shoulder. His black boots were shiny and neatly polished, except around the bottom where they were crusted with reddish mud.

"You marines are all veterans. Even if Achilles was your first drop you've earned that distinction now. So I'm going to give you a good idea of what we're up against. With you and the forces the Pericles dropped off yesterday we've got 1,242 regular troops, about half of which are fully-armored marines.

Most of rest of the frontline assault troops were at Tau Ceti like you, which means you're all under-supplied, and your command structures are shot to hell. We've also got 1,040 planetary militia who are well-trained and equipped. Columbia is a popular retirement spot, so the militia is well-leavened with marine vets. A lucky break. The militia also have 6 tanks...old Mark VI Pattons."

Ok, so we had about 2,300 troops. Probably more than I would have expected, especially considering how urgently they rushed less than 200 of us here. Of course everything depended on what they threw at us. This system was worth a considerable effort, but we just had no way of knowing what the enemy could bring to bear on us quickly or how hard they'd hit us from space before landing.

"We're going to get everyone billeted the best we can, and I'm going to try to give you Achilles people at least a little rest. I just don't know how long we have until we are attacked. It's possible we may not even be attacked," - yeah, sure - "but we will assume that we are a target. We are building defensive works around all the vital installations...trenches, strongpoints, and lots of underground bunkers and tunnels. A lot of that is already in place, and we're going to be working on the defense grid right up until the enemy starts landing."

So that "little rest" was going to be very little.

"We're going to man the positions with the militia and marine supporting units. All the powered infantry, plus the tanks, are going to be organized into four reaction forces. We're going to hide you underground in key spots and throw you at the enemy where you will do the most damage. You're going to be our ace in the hole, a mobile reserve that gives us the chance to surprise the attacker and take away some of his initiative."

A pretty daring strategy. The powered infantry was only a little over a quarter of our numbers, but we were well over half the overall strength and firepower. Pulling us all out of the fight at the start threatened to fatally weaken the defense, especially since the enemy would almost certainly be attacking with powered units themselves. But it gave us a real chance to win a decisive victory if things worked out. If the enemy fully committed to attacking the other units, we'd have one hell of a tactical surprise for them.

"All the Achilles people get the rest of the day to themselves. We'll get you billeted, and then I want you to grab some extra sack time. You're going to need it. Everyone's putting in 12 hours a day working on defenses - remember, a day here is 27.5 Earth hours - but you guys are going to do 8 with an extra 4 hours of rest. Starting tomorrow. Officers and sergeants, stow your suits and gear and report to the control center for a briefing in 30 minutes at 1300 hours."

About half a dozen non-coms had walked up behind him, and a burly sergeant began barking out instructions about getting us settled in. I told my senior corporal to see about the billeting, and I wandered over to where the rest of the unit commanders were already congregating.

A corporal led us to a maintenance shed where we were able to store our armor. I told the AI to pop my suit, and after asking me if I was sure (and I really hated having to repeat myself to a machine) it powered down the servo-mechanisms, and I could hear the latch-bolts sliding open.

The cool outside air felt great, and I climbed out, feeling as always a bit like a snail wiggling out of its shell. My kit was strapped to the back of my armor, and I opened it up and pulled out a uniform and boots. The room was full of naked marines doing the same thing. We got dressed, and our kits were moved to our billets while we headed over to the briefing dressed in wrinkled but clean gray field uniforms.

Mostly the colonel repeated what he had told us on the landing field, but we got a bit more detail. First, we got some hard intel. The enemy was definitely going to attack, and probably within the next two weeks. And it was going to be a significant force. We didn't have solid numbers, but it was a good bet we'd be hard-pressed to hold out.

Second, Colonel Holm had been far from idle. He'd had most of the civilians conscripted into labor battalions to help build defenses. The interlocking grid he had in mind was a lot closer to finished than I'd thought when he first mentioned it. Having just faced something very similar on Tau Ceti III, I wasn't about to underestimate the effectiveness of hardened defenses, especially under a commander like Holm.

Our supply situation wasn't ideal, particularly among the powered infantry units. Because our weapons had access to the energy generated by our suits, we were able to put out a lot of firepower. But this time we were low on ammunition, so we'd have to make our shots count. This was another reason why the colonel wanted to hold us as a surprise attack force. We'd be able to conserve ammo and use it when we could hit the hardest and make it count.

After the initial briefing we went into a question and answer session. The colonel asked for input and opinions, and then surprised me even more when he knew most of our names and could identify us by sight. This guy was one hell of a leader. Sometime in the last day or two he'd accessed the personnel files from the Gettysburg computer and committed to memory the face and name of just about every officer and non-com.

We spent the next two hours or so looking at maps, reviewing proposed deployments and going through a few scenarios for ways our units might exploit opportunities. This was the first time I'd ever been in on an overall battleplan, and it made an impression on me that Colonel Holm not only wanted to familiarize us with it, but he also asked for comments and input.

When we broke up I headed across the landing field to the billeting area. Our troops had been housed in what looked like a dormitory for workers. I had just about enough time to check on the troops before evening mess.

Everything checked out. The troops were all settled in. In fact, most of them had grabbed a couple hours sleep while we were at the briefing. Good. I wanted them to get as much rest as possible while they could. We'd had a lot of downtime on the Gettysburg, but resting on solid ground is different than on a spaceship. Between the variable gravity, the acceleration/deceleration periods, and very cramped quarters, rest on a ship was never very restful, at least it never was for me.

No one was still asleep when the mess hall opened though. Since it wasn't a combat landing we didn't have to do the intravenous feeding before, but they still didn't give us breakfast before we embarked, so it had been almost 24 hours since we'd eaten. Except what we'd stashed, of course. They didn't feed us, but we weren't under orders to avoid eating as we would be before a drop. And marines always have food stashed someplace. I'd eaten a couple energy bars I had stashed, and most of the troops were significantly better scroungers than I was.

After mess I went back to my billet and crashed. I only intended to rest for an hour or so, but I just passed out, and it was morning before I stirred. The rest did me some good, and when I got up I felt quite a bit better than I had.

I got the troops organized after breakfast mess and formed up on the field to get our work assignments. We could move mountains in our armor, but the fighting suit wasn't exactly designed for precision construction work, so we were ordered to report in our fatigues.

There was a curving line of large rocky hills - not quite small mountains - around the outskirts of the capital. Weston was certainly going to be a target of the attack, and the ridge line ran along the flank of any approach to the city. An enemy moving against Weston would be caught between the flanking force on one side and the sea on the other.

Between the hills and the ocean was a broad, flat expanse of plains, mostly used for agriculture by the colonists. It was really the only land approach, so the enemy would have to come that way if they wanted to hit the capital. And most of the planet's power generation and communications infrastructure was centered in Weston. If you wanted to control the planet you had to take the city.

Colonel Holm had constructed an extensive system of tunnels and underground bunkers beneath the hills, enough to hide at least 1,000 troops. Unfortunately, he only had about 600 of us to deploy there, so we didn't waste any time enlarging the network. Instead we worked on camouflaging the whole setup. If we could convince the enemy that they were only facing the entrenched militia in front of the city, we might achieve a real tactical surprise.

The tunnels were hopefully deep enough to avoid being detected by enemy scans, but it wasn't practical to dig far enough down to be sure. So the colonel ordered the hillsides seeded with powered Iridium, which included a sizable portion of radioactive Iridium 192. This would require a large cleanup later, but for now it would interfere with enemy scans of our position.

Rare on Earth, Iridium was one of Columbia's major exports, a fact very well known to the enemy, so hopefully our ploy wouldn't raise any undo suspicions.

We moved supplies and ammunition into the bunkers so they were ready to be occupied on a moment's notice. We even had a basic communications line creating a physical link between the main positions in the event that all our other comm was jammed.

Ten days later we got to test out our deployments for real. The monitoring satellites around warp gate two sent their warning via a relayed comm laser. The enemy was here.

There wouldn't be any naval battle; there wasn't an Alliance warship in the system. Columbia did have an orbital defense station and a string of x-ray laser satellites. The system was mostly automated, but there was a crew, and they had to realize that they were on a suicide mission. Without naval support there was no way that the planet's limited defense array could hold off a battlefleet.

The orbital fort's weapons, though limited in number, were heavier than those on any mobile platform, so the enemy would have to enter the station's range to attack it. At least the crews would get to fight back before they were overwhelmed and destroyed. Small comfort, but something at least.

It took two days for the incoming fleet to reset its vector and reach attack range. By the time they engaged the station, my men and I were deployed deep in our bunkers. I followed the battle in space on the command comm line, with my AI displaying some helpful graphics on my visor.

The orbital station was essentially a missile platform, and

the weapons it fired were multi-stage, with a significantly greater effective range than shipboard equivalents. Before the enemy got to its own launch range, our missiles were already entering their point defense zone. The station fired all 200 of its weapons, and 16 of them found targets. One CAC battleship was destroyed, and four other capital ships were heavily damaged.

The return salvo was a little ragged as only one of the damaged ships was able to immediately fire. But there were still over 300 missiles inbound, and with no maneuverability the result was a mathematical inevitability. The station's countermeasures were very effective. Short-ranged pulse lasers savaged the incoming spread, and point defense missiles detonated, strewing the path of the incoming projectiles with FLAK.

Even with almost 90% interception, 40 enemy missiles hit the fortress, and it vanished in the nuclear inferno. In the confusion we thought that some of the crew managed to evacuate in time using one of the shuttles, but I found out months later that this never happened.

Before the missiles hit, the station activated the laser satellites. Each one of these was a bomb-pumped x-ray laser. One-shot weapons, they were powerful enough to destroy a major ship on a single good shot. There were 40 of them, and they fired within 30 milliseconds of each other.

There are effective countermeasures against laser-fire, mostly torpedoes loaded with a cloud of crystalline debris that we called Angeldust, which reflected and diffused the incoming laser energy. While effective in theory, it is very hard to time the use of a physical defense system against a weapon coming in at lightspeed, and the CAC task force never even got off a shot. Half a dozen enemy support ships were vaporized, and the lead battleship was holed in three places and knocked out of the formation.

The space-based defenses had acquitted themselves well, causing far more damage than we'd dare hoped. The enemy battlefleet was in very rough shape, but it didn't do much for us on the ground. The assault craft had been kept back out of range, and they were completely undamaged. If we'd had a task force available we could have seriously contested the space above Columbia, but all we could do now was sit and watch while they bombarded the surface and readied the landing.

It didn't take long before the enemy was in orbit and the bombing began. I'm not sure whether they wanted the planet intact or if the damage they'd suffered drastically reduced their firepower, but the bombardment was short and relatively ineffective. Our bunker shook a few times as shots impacted nearby on the surface, but we took no real damage at all, and from the chatter on the command circuit I could tell that even the entrenched units on the surface had suffered only light casualties and some minor disorder.

Columbia didn't have much in the way of ground-based defenses, so there really weren't many targets but the troops themselves. It was hard to do too much damage to entrenched infantry from space without totally wasting the planet, so once they'd knocked out the few anti-air batteries we had, the landings began.

Sitting in the bunker I flashed back to the nine times I'd stepped into a launch bay before an assault. Today the enemy was doing that, and we were waiting...as they had for me so many times.

I knew the assault would be virtually unopposed. First, we really didn't have much in the way of effective weapons systems against incoming landers. Second, I knew Colonel Holm wanted to get them on the surface and trick them into underestimating our true strength so we could ambush them. He wasn't about to make us look stronger by putting up a futile defense against the initial assault.

The colonel had managed to hide a couple of surface-to-air sprint missile launchers from the bombardment and, as much for show as for effect, we did launch a bit of an attack on the landing craft. Our fire was actually pretty effective and we took out nine ships, and we forced the rest to scatter into a defensive approach, disordering their landing pattern.

The CAC landers were bigger than our Gordons, each carrying one of their 18-man tac-teams. So that was over 150 casualties before they hit ground. Not bad considering we really didn't have much of an air defense.

The tactical computers were furiously analyzing the size of the landing, and the tonnage and number of assault vessels in orbit to create a projection of the attacking force. When that estimate came it matched my own unofficial one - we were facing a brigade-sized attack force.

A CAC brigade was about 6,500 strong, divided into ten of their tac-forces plus supporting elements. CAC tac-forces were the rough equivalent to one of our battalions. Based on their standard organization, two of those tac-forces would be fully-powered infantry and the rest normal line troops, though the exact setup was mission-variable. There was a good chance they would have a higher proportion of assault units for an attack like this.

The enemy's landing zone was centered on a flat plain about 10 kilometers from Weston, well within range of our infantry's mortars and rocket launchers, which immediately opened fire and caused significant casualties while the attacking units were forming up to advance. Their corresponding formations deployed quickly and began returning the fire. We were entrenched and they weren't, but there were a lot more of them. I wasn't in the line of command to get streaming casualty reports from the surface, but it was likely we were starting to take losses.

The enemy could have deployed a greater distance from Weston, and out of our initial fire range. We hadn't positioned any defenses further out. But they'd decided to trade casualties for time, accepting some additional losses to position themselves to attack immediately. CAC doctrine was considerably more tolerant of losses than ours, and if a battle was won there was little concern for the casualties it took to secure that victory.

The attack force formed up very quickly and began its advance. Impressive discipline, much better than most CAC forces. Not a good sign - these were well drilled troops. Our forces on the surface were going to have their hands full.

The enemy approach was pretty much straight out of the book. Any advance out in the open would become a bloody mess almost immediately, so standard tactics called for unloading everything you could against the defenders to give them something to worry about other than shooting you.

It was also helpful for the attacker to obscure battlefield conditions as much as possible. We had state of the art targeting systems, battle computers, and enhanced optics, but all of these resources were subject to degradation. Dust and smoke interfered with laser targeting, and once the battlefield was full of heat sources clear scanning became much more difficult.

The CAC support units blasted our positions with mortars, rockets, and several batteries of small artillery pieces while their infantry advanced. The enemy troops used the craters and irregularities of the ground to leapfrog their advance, just as we would, but the CAC forces were far less cautious than any of our units. They rushed their advance, covering more ground in each push - at the cost of additional time exposed and heavier casualties.

I certainly didn't approve of their priorities, but I had to admit that they closed the distance to our troops very quickly. Their first wave was barely a kilometer from the first defensive line, and the second was landed and almost formed up.

The troops manning the trenches were mostly militia. About half the unarmored marine units were thrown in for stiffening, and the other half were positioned in the rear as a ready reserve.

The attackers seemed to be suffering losses considerably in excess of projected rates, but it wasn't until they were fully engaged with our forces that we got the full report. The enemy had no powered infantry units and no fighting vehicles. That was a surprise. They still had the numbers to overwhelm our apparent defenses, but they would suffer far greater casualties. Probably three-quarters of the hits that took down one of their troops would have deflected off powered armor.

Oblivious to the enormous losses they were suffering, the leading units began to assault our positions, overrunning the sparsely deployed defenders. Our defensive lines were designed to draw the enemy in so we could hit them from behind once they were fully committed. The strategy worked - almost too well - and the attackers sliced through our first three lines in several places.

The assault force had suffered at least 1,500 casualties, but they kept up the pressure, and the combat intensity increased significantly. The colonel shifted reserves constantly, launching focused counter attacks wherever there was a vulnerability. The CAC support units kept firing even after the lines were intermingled, and they took out as many of their own troops as ours. But they had a 6-1 edge on the surface and could take the losses. We couldn't.

I kept waiting for the colonel to give us the order to move out. The enemy was heavily committed, with only support units and a few guards in the rear. It was perfect timing. But nothing. Not so much as a squad was committed from the flanking force. I couldn't understand. Our troops on the surface were getting shredded, but we just sat.

My AI updated the projections on my visor. The enemy had pushed back to our final line of defenses. We'd bled them, but our units were down to 50% strength and running low on supplies. The situation was beyond critical, but still no orders to advance.

Holm did throw in the half dozen tanks, and they helped stabilize the line at the weakest spot, but it had turned into a bloody knife fight, and we weren't going to win it. I had just asked myself for the tenth time why we were just sitting here when my AI said, in its usual robotic voice, "Landing craft inbound."

Fuck. Another wave. We were in serious trouble.

My visor projections were updated in real time. The incoming ships were landing about ten kilometers back from the initial zone. Damn, if we'd launched our attack they'd be hitting us in the rear. How the hell did the colonel know? Did he have the discipline and will to hold us back on a hunch while he was getting slammed on the surface?

We got the orders now. Prepare to attack the incoming force, but do not give away our position until given the word. We checked weapons for about the fifth time and moved out into the egress tunnels. Waiting in the tunnels we got the update on the new landing force, and the news wasn't good. Four tac-forces, more than 2,000 troops, and all powered infantry. If we'd been committed already we wouldn't have a chance. Now we were just outnumbered 3-1, which was at least better odds than our guys in the trenches had. At least we had surprise on our side.

The enemy advanced straight toward the city, through their original LZ and over the pockmarked battlefield. When they were passing our exit tunnels we sent out our lead units and engaged them on the flank. We had surprise and they had num-bers, so we knew we had to hit hard and make the most of the initial assault.

My team - I'm not sure platoon was the right word for my little group - was positioned in the last wave. I chafed at sitting and waiting while our troops were fighting against such desper-ate odds, but I had my orders. We could only deploy so quickly through these tunnels anyway, so there wasn't really another option.

I continued to watch the battle unfold on my visor, with con-stant updates feeding in. Our flank attack took them completely by surprise, and our lead elements inflicted massive casualties and completely disordered the enemy's left flank. The third wave's advance stopped dead in its tracks, as they attempted to turn and face our attack.

We pushed them back, and our lead units followed up aggressively. Surprise was our biggest advantage and we wanted to keep them off-balance as long as possible. Once they man-aged to regroup and bring their numbers to bear, we'd catch hell. One to one we were better than them, but this fight wasn't one to one, it was three to one.

We also needed to make this a quick fight. We were extremely short on supplies, and the aggressive attack was using up what we had quickly. The ammunition we had was being well used at least. These were tight quarters for a fight like this, and our fire was having tremendous effect.

My group finally emerged from the tunnels into a sunken ravine running perpendicular to the enemy's formation, between the main row of hills and a rocky ridgeline. It was a well-chosen spot, and the ridge shielded us from the enemy and the fight currently going on.

My orders were to set up a defensive position along the ridge. I had an assigned section, with other groups on either side of me. The colonel himself came on the comlink and outlined the plan. The engaged powered infantry forces were going to pull back behind the ridge to regroup. He was hoping to goad the enemy into attacking the ridgeline, where we were preparing a warm reception for them. If they took the bait we'd hit them with everything we had, while the withdrawing units reorganized and formed a reserve.

My section of the line was the most critical. There was a 500 meter break in the ridge where the ground was flat and open. On either side there were large rock formations that made the ridgeline almost impassable, channeling any advance through the narrow opening. A large number of our retiring troops were going to come through there, hopefully with the enemy on their heels.

I sent the team with the heavy rocket launcher to the rear, back on the main row of hills. I told them to find three good vantage points to deploy the launcher where they had clear line of sight to fire both before and after an enemy force got through the gap. I intended to start firing rockets as soon as we had a clear target and to rotate the launcher to a new position after two quick shots to avoid return fire.

I took the 4 autogun teams and put two on each side of the gap, offset so they wouldn't be at risk from each others' fire. We scouted out locations in the rock formations for each gun so they would be shielded until the enemy was through the gap and into the interlocking fields of fire. With four guns firing from two directions that open area would be very hot for any-one coming through.

I stripped the other three troops from each of those fire teams. I took two with me and split the other ten, with five on each side, hidden behind whatever cover they could find. I positioned myself and my two lucky privates along the edge of the open area. I wanted this to be timed right, and I intended to keep a close eye on things. My AI kept feeding me reports on approaching contacts. We had about 140 of our troops heading this way, and it looked like the enemy was right behind.

It was only about three minutes before our units started coming through. They were in good order and well-organized, moving through by makeshift platoons. I wasn't plugged in to the command circuit at a high enough level to track casualties in these units, but I tried to estimate. Our organization was so ersatz on this operation it was hard to tell, but my best guess was they were down to around 50% strength.

The retreating troops were moving toward the edge of the interior hillside and then redeploying to the left and right to support and reinforce my positions there. One of the pivotal battles of the campaign would be fought in that tight little ravine. That is, if the enemy cooperated and did what we expected. Unfortunately, they didn't. I was waiting for my AI to warn me about approaching enemy troops, but when it came it wasn't what I expected. "CAC formations seem to have ceased pursuit and begun to fall back."

What the hell were they up to? My mind raced looking for possibilities. The last of our units were flowing through the gap, but there was no sign of enemy activity. Then, everything happened at once.

All of a sudden it came to me...I knew what was happening. I started to order my two privates to take cover when the com-link came to life. It was the colonel, and he was yelling frantically. "Cain, get out of the gap. Withdraw now. Code Oran..."

That was as much as I heard. There was a blinding flash right in front of me. My visor went dark, automatically shutting down to protect my eyes. A second later the shockwave hit, slamming me, armor and all, hard into a pillar of jagged rock.

I was on my back for a few seconds, stunned. When I tried to move I couldn't. It wasn't more than another two or three seconds before I felt massive weight against my legs as my armor was ripped open by a huge pile of falling rock, then the wave of pain as the boulders pressed down on my injured legs. I could feel wetness; I knew I was bleeding badly. Then the burning started as the massive heat from the explosion began to seep through my shattered suit.

My armor still had some functionality, though. I could feel the injections from the trauma control mechanisms, and almost immediately the pain subsided. I could smell burning flesh, and while I couldn't feel it, I knew the suit was attempting to electro-cauterize my legs to stop the bleeding.

I was lying there in a surreal daze. All I could think was, time to pay for getting missed all those times. My dead comrades came back to me from my memories, saying, "Welcome, brother...we have kept a place for you."

I was still awake, at least I thought so, but I couldn't see or even feel anything. I couldn't move at all; my armor's power plant must have gotten scragged. Battery power could run trauma and life support systems, but it couldn't move several tons of high density iridium-steel-polymer hybrid buried under more tons of shattered rock.

Code Orange. Nuclear attack. Everything was hazy, but I knew it had been an atomic explosion. The colonel had tried to warn me, but we both realized too late. This was a huge escalation. Neither side had used nukes yet, not even during Achilles.

None of it mattered. I felt the darkness start to take me. At least I was spared the slow agony the rest of our forces were facing. I slipped away, choking on the bitter taste of defeat.

Chapter Six

Armstrong Medical Center
Armstrong Colony
Gamma Pavonis III

I woke up in a hospital bed. That was the first surprise. Not
the bed, the waking up. Somehow I had survived, and to this
day I'm not entirely sure how. Part of it was luck, and even more
the amazing technology of my armor, which managed to stop
my bleeding and inject me with enough meds to keep me alive,
despite catastrophic damage to my body and a dose of radiation
that could have fried a kitchen full of eggs.

Years later I found out that another big factor, maybe the
most crucial in my survival, was Colonel Holm. Somehow my
brutalized armor maintained its link with the command net, and
the colonel could tell I was still alive on his readouts. He personally led a search team into the apocalyptic red zone to find me
and pull me out.

I braced for the pain, but there was none. Of course, I
thought. I must be up to my eyeballs in happy juice. Probably
best that way for all concerned. I had no complaints about it.
I lay there groggy and incoherent for a few minutes, maybe for
a few hours. Or days for that matter; I was completely out of
it. Finally I decided to take a look around, so I lifted my head.
Well, I thought "lift," but my head didn't do anything. It wasn't
until I tried to raise my arm, but only managed to turn my hand
a little with intense effort, that I realized I was so astonishingly
weak I could hardly move.

Of course, I thought. The radiation. It was a miracle I was
alive at all, but I was clearly much worse for wear. I looked
around as much as I could manage with the little I could move
my head. The room was fairly large, with high ceilings - over
3 meters. I was definitely planetside someplace; no spaceship
wastes this much volume. The walls and pretty much everything
else were spotless white. There were various machines lined up

next to the bed, and they were all connected to me by some type of tube, wire, or other conduit.

I tried to yell for someone, but my voice was as weak as my body, and all I could manage was a barely audible whisper. I croaked it out from what almost certainly would have been a very sore throat if I hadn't been so medicated. I didn't expect an answer, but I got one.

"Good morning, Sergeant Cain. I am Florence, your medical AI. Your condition is stable, but I must ask that you refrain from trying to speak or move. You are still very weak. I have notified Doctor Linden that you have awakened."

The AI's voice was female, soothing, and probably exactly what I would have designed for the purpose. My first impulse was to start asking questions, but I was so exhausted it just seemed easier to wait for the doctor.

I didn't have to wait very long. It couldn't have been more than a minute before the door slid open and in walked a doctor followed by two medtechs. "Hello, Sergeant Cain. I'm Doctor Sarah Linden, and I'm very happy to finally have the chance to meet you. We've spent a lot of time together, but so far I'm afraid the relationship has been pretty one-sided."

I managed to turn my head to get a better look, and when my teary eyes managed to focus, I was looking at a woman. A very beautiful woman. She was wearing a wrinkled light blue surgical uniform, but she still looked incredible. She had a very pretty face with blue eyes and the sweetest smile I'd ever seen. There were a just a few wisps of strawberry blond hair protruding from the baggy cap that covered her head, but my mind filled in the blanks, and I saw it cascading around her shoulders.

I tried to manage my own smile, and I rasped out the very best greeting I could manage. "Hello, doctor. It's nice to meet you. I'd shake your hand, but I'm afraid I can't lift my arm."

She smiled again. "I'm glad to see you've still got a sense of humor. That's a good sign. Don't worry, you'll be able to lift your arms soon enough. In fact, you'll be able to do everything you could before. You may find it hard to believe right now, but you'll make a full recovery."

I had to swallow hard to try and keep speaking. My throat was parched and it was hard to get any sound to come out. She saw that I was struggling trying to say something, and she walked over and put her hand softly on my shoulder and said, "Don't strain yourself trying to speak. You got quite a heavy dose of radiation, I'm afraid, and it caused a lot of damage to your digestive system. We can't even let you take water orally until we can get in there and fix you up, so your throat is likely to be pretty dry as well." She started to turn to leave and continued, "Try to get some more rest now, and we'll talk more later."

"Wait." I croaked like a frog, but at least I got it out. "There aren't any mirrors in here, at least none I can see."

She turned her head to look back at me. "Why don't we worry about that after you rest a bit?"

"That bad, is it? It's ok, I can take it. Really."

She didn't answer right away, and I could see that her expression was troubled. After a few seconds she tried once more. "I really think we should wait until you are stronger."

I pushed hard and actually managed to completely turn my head to face her. "Don't worry about me, doc. I'll be fine. No matter how bad it is."

She paused but didn't answer.

"Please."

She finally relented and ordered one of the medtechs to do as I asked. He headed out into the corridor and returned a minute later carrying a large, circular mirror.

Doctor Linden made a gesture and the tech stopped. "Before you look, I want you to understand that you are going to be as good as new before I let you out of here. It won't look like it, and it certainly won't feel like it, but you've been through the worst. It's just a matter of time now. Time for us to work through the procedures that need to be done to fix the damage."

I nodded, or as close as I could come to nodding. "I understand." I had to try 3 or 4 times to force the words out audibly. I couldn't move; I couldn't talk. This was starting to piss me off.

She motioned to the tech, and he moved over to the edge of the bed and held the mirror over me so I could look without having to move.

My height is 1.9 meters. In fighting shape I weigh about 95 kilos. But the shriveled, hairless thing staring back at me would have weighed 50kg at most. If it had legs. Which it didn't.

The memories rushed back. The debris landing on me, the sharp pain as several tons of rock crushed my legs, the rush of outside air as my suit was breached, searing pain as my armor's trauma control system cauterized the stumps. That's how I remembered I had lost my legs. And while I found the whole thing interesting, I didn't really care. I suspect I owed that welcome apathy to the same cocktail of meds keeping what was no doubt agonizing pain at bay.

"Don't worry," the doctor said. "Believe it or not, I was telling you the truth. You're through the worst of it. Or at least the most dangerous. You're going to make it, sergeant, and when I'm done you're going to be tearing down the walls to get out of here."

She looked right into my eyes. I wasn't sure whether she was trying to show me she was telling the truth or just making eye contact so I would stop trying to move my head around, but I enjoyed it nevertheless. "I can't promise it will be fun. In fact, I'm fairly certain you will have some pretty uncharitable things to say about your poor doctor before we're done. But you will walk out of this hospital and return to duty. I promise. But now I'm going to put my foot down with you and insist you get some more rest. We'll talk again later, after you get some sleep."

She and the techs turned and walked toward the door. The doc turned and gave me another incredible smile. "Florence, 30 ml Arthramine. Barring any change in condition, Sergeant Cain is to sleep for ten hours."

The AI responded softly. "Yes, Dr. Linden." I could feel the wave of sleep coming over me as the AI injected the drug into my intravenous feed. I wanted to say goodbye to the doctor, but I don't think I got it out in time.

She was true to her word, and as soon as I woke up we talked a bit more. We discussed my injuries and the rather daunting series of treatments I had ahead of me. It took us several sessions to cover it all, particularly since I spent half the time flirting with her. Or doing the best imitation of flirting a half-man who couldn't lift his head off the pillow could manage. I was still extremely weak, and I couldn't really talk for more than a few minutes. I couldn't even stay awake for more than 30 minutes or so.

I enjoyed our talks, but as I was able to more clearly assemble my recollections, I started to get depressed, wondering why I survived when all of my troopers probably died. Doctor Sarah tried to get me to focus on my treatments and not to torture myself about things I couldn't change, but I was determined to beat myself up. She tried her best, and I gave her a smile and told her I would stop, but we both knew I was lying.

My last thoughts on the battlefield before I lost consciousness had been of hopelessness. I was sure I was a dead man and just as certain that we were losing the battle. The enemy's nuclear attack had shattered my position and blown a big hole in our line. I was pretty sure my whole command had been wiped out, and it didn't seem like there was much chance that any section of the defense could stand.

Once I had recovered enough strength to stay awake for more than a few minutes, Doctor Sarah had a data unit brought in for me. She'd managed to get me access to the battle reports for the campaign. I have no idea how she did it, because they were classified, and she wasn't anywhere in the line of command for the Columbia operation. Nevertheless, she did it. So thanks to my kindly and resourceful doctor, I got a recap of the battle. I started to read it with some trepidation, but by the time I was halfway through I realized it was far better than I could have hoped.

First, over half my troopers survived. Everyone I'd put in place behind the rock outcroppings had enough shielding to survive the blast with only minor damage to their armor. Their positions were largely intact when the CAC troopers finally attacked. The radiation and EMP played havoc on the enemy's scanners, and they advanced into what they thought was a hole... only to run into the converging fields of fire I'd set up. By the time they figured out what was going on and pulled back, the Colonel had assembled a force to hit them from behind.

Jax rallied my survivors, and they hooked up with the other groups along the rock wall to sandwich the enemy strike force between them and the Colonel. Caught in a vice and ravaged by multiple fields of fire they melted away. I heard that a few tried to surrender, but it was far too late for that. No more than a handful escaped to regroup with the rest of the landing force.

From that point it was a confused, chaotic melee. Both sides had lost all semblance of order, and it broke down into shattered remnants of units fighting each other. In the end, the home field advantage told. Colonel Holm had integrated local militia scouts into our units, and as it turned out this was a brilliant move. These guys knew every boulder, every vantage point were a SAW could cover the approaches. They ran circles around the invaders, and we tore them to pieces.

When the enemy sounded the recall and pulled back to their landing ships the Colonel unleashed his coup de grace, a nuclear barrage of our own, turning the enemy's rally point into an atomic hell. Not a single ship escaped. The few survivors broke and tried to run for cover, but the colonel sent out search and destroy teams to root them all out. As far as I know, not one enemy trooper who landed on Columbia lived to tell the story.

It was a huge victory, and another heap of glory for the colonel, but was dearly bought. Our casualties were over 60% - closer to 80% if you count the lightly wounded and those with minor cases of radiation poisoning. Columbia itself was another casualty. The inhabited area of the planet was devastated. The enemy had detonated half a dozen battlefield nukes, and we'd hit their rally point with ten.

When the enemy realized what had happened to their strike force they tried to bombard the surface. But Holm had one more surprise waiting for the enemy. He'd hidden several large defensive batteries, and now he had them open up on the incoming missiles. We managed to shoot most of them down, but a big fusion warhead got through and hit one of the coastal towns, leaving nothing but a crater.

I was beyond impressed with Colonel Holm's prescience. Time and time again he'd seem to read the minds of the enemy. But withholding point defense capability while the enemy landed almost 10,000 troops in two waves virtually without opposition? I was awed at the discipline. And, of course, he was right. Those batteries could have shot down some landing craft, but the colonel knew the enemy could still bombard the surface. By keeping these weapons hidden he convinced the enemy we had no such capacity, and when they did try to blast the planet it was one big sloppy salvo, making it relatively easy for us to target and destroy the incoming ordnance. Had they planned the bombardment to counter point defense capability, there is no doubt that many more warheads would have gotten through. As it was, the enemy had expended all their ordnance, and they had no real choice but to withdraw before we were able to get fresh naval forces to the system.

So the colonel had held Columbia in the face of almost overwhelming odds. As to what that salvaged real estate was worth now, that was anyone's guess. The best estimate was that a quarter of the planet's population had been killed, and a lot more were wounded, homeless, and in desperate need of supplies. Certainly, most of the manufacturing capacity, power generation, and other infrastructure had been destroyed, or at least severely damaged.

Nevertheless, it was a victory, and a badly needed one. It was the talk of the hospital once the word got out, and we Columbia survivors were the most highly sought after conversationalists in the Armstrong Acute Care Facility.

There isn't much to do in the hospital but talk to the rest of the recovering partial-soldiers, so we anxiously traded any bit of news about the war or just about any subject other than doctors and medical procedures. Anything to get our minds off the next time some white-clad figure with a sickly, too-pleasant smile would wander in to extract blood or cell samples, particularly since this usually occurred sometime around 4am, about 20 minutes after you finally managed to fall asleep. Unless it was my doctor, of course. I always had time for Doctor Sarah.

My first thoughts of the hospital went something like, "Well, at least no one is shooting at me." In a month I was ready to trade the bad food and boredom for a little incoming fire. It's not like getting shot hurts more than growing new legs. Regeneration hurts like hell. At least for limbs. The internal organs are a lot easier, and since I got some of those too, I have a frame of reference for comparison.

They replaced virtually my entire digestive system, most of which was destroyed beyond healing by the radiation. They extracted the stem cells they needed and grew me new, perfectly compatible organs. Exact copies, in fact, of the ones I was born with, but grown to adult size. The whole thing took about a month, with another couple days to recover from the implant surgery.

Then the fun started. Digestive system regeneration requires what was gently described to me as an "adjustment period," as my brand new guts settled into my old body. There was no rejection as there is with foreign transplants like the one my sister had - these organs were mine, with the exact genetic makeup of the originals.

But they were completely new adult organs, lacking the bacteria and other bits of stuff needed for them to work properly. My system was infused with several batches of new intestinal flora, and my stomach chemistry was adjusted several times. Does any of that sound like fun? It's not.

Once I got through the gut-wrenching sickness and started to feel at least a little human, it was time for me to grow new legs. I know it sounds counter-intuitive that growing a new leg hurts more than, say, new lungs but it's true. They can regenerate organs in the lab and transplant them, while a new leg has to grow on your body. And it hurts like a motherfucker.

You would think that attaching a new arm or leg would be relatively easy, especially since they've been able to re-attach severed limbs for a couple centuries now. But unlike organs, the process for transplanting new limbs has never been very successful. Something to do with developing the leg itself to match the stump. So instead of being cultivated in some glorified incubator, my legs would be grown in place, right on my body, which sounded simple but was in fact significantly more complicated.

One problem was that most anesthetics and pain relief drugs interfered with the growth and development of new nerves. I'd been heavily medicated with pain-killers since I got to the hospital, but that all stopped when they strapped me into the regeneration machine. I got to feel every bit of it, pure and undiluted. Mostly undiluted, to be completely accurate - they did try to mitigate the agony a bit.

They administered pain-control hypnosis and something they called "compensatory neural stimulation," but trust me, none of it did much...sort of like giving you two aspirin before setting you on fire. It hurt like hell 24/7 for the entire six weeks it took for my legs to grow.

Doctor Sarah checked on me every day, spending a few minutes examining the development of the legs, but mostly trying to distract me from the pain, I think. It was a noble effort, and if anyone could have managed it, it would have been her. But this shit really hurt. I was irritable and miserable, and I even yelled at my beautiful doctor a few times, which only made me feel worse afterward.

Florence also spoke to me in soothing tones, and she (it?) got the worst of my frustration. Actually, I found the medical AI to be quite an amazing device. A sophisticated computer system that managed my condition and drug intake 24/7, it was also programmed to help alleviate boredom and provide customized companionship to mending patients. Among other things, she beat me at chess about 30 times. She could also do things like turn a database of past patient comments into a casual conversation. Something like, "I hear the pasta with mushroom sauce on tonight's menu is particularly good. Shall I order it for you?"

By the way...food. It was about halfway through my leg growth that they actually started giving me real food. Not that I wasn't a connoisseur of various flavors of intravenous nutritional replacement formula - I think that's what they called it - but by the time they actually fed me something solid I almost burst into song.

Solid is a bit of an overstatement - the first thing they brought me looked like soupy oatmeal that had been through a food processor, but I could have waxed poetic about it for hours. Any food that entered my body through my mouth and not directly into my bloodstream was A OK with me.

I was strapped into a machine with my torso disappearing into a shiny metal cylinder that extended to just under my sternum. Below the cylinder each stump extended into its own clear plastic tube that would hold and support the new leg as it grew. Inside the cylinder, in addition to the machinery that powered the regeneration, was an assortment of plumbing that attended to by bodily functions while I was strapped in, immobile for weeks.

I was most concerned with - in order - pain, boredom, and going a little crazy because I could hardly move, but I have to admit it was a learning experience watching my legs grow. At first it was just the bone, growing down from the existing stump at a rate of about 6 centimeters a day. I used to stare at it to see if I could perceive it actually growing. I thought maybe I could a couple times, but I was never sure.

The whole process was monitored and controlled by the medical computer. I was growing legs from my own genetic material, but I needed adult legs, not the baby legs I was born with that grew over 15 or 20 years. Organs were regenerated in almost the exact way they initially formed and grown to adult size, albeit at a greatly accelerated rate. A new liver, for example, would start as a tiny one that would grow, much as it does in a fetus and later a child as it ages.

But my new legs were grafting right onto my adult body. The doctors couldn't grow tiny fetus legs and allow them to gradually increase in size. The genetic material had to be stimulated to grow in a certain way directly on my body, and this was manipulated by medical lasers, electrical pulses, and a variety of other tools.

Once my new tibias and fibulas were finished with their development, I was amazed at the spectacle of my new skeletal feet growing. About the same time my upper legs began to grow muscles, cartilage, nerves, arteries, and the rest of the slimy stuff inside all of us. For a while I was a live anatomy lesson - upper leg showing the muscular system and lower leg the skeletal.

I mentioned that all of this hurt, didn't I? I'd describe what new nerves feel like when they are growing, but honestly, I just don't know how to put it into words. It hurts. A lot.

Doctor Sarah would visit me as often as we could, and we'd talk about different things. Of course, I had realized early on that Doctor Sarah was also Captain Sarah, and that she was every bit as much a marine as I was, and outranked me to boot.

It also meant that, as angelic and patrician as she looked, she probably had not had the easiest life before the Corps. Most of us were plucked from one gutter or another. But I didn't ask, and she didn't ask me either. Since the majority of us had shitty backgrounds, it was traditional to keep it off limits. We were all reborn into the Corps, our old sins expunged.

We were both from New York, and had both lived in the MPZ when we were young, but that's as far into that subject as we got. She received her medical training in the Corps, and before that she made a few assaults, though not as many as I had. She asked me about Achilles, about what it had been like on the ground. She'd served on one of the support ships as surgeon, but never made it to the surface. With a little help from Florence, she got me through the boredom and pain and frustration. I think helping me helped her a little too. The war had not been going well, and I can only imagine how neck deep in blood and partial soldiers she'd been every day.

Once the skin had completed its growth my regeneration was declared complete. That doesn't mean I was as good as new though. In theory, my new limbs were exact copies of my old ones, though the reality was a bit more complicated. I hadn't spent a couple years learning to walk with my new legs, and the neural pathways required to move them were slightly different. It took a month of hard physical therapy before I could walk around normally, and longer before I felt really comfortable with my balance. You'd be amazed at the sweat you can work up holding onto parallel bars and willing your new legs to move a few inches.

Once I was up and walking around, it was time for general physical rehab. I was now healthy, more or less, but I certainly wasn't the toned and fit combat soldier I had been. I was 20 kilos lighter than before I was wounded, and it was mostly muscle that was gone. So they put me on an aggressive training regimen, and most wonderfully of all, they finally started feeding me real solid food consistently. I'd worked my way through the mushy cereals and clear soups, and I can't even express how good a sandwich tastes after weeks of slop.

The training was hard and exhausting, but it was a true pleasure. I got outside, breathed the fresh air, felt the sun (suns, actually) on my face. I started taking short walks, but before long I was running half marathons every day. There was a pristine lake on the hospital grounds, and I took a daily swim too. The air, the water, the sun - it all made me feel alive again, a little more each day.

I spent afternoons in the training rooms, going through one strength-building routine after another. As my strength and endurance increased I really began to feel like myself again. I'd been weak and infirm for most of a year, and now I felt as if I'd been truly reborn.

The care I received was amazing, and I have nothing but praise and gratitude for my entire medical team. Doctor Sarah, of course, but also the other surgeons and all the tech and support personnel. I knew the marines took care of their own, but it was incredible to see how much effort was expended on a single wounded sergeant. Back on Earth, only a member of the Political Class would get this kind of treatment, and it would have to be a highly placed member at that.

When they finally declared me healthy and discharged me, I made point of thanking each of my doctors and medtechs before I left. They'd literally given me my life back. It was pretty emotional saying goodbye, but when I got to Doctor Sarah it just then struck me that I wasn't going to be seeing her every day anymore. I would actually see her again many times, but I didn't know that then. She hugged me and tearfully reminded me she had promised I'd be good as new. One of the techs took an image of us and flashed it to our data units. So I took my duffel bag and my picture of Doctor Sarah and me, and I walked out of the hospital into the dazzling sunlight. Both of Armstrong's binary stars were high in the morning sky, and it was as magnificent a day as I have ever seen on any planet.

I took the monorail to the spaceport and boarded the shuttle to Armstrong Orbital. Before I even checked into my billet I reported to the armorer to be fitted for a new suit. My old armor was almost torn to shreds saving my life, but I'd have needed a new set anyway. I looked the same as I did before, but with all the weight I lost and then gained back, not to mention growing new legs, I would have needed new armor. A fighting suit had to fit you like a glove to function properly.

I had 60 days of leave for rest and recreation, but I really wasn't interested. I'd had all the rest I could take in the hospital, and I was anxious to get back into the fight. Plus, I had a bad case of missing my doctor, and I figured hitting ground on some planet or another was the best way to put it out of my mind.

There was a problem with that theory, however. It turned out I wasn't going right back to the battle after all. While I was in the hospital I found out that the colonel had not only nominated me for a decoration; he'd also recommended me for officer training. The day after I was discharged I got the orders. I was on my way to the Academy. The next time I was bolted into a lander it would be as Lieutenant Cain.

Chapter Seven

The Academy
Wolf 359 III

Humanity occupied, to some extent or another, 285 planets and moons located in about 700 explored solar systems. Some of these were fairly robust colonies, generally small but growing rapidly. Others were just remote outposts, usually placed to exploit some valuable resource or to operate a refueling station for ships travelling between systems. A few were core worlds, the first colonies established, which had now grown into sizable populations and modest industry.

The warp gates that connected them were naturally occurring gravitational phenomenon that physicists had yet to fully explain. Some solar systems had only one; the largest number yet discovered was ten. A system with three or more was particularly valuable. It was the kind of place we'd likely be found, there to hold onto it or to take it away from someone else.

I had been surprised at how much classroom education there was in marine basic training. But that was nothing compared to the Academy. The powers that be had obviously decided that to become an officer one must have a head full of obscure knowledge of dubious utility. Or something along those lines. There was math, science, engineering and, of course, battle tactics. A lot of it was boring but relatively easy, and I didn't have to pay too much attention to get through it. The one thing I really enjoyed was the history. And we got a lot of it. Real history, not the manufactured drivel taught in public schools back home.

Our world was the product of the Unification Wars, a series of bitter conflicts lasting 80 years that finally ended with the familiar eight superpowers controlling the globe. The root causes of the wars were many, though so many records were lost over decades of desperate fighting it is only possible to speculate on the relative importance of each.

By the mid-21st century the democracies of the west, which

had been the drivers of 20th century growth, were in rapid decline. Beset with corrupt and bloated governments, bankrupt by decades of appalling mismanagement, and unable to recapture the economic dynamism of their past, they were teetering on the verge of collapse.

The developing nations of the world, while they enjoyed rapidly-growing economies built largely on cheap labor, proved to be somewhat of an illusion of prosperity. Government interference, fraudulent reporting, and a lack of economic flexibility caused the growth to falter, and when the world economy started to crumble, one by one they fell into turmoil and revolution.

There was unrest in Asia, in Latin America, even in Europe. But the Wars started in the Mideast. The Middle East, which had risen to power and wealth by exploiting massive reserves of fossil fuels, was thrown into chaos by the development, in 2048, of commercially feasible fusion power. Within a decade, demand for petroleum had declined 75%, and the price of a barrel of oil dropped from a high of $500 to less than $30.

An astonishingly small portion of a century's oil riches had been invested in anything productive, and within a few years there was mass starvation, rioting, and rebellion throughout the region. Unrest led to riots, which in turn led to open revolt. Warfare erupted in a dozen places at once as despotic regimes clung desperately to power while their starving citizens stormed the barricades.

The nations of the west, no longer wealthy enough to provide substantive aid nor powerful enough to impose their will worldwide, were unable to stem to flow of global unrest, and revolt spread across the globe. Terrorism became a worldwide scourge, culminating in several nuclear incidents that killed millions.

Teetering governments facing rebellion responded with brutal force; those of more stable nations resorted to ever stricter internal security measures until they controlled virtually every aspect of their citizens' lives. Democracy, such that it once was, disappeared from the face of the Earth. The forms were still followed, yes, but the substance of republican government was freely surrendered in the end by scared populations willing to trade any freedom for increasingly unreliable promises of security.

In 2062 the First Unification War erupted not far from the Mesopotamian basin where civilization began, and for the next three-quarters of a century combat raged in every corner of the globe. By the time the wars were over almost 80 years later, 75% of the world's population had perished, and there were only eight nations left on Earth. The superpowers.

They were bankrupt, exhausted, and devastated. Their economies were ravaged, their armies depleted. Finally, when there were no resources remaining to sustain world war, the Treaty of Paris ended the fighting. On Earth.

Barred from terrestrial warfare by a treaty they were too afraid to violate, the exhausted superpowers took their rivalries into space. Earth was prostrate, drained of resources, scarred by nuclear exchanges, and in desperate need of the wealth that could be exploited from distant worlds and asteroids now that the discovery of the warp gate had opened the universe to exploration.

Space is limitless, so at first the Powers explored peacefully, assuming that there was plenty of room for everyone. But the warp gates that allowed speedy interstellar travel were not infinite, and it soon became apparent that some systems were of great strategic value because of their locations and where their gates led. Choke points developed, and before long the Powers were at war again, this time in space.

The Treaty of Paris has been scrupulously obeyed, as all of the governments realize that the next war on Earth will likely be the last. Armies in space, though staggeringly expensive, are small in scale compared to the massive legions mobilized during Earthbound world wars. Our battles are every bit as violent, bloody, and deadly as any ever fought, but the lands we waste are sparsely populated frontier worlds and not cities with populations in the millions.

We were fighting the Third Frontier War, and all of human-occupied space was on fire. The periods between named, declared wars also saw their share of raids and battles, but these were generally intermittent and fought at a much lower intensity level. The Second Frontier War had lasted 15 years, and though not entirely conclusive it had been a marginal victory for the Alliance and its allies. The interwar skirmishes occurring afterward had swung a bit the other way, and our position had weakened, a trend that accelerated during the first few years of declared war.

Depending on the current status of its ongoing struggle with the Caliphate, the Western Alliance had either the largest or the second largest empire of colony worlds. The Central Asian Combine was a close third, and the Pacific Rim Coalition a distant fourth.

Since the Caliphate and the CAC were usually allied against us, we had our hands full, and we were constantly wooing one or more of the other Powers to side with us. Even when we were allied with the PRC we were still outnumbered, and our network of warp gate pathways was exposed and vulnerable to interdiction.

The other Powers were less of a factor in space, though all of them had some network of colonies, and the alliances between them shifted as goals and expediencies changed. The Russian-Indian Confederation was weak in space, but usually allied with us. The Central European League and Europa Federalis were mostly concerned with fighting each other, and would ally with the stronger powers as it suited their purposes. Since an alliance with one usually meant war with the other, it was more or less a zero sum game.

The South American Empire had a tiny group of colonies, but they were clustered together and highly defensible. The Empire rarely aligned with anyone in the major wars, preferring an opportunistic neutrality. Their forces frequently served as mercenaries for the other Powers, and they would often fight on both sides at different times in a conflict - sometimes even at the same time.

Though there were only eight superpowers on Earth, there were nine in space. The Martian Confederation was formed when the early colonists of the red planet broke away from their terrestrial parent nations during the later stages of the Unification Wars and banded together to form a loose union. The Confederation controlled the largest group of developed colonies in Earth's solar system and a small collection of interstellar settlements as well. While only a fraction the size of the other Powers in population, the Confederation had the most advanced technology of any of the Superpowers, and its forces, while small, were well-trained and equipped. Mars tended toward neutrality, but when the opportunity presented itself they were a welcome ally.

All of the Earth governments were authoritarian to some extent or another; only the Martian Confederation was a real republic. The Alliance national bodies - the U.S., the U.K., Oceania, and Greater Canada - outwardly retained republican forms, but they were really oligarchies run by entrenched political classes. Office holders had to be graduates of the Political Academies, and the politicians controlled who was admitted, creating an almost hereditary class system. The occasional outsider could work his way into the upper classes, but such an individual would require the sponsorship and patronage of someone already powerful.

The middle classes, mostly educated professionals of one sort or another, lived a fairly spartan, but moderately comfortable, existence much like my parents had. Few made any trouble because they were terrified of losing their position and falling into the underclass, again as my parents had. It was a system that worked, at least after a fashion and, if innovation, creativity, and freedom were not what they once had been at least civilization survived. It almost hadn't.

For most people a tiny apartment in an area protected from the worst crime, an adequate supply of rations, and cheap entertainment was enough. For those who wanted more there was space. The colonies of most of the Powers enticed those who craved more freedom, those who were driven to create and build. The new worlds attracted many of Earth's best and brightest, and these fledgling societies, so much smaller than the terrestrial nations, tended to be significantly more democratic than the home governments. They were each a part of their Superpower of course, and they relied upon the parent to provide protection and support. But as long as the stream of vital resources flowed back to Earth, the colonial governments were pretty much allowed to do as they pleased.

Most of us in the military were castoffs from Earth society in one way or another. The Corps looked for recruits with a strong independent streak, something that was not conducive to success in the mainstream world. We weren't the mindless robots in serried ranks of armies past. A modern soldier, operating 20 meters from his closest comrade and 20 light years from the chain of command, had to be innovative and ready to take the initiative.

So the traits and behavioral patterns that made for good, well-behaved citizens on Earth tended to produce poor soldiers in space. Most of my comrades were plucked from the gutter or saved from the executioner just as I was. The system worked. It removed people from Earth who were likely to be a problem for the established order and, conveniently, these same individuals made excellent soldiers and, later, good colonists.

In the streets, when I was terrorizing the Cogs as a gang member, I thought of the government as the enemy. They hunted the gangs and executed any members they caught. It wasn't until I got to the Academy that I learned that the government basically ran the gangs.

It all made sense. The gangs served a definite social purpose within the system, keeping the underclass so beaten down there was little chance of rebellion from below. The urban hell they created outside the protected cities also kept the educated workers in line lest they be cast out themselves.

In retrospect it was obvious. The government could have eradicated the gangs any time it wanted to. Most gang members had the same GPS spinal implants that the rest of the population did, so tracking was no problem. And while the gangs were well armed to prey on helpless workers, a company of powered infantry could have swept the Bronx clean without losing a man.

Which brings us to the questions posed in my military psychology class. Why would the Corps provide us such an honest view of how rotten and corrupt the system was? And the follow up question - knowing the truth about what we are fighting for, why do it? Why climb into that lander to risk our lives for such a monstrosity?

We bounced around a bunch of answers for most of the semester, but in the end I think I understood. They were honest with us for a few reasons. First, we were all misfits in Earth culture anyway, but what I hadn't known was that every recruit inducted into the Corps was also in the top quintile of intelligence in the population. Not many of us were going to have a propaganda-induced belief in the system. If we're going to figure it out anyway, or at least partially figure it out, why not just tell us?

But it was deeper than that. The reason they taught us all of this was so we could truly figure out the answer to the second question, "Why do we fight?" Sure, you could go with the argument they'd make back on Earth, that whatever faults our system had, it had saved humanity from extinction. That was good enough for engineers and administrators willing to tow the line to hold onto their marginally comfortable lifestyle. But most of us had suffered on the underside of that system, often in conditions that left us relatively unafraid of extinction.

So why do we fight? We all thought we had the answer to that from the first time we blasted out of a ship and put our lives in the hands of the men and women strapped in beside us. We fight for each other. That's definitely part of the answer, but it isn't the whole thing. Certainly, having decided to fight we do so for our comrades in arms, those who share the mud, blood, and hardship with us. If my brother and sisters are going in, I'm going in. No questions...no ifs, ands, or buts.

But that's a private's answer. Yes, I'm going if my comrades go, but why do any of us do it? Not so the politicians can maintain their power and privilege, certainly. Sure, you can make an argument that the system back home, deeply flawed though it may be, was superior to some anarchic, post-apocalyptic horror, but that isn't the answer either. Not for us. For many of us that nightmare had been home.

We fight for these colonists. Because they are brave and daring and deserve to be protected. Because they are the future. Because the societies they create, small and struggling that they may be, are far superior to the clusterfuck back on Earth, and they are the one thing that gives us hope for a future, for a better system...for one truly worth fighting for.

The colonists are also us, it turns out. Ninety-seven percent of retiring military personnel choose to settle on a colony world. In fact, less than one in three ever return to Earth, even for a visit. The colonial militias of most of the worlds are leavened with retired combat veterans who settled there. This was by government design in the early days, when a system of military settlers was crucial to defending colony worlds, and it simply continued because it worked for all parties.

So here I was, a man who'd seen his family destroyed by the government; who'd crawled through the rubble-strewn streets as a child, eating rats to survive; who hated and despised the political leaders back home. Here it was, in Military Psychology and Motivational Studies class that I realized I actually did have a country, and one worth fighting for too.

Not that mess I left, but the promising and vulnerable infant that had sprung from the dying body of Earth. Those miners on Carson's World, where I made my first assault and marveled at the courage of the colonists who stood up to armored infantry and held them at bay until we arrived. The inhabitants of Columbia, who dug trenches and built defenses and finally grabbed whatever weapons they had and fought alongside us to save their world. The inhabitants who were now trying to rebuild their pleasant community around the radioactive dead zones and other scars of war.

The training at the Academy was definitely not what I expected. I was surprised by all the soul-searching philosophy. In the end, though, I think I understood the reasoning behind it all.

As a private I had no responsibility other than to do my duty and fight like hell. A corporal or sergeant does command others who may live or die as a result of his orders, but typically he is with them and shares their fate closely.

An officer, on the other hand, commands a larger number of troops deployed over a greater distance. Where a sergeant might follow orders and lead a squad in a suicidal attack, an officer may have to command a squad to make that charge, knowing he is sending them to their deaths while he remains at a safe distance.

A good officer has to love and care about his troops, while also being ready and willing to commit them to whatever is necessary, even if most of them won't come back. Even if none of them will come back. And having done so, the officer must stay focused on the rest of the battle without losing any intensity or concentration. Reflection, guilt, and self-loathing had to wait until everyone was safely back aboard ship. The officer needed a clearer picture of what we fight for so he could reconcile why he was sending those troops into a hopeless place.

There was also a lot of training on strategy and tactics of course, and there was military history. Lots of military history. We studied the tactics of every conflict from the Punic Wars on. We reviewed the campaigns of Napoleon and close order squad deployments in the Second Frontier War. I've wondered at the probabilities that took me from gutter rat in the badlands of the Bronx to an expert in Gustavus Aldolphus' volley fire techniques.

I did well with all of the classroom training, and I aced all the exams. But the coursework was only part of the program. There was physical development as well, and if I thought the basic training regimen was tough it's just because I'd had no idea at the time how badly they tortured cadets. We ran and climbed and swam. We did survival marches and pushed ourselves to the limits of endurance, braving heat, cold, hunger, and exhaustion. Officers in the Corps did what they commanded their troops to do, and they led by example.

The Academy was located on a breathtakingly beautiful world called Arcadia, the third planet in the Wolf 359 system. Half a dozen small island continents were dotted across two main oceans. The temperate zones were covered in massive forests of what appeared to be close relatives of Earth pines, though the Arcadian versions were 100 meters high. The windswept, rocky coastlines were dotted with settlements that seemed perfectly blended into the terrain.

The campus itself was situated on a small peninsula along the western ocean, about 100 kilometers from the capital city, also called Arcadia. The buildings were modern and well-equipped, but they were designed to resemble older structures. The exteriors were mostly covered in the gray native fieldstone, and the buildings were connected by stone pathways winding through neatly tended gardens and clumps of woods.

The western edge of the campus ran along a rocky cliff about 20 meters above the crashing surf, and the commandant's office and a number of other buildings were situated along the edge of the cliff with breathtaking ocean views.

We spent plenty of time on the idyllic grounds of the campus, but we also saw our fair share of the planet as well, especially its least accessible, most inhospitable corners. We did training exercises in the arctic northern wastes, conducting war games across the glaciers, without scanners, in blizzards that reduced visibility to two meters or less. We baked in the hot equatorial sun building a makeshift fort to prove we'd been paying attention in combat engineering class.

We did endless computer war game simulations, but we also got out into the field and moved real troops around, mostly local militia pretending to be regulars. As a veteran of Achilles and Columbia I had more experience commanding troops in the field than most of the other cadets. Those two campaigns had the dubious distinction of the highest casualty rates of any in the war so far. I'd seen a lot of my commanding officers taken out, moving me up the chain of command too quickly for comfort.

Fighting with low-power training lasers and simulated blast radii was like a picnic by the lake in comparison, and I accumulated a 6-0 record as pretend commander. I also managed to keep simulated casualties minimal, which was gratifying but also poked at my guilt. My non-simulated casualties hadn't been nearly so low, and a lot of the troops I'd commanded for real never came back...except as ghosts tugging at my conscience in the dark.

The games were useful training exercises, I guess, but I couldn't decide how much so. No question, a hit with a training laser would have been a hit with a mag-rifle, and the battle computer could accurately simulate a blast radius for a fake grenade. But there was just no way to simulate the tension, fear, and stress of the battlefield. I was scared to death when I got blasted out of the Guadalcanal for my first assault, and I was only worried about myself. Oddly, I felt that fear focused me, maybe even made me a better soldier.

But when I had troops under my command the stress was a hundred times worse. It's crucial to be decisive and clear minded, but inside I doubted every decision and second-guessed every order. How does an officer handle that when he has 49 other men and women in a platoon, all depending on his judgment? Our troops were all well-trained. If an enemy popped up in front of them they knew what to do. But when things got out of control and the battle plan started to unravel, they looked to the officers and expected them to have all the answers ready to go. I know, because that's what I had done. My officers had been ready with those answers, and they had pulled me through my battles. I wasn't so confident I would be able to fill their shoes when the time came.

I had served under some outstanding officers, and I was always reassured how they seemed so in control no matter what was happening around us. Now I started to wonder if they were as wracked with doubt as I was? Of course they were, I started to realize. I was scared when I made that first drop, but I did my job because I was trained to do it. I'm sure my officers were plagued by their own fears and doubts too, but just as I did when I was a private, they did their jobs. Because it is what they were trained to do. It is what I was being trained to do.

We were also fitted for our new fighting suits, and we started a rigorous training program in how to use them. Yes, we'd all been fighting in armor for years, but officer suits are different. The sheer amount of data streaming into and out of the suit is staggering, and it takes a lot of training and experience to learn to handle it effectively.

We learned how to prioritize the data and interact with the command AIs in the suits, which were vastly more sophisticated than the ones in our non-com armor. We spent hours, days, weeks going through command net protocols and how to organize communication so the orders and data that had to get through did get through. Interaction with ship-based combat computers, procedures for requesting orbital bombardments, evacuation procedures, nuclear battlefield management, disciplinary codes...we studied it all.

And we studied it all on a highly condensed schedule. We were at war, and worse, we were losing that war, or at least we were hard-pressed and suffering heavy casualties. The Corps needed officers, and it needed them now, so we completed the three-year training program in sixteen exhausting months, with the commandant riding us every step of the way.

The commandant when I was at the Academy was General Oliver Carstairs, and he was a veteran of the First Frontier War. Carstairs must have been over 110 when I was at the Academy, and he had forgotten more about battle tactics then any of us ever knew. The Commandant was old, but he was a marine, and between rejuvenation treatments and sheer tough-as-nails stubbornness he could still put in a respectable performance on the obstacle course. He might not have been able to keep up with a group of battle-hardened 20-something cadets, but he'd have run most civilians into the ground. And he'd seen at least 75 years of action in every war man had fought in space.

I spent a lot of time at the Academy pondering how the Corps had so many men and women of such quality. There was stupidity and foolishness in the military; Operation Achilles proved that if it accomplished nothing else. There was laziness, corruption, and cowardice too, no doubt. But not much.

Before I went through the Academy it always amazed me that

the Corps could be as confident and capable as it was when the nation itself was jaded and corrupt and withering. Of course we were the military of that dying superpower which had so long outlived its prime. But we were also the military of a dynamic new nation, based among the stars, and one with which most of us came to feel far more affinity.

When I got back from my first assault I realized I had found my home. That was when I learned how to fight for my brothers and sisters in arms. But it was at the Academy that I found my pride...and learned how to fight for myself.

The months I spent in officer training did wonders for me, and I felt more confident and capable than I ever had. It was also a pretty good time for our war effort. Despite the fact that we'd managed to hold Columbia - virtually destroying it in the process - the war had been pretty much a disaster right up until I put on my cadet grays.

We'd been standing alone against the Caliphate and the CAC, except for some fairly minor Russian-Indian support, and we were outnumbered and getting overwhelmed. But a few months after I left the hospital and got to the Academy, the navy won a crushing victory at the Vega-Algol warp gate. Two-thirds of the CAC battleline was destroyed, and the remainder was forced back on the defensive. The victory must have been enough ammo for our ambassadors in Tokyo, because the PRC came in on our side just a few weeks later, and our battered forces joyfully welcomed fresh allies to the fight.

The enemy had obliged us by making the same mistakes we had, and they expended their momentum on costly offensives against worlds like Columbia. Eventually the cumulative attrition caused operations on both sides to slow to a crawl, giving the PRC time to mobilize and reinforce our battered forces.

By the time I put on my dress blues for graduation we were ready to start some limited offensives. The ranks had been replenished, and the officer corps was about to be reinforced by the 180 new lieutenants in my class, with another cadre going through accelerated training six months behind us.

Losses had been heavy in five years of war, and most of

us would command units consisting primarily of new recruits. This was a major change from my first assault, when I was the only recruit in my squad, and my fire team leader could spare a veteran private to assign as my babysitter. I'd be lucky if the squads in my platoon had one or two seasoned privates each. The squad leaders, while combat veterans all, would probably be making their first drop as SLs, and they'd need to keep a close eye on all the rookies filling their ranks.

I gave a lot of thought to how I would handle my platoon given these realities. My troops had performed well during Achilles and also on Columbia, but I would have to command raw troops differently. Having veterans like Jax was a huge help to executing any strategy, but I'd be very unlikely to have anyone like that in my new platoon.

Jax himself was otherwise occupied. He'd survived Columbia more or less intact, and started at the Academy while I was still growing new legs. He graduated six months before me, and as I was polishing my gear for commencement he was already off somewhere leading his own platoon.

So through no fault of my own, Jax had leapfrogged me and gotten his commission before I got mine. There are few talents more helpful to a soldier than one for getting missed by the enemy. It was one I'd had for a long time, but it failed me on Columbia.

I didn't realize that I was about to make a jump of my own, and a totally unexpected one at that. I was surprised enough when the commandant invited me to dinner, and I almost spit out my brandy when he gave me the news. I was graduating first in my class and being decorated twice - for Achilles and Columbia.

That wasn't all. I wasn't going to get my lieutenancy after all. Based on my performance at the Academy and my experience commanding troops in the field they were graduating me as a captain. My first platoon wasn't going to be a platoon at all. I was going back to command my old company. There weren't going to be too many familiar faces, but I was going home.

Chapter Eight

AS Bearclaw
Task Force Delta-Omega
Gliese 250 system

"Quiet, Hector...I'm trying to think."

I'm not sure what possessed me to give my suit's AI a name, but that's what everyone else suggested, so I just did it. I have to admit it was a bit more intuitive than calling it PNOV3168, which was the designation it had when I got it. As to why I chose the name of a doomed Trojan hero killed by Achilles, when I myself had survived our own Achilles, your guess is as good as mine.

"I am simply trying to provide you with the information flow required to make informed decisions" The reply was predictable. Hector had a very calm and slightly hushed tone of voice, sort of what you'd expect from a therapist. It was hard to get used to; the trooper AIs had a very robotic sounding voice, and they didn't have all that much to say anyway.

The new officer AIs were the state of the art in quasi-sentient computers, and the designers had decided that giving them a soothing, human-sounding voice and an active personality would reduce stress on officers in the field. I can't speak to the psychology of the officer corps in general, but the damned thing creeped me out. And it talked too much.

"Hector, shut up! If I need something I'll ask for it!" Can you feel a machine sulking or was it just my imagination?

Graduation had been amazing, not just because I was first in my class and was decorated twice, but also because of one extra surprise. Doctor Sarah somehow managed to be there. I don't know how she did it. We'd stayed in touch while I was at the Academy, but war in space is not conducive to scheduling personal get-togethers.

Even better, she had three extra days, and I had two weeks of leave, so we got to spend some time together, some time where she wasn't my doctor and I wasn't her patient. It was amazing, but three days went all too quickly, and the parting was hard. The war was still not going all that well, and I was heading back into the meat grinder. It was a real possibility we'd never see each other again, and we were both all too aware of that fact. But duty called for both of us, and we had to answer.

Now I was back in the fray, and I had my hands full. Commanding a company was overwhelming. I'd led a couple dozen troops before in some very desperate circumstances. But the force under my command now was almost incomprehensible. I had 140 troops, including a heavy weapons detachment and a cache of nuclear warheads. I had more firepower at my beck and call than an army commander in the Unification Wars. I had four other officers under me, each of them as fresh out of the Academy as I was.

Over 100 of the men and women of my company were on either their first or second mission. I managed to fill most of the squad leader slots with experienced sergeants, but there was no question about it; we were a green company. They were well trained, all of them. But training and experience are two different things. When things started to deviate from the plan it was the veterans who held a unit together. During Achilles, and later on Columbia, I'd seen it happen. This time I wasn't at all sure we had enough seasoned troopers to pull us through if things got really sticky.

The mission had me worried. I would have preferred a straight out planetary assault, but that's not what we'd drawn. We were in the Gliese 250 system, and we'd snuck in through a newly discovered warp gate on the far side of the primary star. Gliese 250 was a binary system with a couple of gas giants and nothing much of value except its location and its collection of gravitational anomalies, otherwise known as warp gates. The system was a major choke point for the Caliphate, with six (now seven) warp gates, four leading to Caliphate systems and two out to barely explored areas on the Rim. The seventh, the one we'd found, connected the Gliese system with 12 Ophiuchi, which was our main outer base.

With no decent real estate in the system for a colony, the Caliphate had constructed a massive space station to serve as a refueling depot and transit facility. I can't even imagine what it cost them to build something this size with no in-system population or even a rocky planet for ores, but Gliese was a hugely important nexus for them, and they needed something that could handle the traffic coming through.

The system was buried well within their territory, or so they thought, and the station was only lightly armed. Our deep survey of the 12 Ophiuchi system redrew the strategic map in an instant, and it gave us a highway right into the heart of a major Caliphate sector. Once they became aware of the new warp gate, Gliese 250 was also potential launch point for a Caliphate invasion of 12 Ophiuchi and our systems beyond. In our hands it was a dagger thrust right into a previously secure sector.

The war had slowed to a stalemate as both sides licked their wounds and struggled to replace lost ships and soldiers. But now we had a chance to launch a major surprise attack and throw them back on the defensive. Step one - take that station.

We wanted it intact, so the idea of just sending in a battlegroup to blast it to rubble wasn't an option. Instead, the plan was to knock out its defensive array with a pinpoint bombardment and then board the thing. My company was supporting two teams of SEALs, who were going to do a deep space entry and secure a docking portal. After that, my men and women would swarm onto the station and take it deck by deck.

Intelligence had provided us with a fairly detailed analysis on the specifications and capabilities of the station. It was a white metal cylinder about ten kilometers long and two wide, and it slowly rotated along its central axis, producing artificial gravity for the outward sections. It's otherwise smooth surface was dotted with long, slender protrusions - umbilicals for docking spaceships. The station could handle at least twenty large vessels docked at one time, but when we hit it there were only three freighters and no warships.

It orbited the outer gas giant, a massive world twice the size of Jupiter, and we were able to mask our approach by coming in from the far side of the planet. Our entry point was clear across the system from any of the known warp gates, so there was no sensor grid to detect our arrival. Shielded by the magnetic field of the enormous planet, our squadron whipped around in orbit and got off the first shot, knocking out the station's sensors and main batteries.

We had four ships - two heavy cruisers and two fast assault ships. After they blinded the station and knocked out its weapons, the cruisers, Washington and Chicago, took up a defensive position in case any inbound enemy ships turned up. Then it was up to us.

The Bearclaw launched two assault shuttles carrying the SEAL teams while half my people buttoned up into the other two. The rest of the company was on the Wolverine, suited up and loaded onto two of her four shuttles. There was another company of reserve troops on the Wolverine, scheduled to board after my people and garrison the station after we'd captured it.

I was bolted in place in my assault shuttle, but my suit was powered up, and my AI was locked into the ship's battle computers, so I was able to follow the SEALs as they began the assault. Their shuttles stopped and hovered just a few hundred meters from the target, and the bays opened and released the SEALs into space. These guys were trained for insertions from space, and they were some of the craziest sons of bitches I'd ever met.

The SEAL armor was bigger and bulkier than ours, with propulsion systems to allow them to maneuver in space. I had Hector project an image of the teams approaching the station, and I watched as the first of them manipulated their thrusters to make contact with the station without slamming into it. I was impressed by the fine control these guys had, as SEAL after SEAL impacted gently and went right to work.

The first team's mission was to blow a precision hole in the station's hull to get inside and defend that position while the second team fitted a portable docking collar that would allow our shuttles to connect and offload my people, so we could take the place deck by deck.

The SEALs worked quickly and confidently, and within five minutes they'd set their charges and pulled back to what the computers insisted (but I doubted) was a safe location on the hull. Thirty seconds later the Bearclaw's computer triggered the series of charges, ripping a neat, nearly circular four meter hole in the station's hull. A few seconds later the SEALs were climbing over the lip and disappearing inside.

The second team was approaching the station, almost in position. Six of them had hold of the docking collar, and they skillfully guided it into position around the gash in the hull. Setting the collar took a little more time than placing the charges, and it was about fifteen minutes before our shuttles got the go-ahead to begin the approach.

The SEALs inside didn't run into any resistance at first. The area beyond the insertion hole was now vacuum, so any security personnel on the station would have to suit up before they could try to respond. By the time they got organized and attacked the foothold, our first shuttle was inbound, and the SEALs only had to hold out for ten minutes or so.

Although outnumbered, the team was well-trained and equipped, and they were able to beat back two assaults with relative ease and minor losses. Before the third attack came my people were swarming aboard and launching our own assault that wiped out the entire security force threatening the landing area.

My first shuttle had landed in vacuum conditions, but after we'd secured the area we took the time to pressurize the now-sealed off section. The second group came aboard in a much more orderly manner, and I organized my sections to move out and begin to secure the station.

The area we were in was a storage facility, large and connected to what we believed to be several main arteries through the station. We'd entered through the "top" of the station, and we were close to the axis, where there was low gravity. Our intel was far from complete, and battleops had given me discretion on how to proceed. I sent one section through what I believed to be a maintenance conduit with instructions to find and take control of the main power plant. They had our best guess as to where it was, and I sent my most experienced junior officer, Lieutenant Frost, to command. Frost had been in Achilles too, and afterward he fought at Sandoval, which wasn't the blood-bath Columbia had been but was no walk in the park either.

The SEALs were too heavily armored to move quickly through the station, so I ordered them to stay and defend the landing area and act as a mobile reserve. They didn't like staying behind, or they didn't like taking orders from me. Or maybe both. But they were pros, and they were under my command, so they followed orders.

I took the rest of the company up through was appeared to be the main transport tube to the surface areas. The entrance to the tube was 60 meters above our position, but in this grav-ity all we had to do was jump and be careful not to smash too hard into the ceiling. It took about ten minutes to get everyone through the hatch. We had a couple of people jump too enthu-siastically and inflict some light damage to their suits, but no major problems.

There was a single large tube, which lift cars normally tra-versed, flanked by two smaller passageways with metal ladders. I figured they'd have shut down the lifts, so we split into two groups and started to climb up the ladder. Every fifty meters or so we'd get to a landing with hatches leading to other stor-age and work areas. We ran into a few maintenance bots and a couple station workers, but no organized resistance.

As we got higher, the climbing got a bit tougher, though of course it was not really very difficult in armor. The gravity increased the closer we got to the surface, and now you could really fall if you lost your grip, and maybe take out a bunch of your comrades as you did. I reminded everyone three times - or maybe four - to be careful. The decks got much closer together as well, and now there were landings every ten meters. When we got to the level we thought housed the main data center we got into our first real firefight.

The landing here was fairly large, with four doorways leading out. There were security personnel at each of these, firing at us as we emerged from the transport tubes. The security officers had light energy weapons, very effective at short range against lightly armored targets, but it took a direct hit at very close range to do any significant damage to an armored marine. We were close. In fact this was knife-fighting range for us, and since we were at a big positional disadvantage, instead of conducting a lengthy exchange of fire I ordered a charge against all four entryways.

"Charge and take the enemy positions as you emerge. Tube one, alternate. Odds take the north portal, evens the east. Tube two, odds to the south, evens to the west. Now!" North, south, east, and west were pure constructs, of course, familiar reference points assigned to directions by our battle computers.

I was about halfway down the transport tube in the middle of our formation where my training told me I was supposed to be. My gut told me otherwise, and I couldn't wait to get off this ladder and into the fight. Hector projected a schematic of the battle inside my visor. I could see my people, a series of blue dots, moving quickly from the platform into the corridors beyond the hatches. I could see red dots - the enemy - falling back slowly.

The fight was over quickly. This was the first time in all my assaults I'd seen true hand-to-hand fighting. We didn't often get this close to the enemy, but these confined spaces were very different from the usual battlefield. The station security troops wore body armor, but it was no match for our powered suits. My troops were also armed with close quarter blasters - our mag-rifles would have torn the station structure apart, and we wanted to capture the place, not turn it into rubble. The pulse laser blasters were powerful weapons, but their intensity dropped off quickly in atmosphere, making them at best good for short-range work.

Our weapons were far more effective against their unpowered armor than theirs were against our powered suits, so we were able to charge into their fire, taking only a few casualties. Once in hand-to-hand range we finished the job with our molecular blades. The blades were a sort of bayonet that retracted into the arm of the fighting suit when not in use. About 30 centimeters long when deployed, the blade was honed down to an edge just one molecule thick, which could cut through virtually anything, especially with the enhanced strength of our suits behind it. In a few cases the troops didn't even bother with the blades. A nuclear powered fist was enough to take out a lightly armored defender, and there were a few crushed skulls among the casualties.

By the time I got up to the platform it was all over. We had three casualties, two minor wounds with some suit damage, and one KIA, hit by a lucky shot that burned through the armpit of his suit. Our armor was tough everywhere, but it was weakest at the joints, where mobility required some concessions from protection.

I walked over to the northern corridor to check things out, and I found a blood-soaked slaughterhouse. There were a few charred bodies, the victims of our blaster fire as we came in, but most of the work here was done with the blades, and that worked was effectively done. There were severed limbs, bodies sliced in half, or nearly so, and bloody, unidentifiable bits of flesh everywhere. The walls were literally dripping with blood, small rivers of droplets slowly sliding down the smooth plasti-steel. Further down the hallway there were at least half a dozen bodies, victims of blaster fire as they tried to run. The other corridors were similar, and the south was worst of all, with the body parts piled so high we had to drag them out onto the platform so we could get past and head down the corridor.

It was the south corridor I expected to lead to the data center, and the heavier enemy presence there seemed to confirm my suspicions. Taking the data center was a primary objective on its own, but I had my own tactical plan as well that required its capture.

I left a squad at the platform to protect our rear and took the rest of the command down the south passage. We moved slowly, carefully. This was like urban street fighting, but even tighter. We passed numerous doors, each leading to another room or corridor. Every room had to be checked - I wasn't about to leave an enemy platoon unmolested in our rear.

We had a canister of small charges that were just powerful enough to blow open the hatches without causing a lot of other damage. The majority of the rooms were empty, but we did run into a few occupants, mostly techs of some sort at work. War is a harsh business, and we didn't have time to deal with prisoners, so we did what we had to do and moved on.

Suddenly an arc of electric-blue light ripped into our front rank, practically blowing one of my troopers to pieces. I ordered return fire, but the corridor was just wide enough for three people abreast, so it was hard to bring too much firepower to bear. About ten seconds later another blue bolt hit Corporal Wells, boring a neat 10cm hole through his chest.

"Open up the rooms, and take cover," I barked.

There were six rooms along the stretch of corridor we occupied, and we dispersed into them. I stayed in the corridor and directed everyone near me to the closest room. The blue beam continued to fire about every ten seconds, and it took out another one of my troopers and then just missed my head before I dove into one of the rooms.

I assigned two troopers to each doorway to return fire from cover. The enemy began to return fire as well, but it was all pretty ineffective. I think we took out two of them, and one of my guys was grazed in the arm.

This wasn't going to cut it. We were pinned down. My whole plan was based on speed and now we were sitting here stuck in the mud. I was pretty sure that was a portable particle accelerator out there, probably drawing directly from the station's power core, and Hector confirmed my analysis. The thing could fire every ten seconds or so. We could rush down the corridor, but we'd take a lot of casualties. The weapon was powerful enough to take out two or three targets each shot at close range.

"Hector, connect me with Lieutenant Frost."

"Frost here, sir."

"Lieutenant, give me a report. Have you reached the power core yet?"

"No sir. I'm pretty sure we've located it, but we have heavy resistance. I can expedite, but it will cost."

"Negative. Continue your plan for now, but if you aren't in there in fifteen minutes then take it at all costs."

"Understood. Frost, out."

Ok, so we were bogged down at the power plant too. If I didn't come up with an alternate plan we were going to end up frontally charging both positions, and a lot of my troopers would never get off this station.

I thought for a few minutes, and an idea started to form. We had four cutting lasers. The walls between compartments weren't armored. Maybe, just maybe we could cut through and advance from room to room.

I got on the link with my officers and non-coms and explained the plan. Unfortunately, one of the troopers with a cutting laser had been a casualty, and another was with Frost's group. So we only had two to work with. Private Hemming was with me in the forward-most room, and Private Black was the same side of the corridor one room back. I had Black start cutting his way into our room, while I got Hemming working on the wall between us and the next room. I had four troopers flanking Hemming; we had no idea what was waiting in that next room.

The cutting lasers were designed to draw on our suits' power plants, and they were quite strong. They cut through the interior walls of the station easily, but there were pipes and conduits of all sorts, so as we cut we'd sever them, creating showers of sparks, water, and steam. None of it was a threat to us in our suits, but it made quite a mess.

It took about three minutes to cut a hole large enough for a crouched man to get through. As soon as the cutting was done the marine with the torch would back away and one of the troopers on guard would kick the loose section of wall, and another would look through, weapons at the ready. All together it took us maybe five minutes to get from one room to the next.

Of course, we had troops in rooms on both sides of the corridor, and we were only cutting our way forward on one. My thought was to get far enough ahead to get around the projector and take it out, and then the rest of the company could advance down the corridor. But the rooms were small, which meant more walls between us and our destination. After twenty minutes we'd gotten through three, but unless they got a lot larger we were looking at ten or twelve more. This was taking too long.

I was just about to bite the bullet and order a charge down the corridor when Frost commed me.

"Captain, we're in the power center. We took three casualties, no KIAs."

I let out a little sigh of relief. "Excellent, Frost. Good work. Can you cut off power to specific sections of the station from where you are?"

"Sir, I'm not sure. I am in the main control center now, and I have Jarvis working on the computer, but I don't know how long it will take him to breach the security."

We didn't have time to try hack our way into their control system. "Frost, is there a manual cutoff for the whole thing? I don't want to shut down the reactor, just cut off the power flow to the grid."

"Stand by, Captain"

He was silent for about ninety seconds, and then he came back on and said, "Yes, there is a main cutoff, but I'm not sure what will happen if the whole station loses power."

He was right, of course. We had very incomplete information. I had to assume all the vital systems had some type of backup power, but there was no way to be certain. If I was wrong we'd lose life support and who knows what else. But I was pretty sure that projector in the hall was connected directly into the station's power grid. On the battlefield that type of gun would be on a tank or other vehicle with enough energy generation to power it. But the only way they could have rigged it up here is by drawing directly from the station's reactor. Cutting off power would shut the thing down. At least I hoped it would.

"Frost, on my command you will cut off power to the entire station."

"Yes sir." He paused for a few seconds and then said, "Captain, we have station security forces attempting to counterattack us here."

Shit. "Is your position in danger?"

There was a short silence, probably Frost evaluating reports from his troopers. "Not presently sir. I have pickets posted at all approaches. We're exchanging some fire, but I don't think it's a serious threat at this time."

"Ok. Prepare to execute power shutdown on my command. Duration sixty seconds, and then restore."

He acknowledged, then I told Hector to get my officers and non-coms on the line. I explained what I wanted to do. First, we were going to make a run for that projector and take it out before the power came back. Then, by squads, we were going to get down that hall as quickly as possible. I designated one squad to remain in our initial position and a second to follow behind the charge, checking out each of the rooms along the way to make sure we weren't leaving hostiles behind us. The first squad would support them if they ran into anything they couldn't handle on their own.

The initial run down the corridor was the riskiest part. I had no way to be sure that thing was hooked up to the main grid, or even if it could hold a charge for another shot if it was disconnected. Whoever led off down the corridor could easily end up being fried, and if anyone was going to take that chance based on my crazy scheme it was going to be me.

It was stupid, I knew that. I was the field commander, the first time I'd been in charge of an overall operation, and going out and getting myself killed in the middle of the fight was an idiotic thing to do. I was about to ignore everything I learned at the Academy too, but I just couldn't order anyone else down that corridor. Not after Achilles and Columbia. I'd sent too many men and women who trusted me to their deaths, and now it was my turn.

I laid out my plan and got the expected chorus of protests, but I told them it was decided. I'm sure they all still disagreed vehemently, but they also knew when to stop arguing with their commanding officer. Hector, on the other hand, had no such limitations, and after I'd finished with the briefing he added his commentary. "You do understand that this is a foolish decision based on your misplaced feelings of survivor's guilt, do you not? You are jeopardizing this mission by actions that have no basis in regulation or tactical expediency."

I wondered what it had been like in an age when computers just did math and kept their mouth shut. "Not another word, Hector. We're done discussing this." I half expected yet another argument, but for once he shut the hell up.

I waited until all the units were organized, and I told the squads that would be following me to advance as soon as the power was restored, and after 75 seconds in any event. Then I had Hector connect me with Lieutenant Frost. "Status report?"

"Enemy is still attempting to retake the power center. We have a low-intensity firefight in two of the approach corridors, but no serious threat at this time. I have two wounded in recent exchanges. Best estimate is approximately 20 enemy casualties."

"Very well. Are you ready to execute the power cutoff?"

There was the slightest hesitation, then his answered, slowly and deliberately. "Yes sir. everything is ready." He was worried about what unexpected effects the power shutoff might have, but he didn't say anything about it.

"Have you briefed your troops in the corridors?" I didn't want any of our people getting surprised in the middle of a fight.

"Yes sir. My entire command is ready."

I moved to the doorway, and activated my mag-rifle. The rest of the troops had only blasters, but the officers and ser-geants had mag-rifles as well, just in case they were needed. The velocity of the mag-rifle projectiles would wreak havoc on the station interior. But I needed to clear that hallway, so whatever collateral damage was done to the station was unavoidable. Plus, we weren't near the exterior, so at least I wouldn't blow a hole in the hull and decompress the entire area. I peered out cautiously into the corridor, and then I ordered Frost to cut the power. There was a delay of 3 or 4 seconds and then the lights went out, and then the entire place shook fiercely.

I held on to the open doorway, but I could hear everyone else slipping and sliding around. The station-quake was brief - I supposed that the station-keeping drives that maintain the rotation and orbit were affected by the power outage, which I later learned was exactly what had happened. If the power stayed out for too long the rotation of the station would slow and we'd lose the artificial gravity.

But now I had something to do, and I swung myself around the doorframe and bolted down the corridor. The sooner I got down there the better. Running in a confined space isn't easy in armor. Your legs are so strong that unless you're really careful you tend to start jumping. Staying low and moving with speed took a lot of practice, another reason why I was doing this. I don't think anyone in the company had the hours in a suit I did. I had my infrared scanning suite on full, so I could see there were enemy troops ahead. I must have surprised the hell out of them, because I was halfway down the corridor before they started firing. Most of the shots missed me, but a couple hit my armor, with no significant effect. I opened up with the mag-rifle at the max rate of fire and sprayed the entire area. I could hear screaming and scuffling around, and their fire stopped completely.

I made it almost up to the gun, which I could make out by its residual heat signature, but I was slowed up because there were four or five bodies on the ground in front of it - victims of my fire. There were crackling and hissing sounds all around, but no live enemies.

"Light, Hector," I snapped, and my sometimes surly, but more or less obedient AI turned on my helmet light. The gun was a semi-portable particle accelerator, just as I thought. There was a heavy insulated conduit at least 12cm in diameter connecting it to some sort of power hookup in the wall.

"Ten seconds to power restoration." Frost's voice on the link.

I grabbed the conduit and ripped it out before the power came back. I knocked the gun over and sprayed it with fire from my mag-rifle. At this range the projectiles ripped through the gun and the floor below. When I stopped firing, the thing was a pile of useless junk. It wouldn't kill any more of my troops now.

Just then the double doors behind opened up and security personnel streamed through. The lights came back on, and the system shook again, though not as hard as before. I managed to stay standing in my suit, but the station troops were all knocked off their feet.

"Hector, blade."

My molecular blade snapped out of the sheath in my arm and I started slashing at the enemy, trying to take out as many as I could before they overwhelmed me. With the strength of my suit behind it, my blade sliced effortlessly through their armor and bodies alike.

But they kept coming through the doorway, and I was pushed back against the wall. eventually one of them would get a blaster shoved into a weak spot in my armor. I knew my lead squad was on the way down the corridor, but that few seconds seemed to go on forever. I was just about to go down under the attackers when I saw my troops wading into the enemy from behind, blades slashing all around.

It was nasty business, and it went on for a while, because the narrow confines kept the frontage small. Finally, we finished them off in the corridor and pushed our way into the room. The data center was a huge open area, with a ceiling several levels high with catwalks around the edges.

Once we pushed into the center the remaining enemy troops lost heart and broke. Some tried to run, but most of them were gunned down before they made it out. A couple got away, and it wasn't important enough to detach a squad to chase them down. The rest surrendered, and since we were finally in a place where we could get a little more organized, I told the troops to take prisoners.

First things first. I detached a platoon to check the room thoroughly and find every way in and out, posting a team at each entrance. Then I ordered Lieutenant Sanchez to figure out how to operate station communications from here.

After I'd taken care of business, I commed Frost to see how things were going down there. Everything seemed under control. The enemy was still posted around his position, but they seemed to have given up on assaulting it. They were exchanging light fire, but the situation was stable. I checked with the SEALs at the entry point too, and everything was quiet there. They would have advised me if anything had happened, of course, but I wanted to make sure.

"Hector, send the signal for the support company to prepare for launch."

"Acknowledged."

I walked over to where Sanchez' was sitting at a workstation. He looked up and said, "I think I can access the communications system and make a station-wide announcement. But it's going to take a team of specialists to actually get control of this system if you want to affect life support or other systems."

I didn't expect anything different. Fortunately, we had just such a team waiting with the support company. Plan B was to send a force to seize a landing bay and get the reserves and tech support crew onboard. But first I was going to try Plan A.

There was a lot of fanaticism among Caliphate troops; their front line Janissaries almost never surrendered. But these were just routine security troops posted far back from what was thought to be the front line. They were just conscripts, and they'd been roughly handled so far. I had no idea about the command structure here - intel had been really weak in that department - but if their troops were ready to give up there wasn't much the command staff could do. If a Caliphate station commander and his officers wanted heroic deaths I was more than willing to oblige, and if their troops were ready to drop their weapons I was just as happy to let them do it.

"Hector, I want you to translate everything I say into Arabic and feed it into the communications system. Understood."

"Yes captain. What part of that did you feel was beyond my computational capability?" He hadn't been obnoxious for a while, so I guess he was due. They really needed to work the kinks out of this AI personality programming.

"Sanchez, I want you to plug my AI link into the com system, and put us on stationwide broadcast."

"Yes sir." He paused for a few seconds, looking briefly at the screen in front of him. "That will just take me a few minutes."

While Sanchez set up the communication, I checked on our overall status. We had about 30 prisoners, and they'd been disarmed and stripped of their body armor. They were locked in a storage room, and there were two guards outside the room and another monitoring on video.

All of the entryways were guarded, with a picket placed down each corridor and a fire team at every entrance. The rest of the troops were formed into a reaction force to meet any threat that might develop. I checked again with Frost, and his situation was largely unchanged. The enemy had withdrawn from several of the approaches to the power facility, with only sporadic fire from the others.

"Ready, captain. You are on systemwide communication."

I nodded to Sanchez, though gestures of that sort were pretty pointless in armor. "Attention Caliphate personnel. This is Captain Erik Cain, U.S. Marine Corps, Western Alliance Military Command. Presently, my forces are in control of both the power generation facilities and the main computer center. As you are aware from our recent demonstration, we can cut power to any areas of the station we wish."

I paused for just a second. I was actually speaking to Hector, and he was repeating what I said in Arabic on the com line. I was distracted briefly by the realization that he was using my voice and not his. Nice touch, Hector, but a little creepy too.

"We effectively control the station at this time. We have sufficient force to occupy the entire facility deck by deck if we need to." Ok, that was a lie, but worth a try.

"Even in the event that, for some reason, we are unable to take possession of the entire station, local space is totally controlled by our warships. Your defense grid has been destroyed, and if we are unsuccessful in taking the station our orders are to destroy it. We have the firepower to do just that." That much was true.

"You can fight on, but I have neither the time nor patience to allow this battle to go on any longer than necessary. If my troops are forced to take this station level by level there will be no quarter offered to any Caliphate personnel. If the station is surrendered immediately I will guarantee the safety of all inhabitants." Ok, this was a gamble. If they surrendered, it paid off. But if they didn't, I just gave them a reason to fight like banshees.

"If you surrender, all prisoners will be given the option of repatriation to the Caliphate at the soonest possible opportunity." I didn't really have the authority to offer repatriation to POWs, but I was pretty sure that central command would back me up. Especially if I captured the station with light casualties. If not, I was perfectly willing to lie to save the lives of my troopers.

"Alternatively, surrendered personnel will be given the opportunity to request asylum in the Western Alliance." Caliphate personnel were "encouraged" not to yield, and things could be difficult for anyone, especially a commander, who surrendered. I wanted to give them a good option. They weren't all religious fanatics.

"You are not frontline military personnel. I have no desire to have my fully-armored assault troops hunt down and kill everyone on this station, but I will. I will." I paused to let that sink in. "I am prepared to accept a surrender within the next ten minutes. After that period there will be no quarter, no mercy, no cessation of the attack. You have ten minutes. After ten minutes we will accept no incoming communications."

I made a motion for Sanchez to cut the broadcast. In a few minutes we'd know if it was going to be easy or difficult. Meanwhile, I signaled for the backup company to launch. If the station surrendered they could land in one of the bays almost immediately and assist in managing the surrender and taking control of the station. Otherwise, I'd assemble a recon force to take the nearest bay so we could get them aboard. I'd need the numbers to fight my way through every section of the station, and I'd want the tech support crew to help us utilize control of the computer and power generation centers.

I suspected that the commander's inclination would be to fight on, and that's why I broadcast my message live. His conscript troops were probably not as anxious to die, and the huge number of civilians on board even less so. As it turned out, I didn't have to wait anywhere near the whole ten minutes.

"Incoming message, sir." Sanchez on my comlink.

"Send it to me. Hector, translate, please." But I didn't need Hector's help. The response was given in accented, but clear English.

"Captain Cain, this is Sub-Commander Ahmedi. The commander has elected to pass on to the afterlife. An honorable death. As acting commander I offer the immediate surrender of this station and its personnel subject to the terms offered. I await your further instructions."

"Hector, translate my reply. Sub-Commander, I am pleased to accept your surrender, and I commend you on choosing to avoid a continuance of hostilities, which could not have altered the outcome of this engagement but only caused needless bloodshed. Please stand by for further instructions from my officers." I just stood there for a few seconds, letting out a sigh of relief. War is always bad business, but I was grateful, for once, to have most of the troops I led in coming out with me.

"Sanchez, secure a landing bay so we can bring the support elements onboard. Closest one to here. Coordinate with the sub-commander, and send a squad down to secure the area. Tell the sub-commander to release all security on the computer system so you can pull up schematics. Once we have the reserves deployed, have the Caliphate troops report to a suitable assembly area and supervise the disarming."

I barked out a number of additional orders, and having made the arrangements to secure the station and its personnel I took a few minutes to reflect. The surprise attack on the Caliphate Station Persaris was a complete success. We had six dead and seven seriously wounded, a casualty rate of less than ten percent, and a welcome change from the abattoirs of Achilles and Columbia. I'd completed my first mission in charge of a company, and, moreover, as the overall mission commander. Maybe I could do this after all.

We spent another week on the station, mostly helping to

organize our skeleton operations crew and supervise the detention of the prisoners. There were only 157 surviving security personnel, but I wasn't taking any chances, so all 2,000 or so occupants of the station were treated like combatant detainees. It was nothing but a rest for us. Our armor was shuttled back to the Wolverine, and we were fitted out in fatigues with light hand weapons.

Just before we left a new task force arrived, carrying a battalion of regular infantry and a full complement of technical and operations staff. Five cruisers joined the two we already had, forming a strong defense against an enemy attempt to take the station back. Freighters and repair ships also arrived to repair and upgrade the system's defenses, and a large transport docked to collect the prisoners.

I had the company assembled in one of the large landing bays to prepare to shuttle to Wolverine. When I walked in, Sanchez and Frost had the men lined up on either side of the bay. As soon as they saw me they started clapping and chanting my name, all of them. I raised my hands and tried to gesture for them to stop, but they just kept it up. As I was looking around the room, I noticed the SEALs where there too, clapping and yelling with the rest.

Chapter Nine

Space Station Tarawa
Gliese 250 system

Major Cain. It still sounded strange to me. I remember the first time I saw a major at Camp Puller. He seemed so imperious and so totally in command, I was in awe. Was that me now?

I outranked the officer who recruited me, or at least his rank at that time. Actually I'd found out that Captain Jack had ended up as Colonel Jack, and that he'd died during Achilles. I didn't know at the time, but he was commanding the rearguard that covered us all as we escaped, and he was almost the last man hit.

I glanced at the organizational chart. A battalion. Over 500 troops, all under my command. We were going in as part of a brigade-sized attack, which would be the largest operation since Achilles. I was strangely calm, although the prospect of commanding so many troops in battle was daunting.

A look at the top of the org chart made me feel a bit better. Brigadier General Holm was commanding the operation. Holm had taken an interest in my career, and I didn't doubt I owed my rapid advancement since the Academy to him, at least in part. I hadn't served with him since Columbia. In fact, until a few days before, I hadn't even seen him since that battle had started, though I'm pretty sure I owed my survival to his efforts to find me when anyone else would have given me up for dead.

Although smaller than Achilles, this was still a major operation, and it got me thinking about the evolution in battle tactics over the last 75 years. Early fighting in space was conducted mostly by local militias, with very small units of regulars attached for stiffening. Even during the First Frontier War, it was rare for more than a platoon of regulars to be involved in any one battle. This was true colonial warfare, not unlike what transpired in the early days of the European wars in the New World. It was just too expensive to move around large bodies of troops in space. The navies were small, and they simply did not have the capacity to transport major units. Certainly, all these early battles were fought without tanks, artillery, and other support elements.

The colonies were smaller then, too, and there were a lot fewer of them. The thin populations were generally spread around wherever there were resources to exploit, and true cities and towns were rare. Taking a planet usually required no more than attacking a few clusters of settlements.

The spheres of influence of the Powers were much more in a state of flux, and many worlds changed hands repeatedly. Hostile colonies were all mixed together, sometimes even in the same system, and there were no real borders or rational lines to defend. The treaty that ended the First Frontier War started the process of rationalization. The Powers were each more willing to concede systems they knew they'd have trouble holding anyway, and a natural trend toward consolidation began. The skirmishes in the years after the First Frontier War accelerated the process, as the Powers grabbed whatever exposed enemy worlds they could when the opportunity presented itself, and scaled back on defensive efforts for poorly located systems.

By the time full scale war broke out again, each belligerent had a more or less defensible cluster of interconnected colony worlds. The Second Frontier War was a definite progression from the first in scale and intensity. There were still plenty of small skirmishes over petty colonies, but by this time each side's core worlds had begun to develop into significant populations. Although the battles were still small, and the militias who fought in them would continue to be important, this war was decided by regular troops fighting over key systems.

Larger populations, stronger planetary defenses, and militias leavened with retired veterans all necessitated a strengthening of attacking forces. Combined arms returned to warfare as strike forces began to be supported with tanks and field artillery. The complexity of war in space was increasing, and tactics and training went along in lockstep. By the end of the Second Frontier War it was not uncommon for strikeforces to consist of an entire battalion supported by a couple tank platoons. Atmospheric fighters were also deployed in large battles, often launched from orbiting assault craft. The decisive battle of the war, at Persis, saw over 5,000 troops engaged on each side.

Nevertheless, the typical engagement involved fewer than 500 troops on a side, and heavy support units were still rare. Things were evolving, but war in space was still hellishly expensive, and resources were always stretched thin. The years leading up to the Third Frontier War saw a return to very small actions, but when things began to escalate toward outright war, the battles became bigger again. Our attack on Carson's World involved an entire battalion where 40 years earlier a platoon or two would have sufficed. There was another reason why so much force was deployed to that seemingly insignificant planet, but I wouldn't find out about it until years later.

As the Third Frontier War heated up, the battles continued to increase in size and complexity. Colonies, especially core worlds, had become large and wealthy enough to build some indigenous industry and upgrade their local defense capabilities. All of a sudden we were attacking planets that had tanks and artillery as part of their local forces, compelling us to respond in kind.

We were learning this new reality on the job, and paying in blood for our lessons. One reason that Operation Achilles was such a disaster is that no one had ever mounted so large and complex an assault in space. In fact, it had been more than a century since a battle this size had been fought on Earth. No one in the command structure had any experience in coordinating a combined arms assault at that level. Still, we came fairly close to pulling it off. Like everyone else who was on the ground, I'd come to regard Achilles as a display of command incompetence. It was only later, when I studied the whole operation at the Academy, that I realized just how close we had come to success. If we'd been able to maintain space superiority we probably would have just managed to take the planet, possibly ending the war right then. Our forces were devastated, but the defenders had been nearly wiped out.

So now I was heading for a briefing on this new campaign. After we took the station at Gliese 250, my company rejoined the battalion for twin assaults on Dina and Albera, two moons circling a gas giant in orbit around Zeta Leporis II. Fruits of our victory in Gliese, from which they were a single transit, the twin moons were major mining colonies of crucial importance to the Caliphate's war effort.

The battalion attacked Dina first, then we regrouped and reinforced before hitting Albera two weeks later. Without controlling Gliese 250, the enemy had a very circuitous route through CAC territory to reach the Zeta Leporis system, so it would be difficult for them to mount a counterassault any time soon. Both battles were tough, close quarters affairs fought mostly underground. The colonies were solely engaged in mining the rare ores that were plentiful in the crust of the two moons, and all of the habitable areas were located well below the surface where they were shielded from the massive radiation produced by Zeta Leporis I.

It wasn't unlike the battle on the station, but there was no single installation we could grab and compel a surrender, so we had to fight it out chamber by chamber. The moons produced vital war materials, and they were garrisoned by regulars, not second rate security forces like the station. We had quite a fight on our hands.

Halfway through the battle on Albera, I ended up as acting battalion exec when Major Warrick went down in a firefight. She wasn't badly wounded, but her armor was scragged, so she was out of the action. Captain Torrance had been acting executive officer, so he moved up to take command of the operation. He bumped me up to exec even though half the other captains had more seniority.

The toughest part of the fight was right near the end on Albera. The enemy had back held a tac-group of Janissaries we didn't even know was there. Roughly equivalent to a reinforced company of ours, they were completely fresh, and they hit us when we were tired and low on supplies. Eventually I took the battalion reserve and we found a way through the tunnels around to the other side. Once we hit them in the front and rear simultaneously their position became untenable, but they still fought on. Janissaries almost never surrender, and we had to wipe them out. It cost us.

Despite the serious losses, the victories were complete, and
with Gliese and Zeta Leporis we had taken two vital Caliphate
systems in less than four months. They'd have to try to take
both of them back, which at least would keep them too busy to
attack any more of our worlds for a while. I suspect that was
the major reason we attacked the moons. I seriously doubted
we'd be able to mount a credible defense of both systems, and
since our only access to Zeta Leporis was through Gliese, it was
an easy choice which one to try to hold. Our prospects were
improving, but we were still playing catch up, and we were short
on resources across the board. When we pulled back to Gliese
250 to refit and regroup it was immediately obvious we were
going to make a play to hang onto the system and its massive
space station. The place was swarming with naval units - the
biggest fleet I'd seen since Achilles. The station itself was a
beehive of construction work, and it was now surrounded by a
ring of defensive satellites and weapon platforms.

When we returned from Zeta Leporis we looped around the
orange Gliese primary and decelerated at full power. It made
for an uncomfortable ride, getting slammed into our accel/decel
couches the whole time, but it got us docked quickly. We all
needed some rest, and while the station wasn't the ideal place
for leave, it was still a chance to rest and recuperate with no one
shooting at us. Unless the enemy attacked while we were there,
of course.

The station, renamed Tarawa, was amazingly organized
considering it had only been four months since we'd taken it,
and we had billets assigned when we arrived. I dismissed the
company and headed to my assigned quarters, planning on an
extended period of sleeping without being crushed to death by
6G deceleration.

My quarters were quite large and comfortable; I was really
coming up in the world. Rank does indeed have its privileges,
and frankly I was starting to enjoy some of them. I flopped
on the bunk and was just about to order the AI to turn off the
lights when the door buzzer sounded.

"Open," I barked at the AI. I wasn't really in the mood for visitors right now. All I really wanted to do was sleep.

"So look how far my resourceful sergeant has gone." The voice was familiar and the voice cheerful.

I jumped up. Standing there in my doorway was Elias Holm. No longer Colonel Holm, as evidenced by the single polished platinum star on each collar. I stood at rigid attention and gave him my best salute. "General Holm, sir! I am very glad to see you sir. I believe I am greatly in your debt...in more ways than one.

He smiled warmly. "Please, please. No standing at attention. You're making me tired just looking at you. At ease." He looked the same, more or less. Maybe a little more gray in his hair or another line on his face. I realized with a start that between the hospital, the Academy, and my campaigns since, it had been well over three years since I'd last seen him on Columbia.

He motioned for me to take a seat. "Let's sit and relax. We can catch up a bit. I brought us a little refreshment." He held up a small bottle of caramel-colored liquid. "Cognac, straight from Earth, imported direct from Europa Federalis. Got it as a gift." I guessed that that little bottle would have cost a month's pay. To be honest, I wasn't much of a drinker, but I wasn't going to turn down the general. Besides, he brought the good stuff. If ever there was a time...

I hadn't really checked out my quarters at all, but I asked the AI for glasses, and a small cabinet in the wall opened. Inside were a dozen glasses of various sizes. I took two that looked suitable and brought them over to the table. The general popped open the bottle and poured.

"Erik," he said, "I am very proud of what you have accomplished. I had a strong feeling about you on Columbia, and your performance there and since has reinforced it. You've done solid soldiering, my boy."

I found praise hard to handle sometimes, but this was the one person in all of human space I most wanted to please. Ok, he was probably number two, but I respected the hell out of General Holm, and it meant a lot to hear all of this. "Thank

you, sir. I've tried to do my best, though I must confess I sometimes feel out of my league and just lucky when things work
out."

He snorted. "Erik, let me tell you a little secret as part of
your initiation to the brotherhood of command. We all feel that
way. If you didn't, you wouldn't be worth a damn as a commander. But you've dealt with it all, and you've risen to meet
every challenge thrown at you." He raised his glass. "To the
Corps. And to our brothers and sisters who are no longer here."

I grabbed my glass and clinked it against his. "To our lost
brothers and sisters." I took a sip and felt the heat of the cognac
sliding down my throat.

"I brought you something, Erik. It's not 100% by the book,
but I figured it wouldn't hurt anything for me to bring these."
He slid a small box across the table. I picked it up and opened it.
Inside there were two small round platinum circlets. A major's
insignia.

I was speechless for a few seconds, and then I managed to
stammer out a few words. "I'm not ready. It's too soon."

"Look Erik, you're ready. I have total confidence in you, and
I want you to lead one of the battalions in my new offensive. I
know you've come up quickly. The fastest in Corps history, in
fact. Though I don't suppose that helps your confidence any."
He let out a little chuckle. "But you know better than anyone
how many losses we've suffered. We just don't have the extra
years to waste. We're desperately short of capable command
personnel, and it's all the more crucial since so many of the
troops are green. So accept your promotion stoically, because
we both know that when the time comes you'll do what needs
to be done."

He grabbed the bottle and refilled the glasses. "Have another
drink, because the promotion isn't all. You're being decorated
again. Twice. Once for taking this station and again for the
moons campaign. And you're getting the platinum star cluster
for that stunt you pulled in the corridor here."

He paused to let that sink in. I just sat there silent, dumb-
struck. "It reminded me of your adventures on Columbia. I

noticed back then that all your troops were in heavy cover, but you were standing out in the open. You ate a nuke for that one. I'm sure you remember. Those were magnificent displays of valor. I salute you." He raised his glass and drained it. "But that's the end of it. I don't want to see you pull anything like that under my command. I need you as a commander, not a fallen hero."

I started to argue. "But general, the situation was..."

He held up a hand and stopped me. "Erik, you are one of the most intelligent soldiers I've ever seen. Think about it. You know I'm right. You indulged yourself on the station. You assuaged your guilt over the men and women who've died under your command by taking on the most dangerous task yourself. Believe me, I understand it. I would have wanted to do it too. But in the end, you made yourself feel better and jeopardized the mission to do it. You were in command of the whole operation, not just taking out one gun. In another place or another time things might have been different, but at that moment, on this station, your life was more important than that of anyone else. You could have sent a private or corporal down that corridor, and if he or she got killed you could have sent another. But you had no right to go yourself."

He paused very briefly and continued, "Erik, this is what we do. We're professionals, all of us. Making these kinds of decisions, it's our job. Your troops understand this, but you need to as well. Don't think that we don't all feel the same way. The ghosts talk to me too, so I know exactly how you feel. But you need to deal with it, because it's only going to get worse. You're one of the most promising young officers I've ever seen, and you've come along at a time when we desperately need good commanders. You're going to be leading many more troops, Erik, and a lot of them are going to die. You need to be ready, and you can't feel you need to throw away your life to atone for some imagined sins."

We were both silent for a good while after that. I nursed my drink and thought about his words. He was right, I knew he was right. But it wasn't easy. It was one thing to ask men and women to follow you into danger, but quite another to say, you and you, go into that death trap while I stay here. He was also right that I'd have to get past it if I was going to be an effective officer. They tried to cover this whole topic at the Academy too, but you really couldn't understand it fully until you'd lived it.

The general was silent. He knew I needed a minute to think, and he gave it to me. He took the bottle and filled our glasses and then sat quietly, staring at his cognac but not drinking.

Finally I broke the silence. "I know you're right, general. I can't tell you how much I appreciate your taking the time to talk this through with me. I'm having a hard time dealing with the losses. We were lucky and had light casualties here, but then the moons campaign was another bloodbath. Not as rough as Achilles or Columbia, but bad enough. Lots of empty seats on the shuttle coming back. I want to thank you for handling this privately and not through disciplinary channels. And for all the other ways you've helped my career."

He laughed softly. "Erik, this isn't disciplinary at all, private or otherwise. You are one of the best marines I've ever seen. Consider it help with your continuing education and development. Maybe I'd like to see you sidestep some of the things I learned the hard way. You're less of a drinker than I am," - he looked at my full glass and laughed again - "but I was less of a drinker myself a few thousand ghosts ago." He drained his glass. "But look at it this way. You've created one hell of a blood and guts reputation for yourself. I think your troops would raise you up on their shields and declare you emperor!"

We both laughed, and having gotten past the "official business," we sat for a long while and talked about all sorts of things delightfully devoid of military significance. We even crossed the boundaries somewhat and discussed a bit of our pre-corps pasts, but that was the cognac talking.

I learned a lot about the general that day, not the least of which is that he can drink me under the table. We polished off that very expensive bottle, which left him still in decent shape and me barely able to stand. He helped me over to my bunk and pulled off my boots. On his way out he ordered the AI to shut off the lights. That was the night I got tucked in by the marine corps' biggest hero.

So now I was here, reviewing the battalion I would be commanding, shiny new major's pips on my collar. It was a new unit, and most of the privates were fresh out of training. But the general had arranged for my old company to be transferred to my new command, so I had some familiar faces. He'd also given me authority to issue battlefield promotions to non-com positions, so I was able to take a lot of my veteran privates and make them team and squad leaders. I had a couple I wanted to send to the Academy, and the general approved them all, effective after the campaign. He didn't want to lose any experienced personnel from the mission, and I agreed completely.

I spent three days reorganizing the battalion. I tried to get an experienced private in every fire team, but I just didn't have enough. So I made sure each squad had at least one and that any team without one had a very experienced non-com in charge. I couldn't commission new lieutenants, but I could put a few veteran sergeants in command of platoons. I ran it by the general, and he told me to do whatever I thought was best. He also approved my request to bump Frost and Sanchez to captain and give each a company. Sanchez took a hit on Dina, but he'd be back to duty before we shipped out. By the time I finished rearranging things I was pretty happy with the results. I would have loved another experienced officer or two, but you work with what you've got.

A week before we were set to ship out I got one more surprise, courtesy of General Holm. I had just finished a final briefing with my platoon commanders and was heading out to the dining hall, when a familiar figure turned the corner and said, "Well if it isn't Major Erik Cain, the war hero."

I couldn't restrain my shocked smile. "Captain Darius Jax! How have you been, old friend?" I walked up to him intending to shake his hand, but somehow it turned into a big bear hug.

He flashed me a broad smile. "Tried to get myself killed on Alpha Leonis IV, but otherwise pretty fair. Of course, who can keep up with the legendary Major Erik Cain?"

"That will be quite enough of that, thank you. Come on, let's head down to the officers' club and get some dinner. We've got some serious catching up to do."

We hopped on the lift down to the club and worked our way through a couple of dinosaur-sized steaks as we took turns recounting the events of the past three years. Jax had been badly wounded during the Alpha Leonis campaign and got the pleasure of regenerating an arm, which gave us something to commiserate about. When he mentioned he was at Armstrong I thought he might have met Sarah, but the medical center was enormous, and their paths hadn't crossed.

The best news, as far as I was concerned, was that Jax was assigned to my battalion. The general, who had been impressed with both of us on Columbia, had apparently been mentoring his career as he had mine, and he arranged to have Jax transferred to serve under me. His captain's bars were shiny and new, but I decided right on the spot to make him my battalion executive officer. He had never commanded a company in the field, so putting him a heartbeat away from battalion command was unorthodox to say the least, but I knew Jax, and I knew that he could handle it. I knew I could trust him.

After expressing the obligatory concerns about his readiness for the position, he accepted. We shook on it, and business concluded we spent a long night talking and reminiscing. Jax and I had fought together in Achilles and on Columbia, two back-to-back bloodbaths, and each of us had been able to count on the other. It created a real kinship between us that was hard to explain but very real nonetheless. I have always been a loner, and Jax was close to the only person I would have called a friend. My personal relationships were few. Sarah, of course. And the general, who was rapidly becoming like a father to me.

Getting back to business, I felt a lot better about the battalion. With Jax, Frost, and Sanchez as three of my captains, and my veteran NCOs from the old company spread around as platoon execs and section leaders, I figured we'd be able to manage just fine, even with the high proportion of green troopers.

The campaign itself was a significant undertaking. The brigade was going to assault three systems, one after the other, only the second time a strike force had been given multiple targets. We'd be reinforced and resupplied between attacks, but we were going to hit all three in rapid succession, with very little time between to rest and refit.

As the war grew in scope, central command was planning more in terms of this type of sustained, multi-planet campaign. We had just completed the first one - the attacks on Dina and Albera, but they were two moons of the same planet. This was much vaster in scope, with almost ten times as many troops and three enemy worlds in different systems.

The entire campaign represented something of a doubling down on holding Gliese 250. We were attacking a group of systems known as "The Tail," a chain of three stars with no lateral warp gates at all, just one in and one out until the last system, which had only the one. The entire thing was a dead end, with no discovered route in or out except through Gliese. That made the systems easy for us to defend once we took them. As long as we held Gliese, the worlds of the Tail would be safe from attack. Of course, if we lost Gliese and didn't take it right back, the systems and any forces deployed down that dead end were cut off and as good as lost. They'd fight, of course, but trapped with no hope of resupply or reinforcement they'd stand no chance. If the enemy took Gliese back while we were still in the middle of the campaign, we'd have a disaster on our hands as bad as Achilles.

With no usable real estate in the system, the battle for Gliese, if and when it came, would be a naval affair. The little maneuver we'd pulled off to grab the station was only possible because it had been a surprise attack, and there were no Caliphate naval forces posted in the system. But now the navy had done everything it could to bring force to bear, and if the Caliphate came back they'd have one hell of a fight in space. And I do mean one hell of a fight. As long as our invasion force was deployed down the Tail, Gliese would host the biggest concentration of naval force deployed anywhere since Operation Achilles.

We even had an allied PRC task force in-system to bolster

our defenses, which was a new level in cooperation between the two powers. In addition to bringing 8 cruisers and a number of support vessels, the armada delivered Captain Akio Yoshi, an observer and liaison officer who would be coming with us on the campaign. The general attached him to my battalion, and asked me to make him as comfortable as possible.

I took the general's charge seriously, and checked and rechecked all the arrangements. I inquired about his billeting arrangements and found that he'd been assigned VIP quarters, which were quite a bit larger than my own. I checked them out to make sure everything was ready for his arrival, and I assigned a private to act as his orderly and assistant while we were on the station. I tried to arrange for one of the officer's clubs to have some Japanese dishes available while he was here, but since we'd only taken the station a few months ago, the supplies were still fairly limited, and they couldn't really accommodate my request.

I had a basic course in Japanese at the Academy, but the language curriculum was one of the things that had given way to the wartime acceleration of the training program, and my resulting ability to stammer a few words did not exactly facilitate communication. I was as likely to call his mother a rhinoceros as I was to offer a respectful greeting, so I took a portable AI with me when I went to the landing bay just in case his English was no better than my Japanese.

I could have saved myself the trouble. After we exchanged our respective salutes he greeted me warmly, in perfect English. "Major, I am glad to finally meet you. We in the PRC have heard much about your exploits, and I have been a particular fan. I am most honored to be your ally, and I sincerely hope one day to be your friend."

He extended his hand, and I grasped it firmly. "Captain Yoshi, I am very glad to meet you as well, and quite grateful that your English is far better than my Japanese."

He laughed heartily. "My father was the PRC ambassador to the Alliance for almost ten years. I grew up in the Georgetown Sector of Washbalt. No doubt one reason I was assigned to this duty."

"Well that should make things much easier on me. I'm from New York myself." I motioned for the orderly to collect the bags. "You must be exhausted. Let's get you settled into your billet. The private will bring your baggage to your quarters immediately."

"I would be most grateful, Major. And if I may make a request?"

"Certainly, Captain Yoshi, what can I do for you?"

"It's been a long day, and I'm starving. Is there anywhere on this station that makes a good burger?"

I started to answer him, but couldn't stifle my laugh. He looked at me quizzically, so I explained about my misadventures with the officer's club kitchen, and we both laughed again.

"Your efforts were most kind, Major, but you needn't worry. Ten years on your east coast, remember? If I can get a good rare burger and a pepperoni pizza with a decent beer to wash it all down I'll be just fine."

We had another laugh, and then we downshifted into small talk as we made our way to the officers' club, where we had two rare burgers that Akio pronounced, "quite excellent considering where we are."

We got along immediately, and while there was very little common ground between his privileged background and my, shall we say, grittier past, it turned out we were very similar in many ways. We agreed to dispense with the "major" and "captain" stuff, except in front of the troops.

I learned a little more about the liaison program over the next few days, and I thought it was a great idea. In the past allies tended to operate in overall cooperation, but generally undertook their own separate operations with minimal joint planning. Combined task forces, like the one taking shape in Gliese 250, were quite rare, and any suggestions at embedding allied liaison officers into active strike forces would have elicited shouts of "espionage!"

But mistrust was starting to give way to necessity. Since the Unification Wars, there had been no formal, long-term alliances or treaties between any nations. Certainly, some of the powers were more likely to support others - us and the PRC or the Caliphate and the CAC, for example. But there were no long-term arrangements, and each war set off a desperate scramble to attract allies, with the belligerent powers offering their prospective new friends all sorts of choice bits of the enemy empire in return for joining the fight.

But the scale of war in space was increasing, and it was becoming more crucial to have long-term allies. No power was strong enough to stand alone. The CAC and the Caliphate had as close to a permanent alliance as existed, which put enormous pressure on us. We could have handled either one of them, but not both. As both were usually fighting against us, and the PRC was the blood enemy of the CAC, an alliance made all sorts of sense.

For six years we had fought both the CAC and the Caliphate alone, and our defeats were largely the result of being spread too thin. If the PRC had entered the war at the beginning, the strategic situation would be enormously different. We might have even won the war by now. But there was still tremendous distrust between the superpowers, and these wheels turn slowly. Maybe it starts with two officers, a couple of hamburgers, and a night spent drinking too many beers.

Akio fit in very well, and he got along with everyone. He was very friendly and easy-going, but when I pulled up his file and read it I realized that this guy was one hell of a fighter too. In the couple years since the PRC had entered the war he'd been in five assaults, the last two as a company commander.

His first assignment was commanding a platoon protecting an exploratory expedition on a newly discovered planet. The CAC, which also claimed the system, sent in two companies to take out the whole group. Akio's platoon dug in and held out for 5 days against five to one odds before PRC naval support arrived and the CAC forces withdrew. He had 65% casualties and was wounded twice, but he held the place and kept every civilian member of the expedition alive.

I was going to have trouble keeping this guy a safe distance back from the fighting, I could see that now. And I didn't want to end up having to tell the general how I got the PRC liaison officer scragged.

Chapter Ten

AS Belleau Wood
Task Force Crocket
En route to Iota Draconis system

The order of battle listed 6,307 troops, including the general and Aoki. It took three days to shuttle us all to the waiting transports, and another two to get all the equipment and provisions loaded and the ships underway.

My battalion was assigned to the Belleau Wood, which was eerily familiar, since it was a sister-ship to the Gettysburg. We filled it up this time though, and things were pretty crowded. I had a cabin with an adjoining office this time instead of a bunk in the non-com berthing area. Another of those privileges of rank.

We were accelerating at 1g, so we didn't have to strap into the acceleration couches, at least not yet. It would take a couple days to get the fleet into formation, and until then we'd have a comfortable ride. I used the time to get everyone settled in and put together a schedule of workout and training sessions. When they weren't strapped into the couches or asleep, I wanted them kept busy. God, when did I turn into an officer?

The fleet was impressive. Ten large assault ships of the Gettysburg and Arlington classes, and twenty-four smaller transports and supply vessels, protected by a nine ship task force built around the battleship MacArthur. We were lighter on warships than we'd normally be for this big an op, but that's because they were staying in Gliese to protect our rear.

Eight days later we zipped through the Iota Draconis warp gate and burst into enemy space at .05c. We didn't expect any significant defending naval forces, but the task group went in ahead anyway, the transports lagging behind. If we guessed wrong, and there was a Caliphate fleet down the Tail, there was no point in losing a brigade before they even touched ground.

As expected, there weren't any warships in Iota Draconis,

but the MacArthur's group did capture four large freighters filled with rare ores from further down the Tail. The ships had been trapped at Iota since we'd taken control of Gliese 250.

Iota Draconis II was the largest colony of the three we were going to assault, and the orbital defenses were a lot tougher than anticipated. The fleet took them out, but the MacArthur took significant damage, and one of the cruisers was holed in multiple places and knocked out of the fight indefinitely.

This was the first time I'd served under General Holm in an attack, and the landing was the most meticulous thing I'd ever seen. Every aspect was perfectly timed, with the general closely monitoring each detail. A single regiment landed in the initial wave, with a reserve battalion suited up and ready to reinforce if necessary. My people stayed onboard, and I found it difficult to sit in my office and watch the battle unfold without me. I'd invited Jax and Aoki to monitor progress with me, and we sat silently for a long while, each of us unsettled at sitting on a ship while troops were landing on an enemy world. Finally, Aoki broke the silence. "I have never seen a landing so perfectly executed. General Holm truly lives up to his reputation."

"I've never met any officer with a mind like his." I looked up from the screen over to Aoki. "He sees everything, and he anticipates every possibility. I still don't know how we managed to hold Columbia, or how he knew the enemy had that third wave coming. Jax and I were only sergeants at the time, but Holm was aware of everything that was going on during every minute of that battle. And with all he had going on at the end he still had the time to track one wounded sergeant and send out the party that pulled me from under a pile of radioactive debris."

"He did more than that, Erik," Jax said. "He led the search party himself. We counter-attacked right after we repulsed the enemy advance - your emplacements were spot on, by the way...I've never seen troops melt away like they did in those fields of fire. We ended up four or five klicks from our starting point by the time the fighting was over. I was sure you were dead, but the general - colonel then - commed me and said you were alive and ordered us to head back and find you. By the time we got to you he was already there, with two medics and a couple squads of infantry searching."

I hadn't known the whole story before then, and I sat there quietly for a few minutes thinking about it. All three of us were silent, in fact, until the first units started to hit ground.

The assault went very much according to plan. The planet, which the enemy called Al'Kebir, was one large landmass dotted with small lakes and seas. It was hot, almost too hot to sustain habitation, but like so many worlds on the rim, it was rich in resources rare and valuable on Earth, so men lived there. The assault was a complex one. On most colony worlds the limited populations were clustered in relatively small areas near resources or the original settlements. But Al'Kebir was mostly barren desert with dense areas of rainforest surrounding the many small landlocked seas. The rainforests were full of dangerous plants and animals, but also a wide variety of useful and valuable resources. The population was dispersed into the small, moderately habitable bands between the rainforests and the surrounding deserts. There were no major cities or towns, just tiny villages spread in the habitable zones all over the planet.

This invasion would have no battle lines, no major objectives, and no concentration. It was a series of widely scattered search and destroy missions intended to wipe out the garrisons and take control of a hundred tiny villages. We knew there were regulars stationed on the planet, though intel didn't think there were any first line Janissaries. The native troops would probably be a cut above the average colonial militia - they usually were on these inhospitable worlds.

We had 1,800 troops in the first wave, all powered infantry. There were ten initial LZs, located in the deserts, each about about 15 klicks from one of the habitable zones. The primary maneuver element was the platoon, and the companies were spread out over a wide area. The invasion forces went from village to village, systematically taking each and then moving on to the next target. Localized rally points were set up to evacuate the wounded and deliver resupply to the committed units.

Things went pretty well. The regular garrison troops

defended the villages, but they were second line troops and
heavily outnumbered. Also, unlike the Janissaries, many of
them were willing to surrender rather than be wiped out. It
was the locals and not the regulars that gave us the hardest time.
They withdrew into the rainforests, forcing our troops to follow
them into the dense terrain to root them out. Combat in the
jungles was difficult and slow. The fighting suits protected our
troops the biggest dangers of the environment, but the swamps
and quicksand were huge impediments to maneuver. Finally, the
general sent down some teams with heavy incendiaries, and we
leveled the jungle wherever there were heavy pockets of resistance. Quite a few of the defenders were incinerated in these
attacks, and most of the rest surrendered rather than face the
same fate.

The destruction of large stretches of rainforest would damage the planet's economy, perhaps permanently. But this was
war, and we did what we had to do. The mop up took another
week, but the planet was ours. It was an unpleasant battle for
the troops that fought it, but our losses were actually fairly light.
The locals in the jungle gave us fits trying to run them down,
but they didn't have the weaponry to inflict heavy casualties on
our assault units.

We burned through a lot of ammunition and supplies, however. - about 40% over projected expenditures. Since this was a
campaign with three objectives, budgeting our supply was crucial. The moons campaign had been the first multi-objective
operation we'd mounted; this was the second. It marked a significant expansion of scope in strategy and planning. Instead of
targeted a single world and launching an assault, our operations
were starting to fit more into an overall strategic plan. We were
no longer taking A because it was a juicy target; we were taking
it because it led to B and that led to C.

We had about 60 dead and 175 seriously wounded. One of
the transports was detached to take the wounded and prisoners
back to Gliese, and the task force reformed and made a course
for the only other warp gate in the system - the one to 79 Ceti.

The transit took six days, and then we decelerated into the 79

Ceti system and revectored toward our target, the fifth planet. I have landed on many worlds, some virtual paradises and others difficult environments, but 79 Ceti V was the most hellish world I've ever experienced.

The system's seventh planet was an enormous gas giant, with almost 100 times the mass of Jupiter, and the forces exerted by this gargantuan neighbor distorted the orbit of world number five. Highly elliptical in nature, the resulting path around the sun caused the planet, called Eridu by its occupants, to be bombarded by intense heat and radiation during its long summers and to become a frozen wasteland in winter. The atmosphere was noxious, though not immediately lethal. But between the overall environment and the massive radiation from both 70 Ceti and planet 7, Eridu was one of the unhealthiest environments ever occupied by man.

However, the planet had large, naturally occurring stable isotopes of certain trans-uranic elements, exotic materials that existed only in trace quantities in laboratories on Earth. These elements were extremely useful in starship drives, and they were almost incalculably expensive. Eridu was the only known location where these elements occurred naturally in significant quantities, and where there is such value men will find a way to extract it.

According to intel reports, the planet was primarily inhabited by bonded workers, citizens of the Caliphate who had committed some offense or failed to pay a tax and were sent to Eridu to work off the debt. Poorly equipped with protective gear and working under dismal conditions, the median life expectancy for a new worker was less than eighteen months. Few who were sent there ever returned.

The supervisors lived in better shielded quarters and were equipped with superior protective suits. They were rotated out after a two-year assignment, generally quite wealthy after their stint. With no permanent population, there was no militia or local defense force, and the planet's garrison consisted entirely of regulars. Because of the savage environment, the garrison was 100% powered infantry, which meant we were likely to have a significant fight on our hands.

My battalion made up the lead assault wave. Eridu was the toughest objective of the campaign, and the general was counting on me to make sure the landing went smoothly. Or as smoothly as possible. Landing on Eridu was not an easy task. It was mid-winter, and the planet was wracked with massive ammonia blizzards. The dense, radioactive snow played havoc with scanners, but was even tougher on visibility. We sent down three automated drones, each with a very high-powered beacon that would serve as guidance for the landers. One of the robot probes crashed, and the second had a very hard touchdown but managed to deploy its beacon. On the third we got lucky; it landed perfectly.

We used the two functioning beacons as ground zero for two groups of landers. The general left all the details of the landing up to me, and I decided to bring down two companies in the first wave, and after they had landed, send in the battalion assets and the third company.

I went in with the first company, though I suspected I might get a lecture about it after the battle. If my troops were going into this hell, I was going with them. It was a rough ride down, but my lander made it without any damage. A few of the others came down hard and eleven troops were wounded. One crashed, killing all five occupants.

The conditions were even worse than I expected. Visibility was less than ten meters, and even with Hector constantly enhancing the constructed images, the data from my scanners was fuzzy and difficult to read. The wind was fierce, and I could feel myself pushing against it even in my suit. It would have blown an unarmored man away like a dry leaf.

I had assigned one platoon from each company form a circular picket line all around the LZ. I didn't seriously expect the enemy to come out of their bunkers to fight us here, but long-range scanning was next to useless, and I wasn't going to risk a surprise. The rest of us cleared the LZ. The Gordons were shot, but they had enough juice left to lift off and fly a few klicks before crashing. I wanted the landing zone clear. Dealing with the conditions was bad enough; I didn't want the second wave having to deal with the debris from the first. God damn it, I wasn't losing any more of my troops in crashes we could avoid.

We had a couple of hard landings and a few more minor wounds, but the second wave made it in with none seriously hurt. I formed the battalion up with two companies abreast, covering a frontage of about 6 klicks. I had a company and the battalion assets in reserve about three klicks back.

There were two major mining operations on the planet, and they were the only population centers. We were assaulting one of them, and as soon as we were engaged, the 2nd battalion would commence their landing against the other one.

Our advance was slow. Even in powered armor, it's not easy to make time slogging through waste deep ammonia snow, with almost no visibility and your scanners only half working. I didn't want any stupid accidents causing unnecessary casualties, so I kept the pace very deliberate.

We had a rough projection of the location of enemy bunkers, but we really had no idea what they'd managed to do since we burst through the warp gate and triggered the alarm systems. We didn't even have a reliable estimate of enemy strength. Their visibility and scanning would be as fouled up as ours, but I figured they'd probably have some type of detection net set up. I gave orders for any squads that drew fire to fall back and report.

I wanted to be in the forward line, but I knew the general didn't want me there, so I took position back with the battalion assets. Not that he'd know unless I got hit. We had verbal communication with the fleet, but the radioactivity and the vicious storm cut the normal link with the battle computers on the flagship. We were on our own, much more than any strike force I'd been part of.

We got to within one klick of where we had intermittent readings of some type of energy source, when automatic fire ripped across the frontage of one of my squads. They followed orders and pulled back, carrying their two casualties with them. The guys who were hit were just wounded, but both of them died before their comrades got them back to the medic. The

cold and the atmosphere were a rough combination for the
wounded to survive.

I commed the entire battalion and told them to prioritize
patching the armor of wounded personnel. The suit's trauma
control would stabilize most wounds, at least for a while. But
it wouldn't help if the injured marines were exposed to the elements for too long. The suits did have a self-repair system, but
it was only good for patching small breaches. We had adjustable
patches that could be used for temporary repair jobs, but they
had to be applied manually, usually by someone other than the
wearer of the damaged suit.

I ordered a platoon to move around the flank of the position
that had opened fire, but they took fire from another direction
and pulled back with one man down. Trying to flank the second
enemy position we took fire from a third. I had Hector chew-
ing on the probable locations, and he projected that there was
an enemy position every 1,000 meters along a circle 3 klicks in
radius out from the settlement. I had him transmit his best cal-
culated locations to the platoon commanders.

We still had no idea how big or well armed the strongpoints
were. The fire was heavy, a SAW or equivalent at least, maybe
something bigger. Frontally assaulting these things was going
to be expensive, maybe even impossible in these conditions. If
we could get clear line of sight we could try to take them out
with heavy weapons fire, but a direct hit in this storm would be
dumb luck.

I had a plan, but it dug at my weak spot. It wasn't exactly
a suicide mission I had to give out, but it was close enough to
gnaw at me. Unfortunately, it was the only decent idea I could
come up with. "Hector, give me the four most experienced
scouts."

"Garrison, Evers, Connors, and Rodriguez have the most
months of service. Garrison, Harris, Connors, and Janek have
the most assaults. Alvarez has fewer assaults and less time in
service, but has been in two battles on worlds with extreme cold
conditions. Recommendation of four most qualified candi-
dates: Garrison, Connors, Janek, and Alvarez."

Wow. Not even one obnoxious remark. Hector was mellow-ing. I guess he was getting old like me. I thought for a second before making my decision. "Ok, Hector. Put me on com with Garrison, Connors, Janek, and Alvarez. Get Captain Frost on the line too."

"Of course." His reply was immediate. "I am glad to see you accepting my recommendations. I anticipated some emotion-based need to adjust my determinations."

Oh well. Spoke too soon about Hector. "Just do it."

There were a few seconds of silence while he established the links. "You are connected with the requested parties."

I just launched right into it. "I have a mission for the four of you. We need to breach this ring of strongpoints, and we don't have time to take potshots at them in this storm. I'm going to use specials to take them out, but we need better targeting than we have. These things are reinforced, and if we're going to use warheads with low enough yields to allow us to advance immedi-ately we're going to have to land them right on the mark.

"I want you to move out in two pairs, each toward one emplacement. We're going to start popping grenades and rock-ets at them to get their attention, and you are going to sneak up and get close enough to hit the structures with a laser sight. You're going to have to get really close, even with a high-pow-ered laser - maybe 20-30 meters. I want you to take your time on the approach. Crawl the whole way; don't raise anything high enough to get it shot off.

"Here's the tough part. They're going to have the same trou-ble scanning you as we have with them, but when you hit them with that laser there's a good chance they'll detect it. We have no idea what's behind that outer ring, but I want this whole thing to be a surprise, so I can only give you 5 minutes to get out of the blast radius. You guys crawl back as fast as you can, but at 4:45 I'm going to give you the warning, and you hug the ground as tightly as you can.

"I'm sending two companies through the gap as soon as the shockwave passes, and we're going to charge right into what-ever is behind these bunkers before they have time to react. It's enough time for you to get away from the blast, but just barely. So once one of you gets the sighting on a structure I want both of you on the way back instantly."

I paused a few seconds to let them process what I was saying. "One other thing. When you have visual and think you can get a laser spot, check in before doing it. We've got to get both teams in position before anyone paints the target. That 5 minutes starts when the first beam hits, so if the other team isn't in position they're not going to have time to get the spot done and get out in time. I know this is high risk, but it's the only way we can get through these defenses without getting half the battalion shot up. Any questions?"

I didn't expect any, so I wasn't surprised when there were none. Just four quick "no sirs." I had Hector terminate the link, then told him to get Frost back on the line.

"Frost here, sir."

"Dan, I want you to supervise the scouts. Split them into two pairs and monitor them every step of the way. I'm going to supervise the firing myself. Five minutes to the second after we get the first spot those nukes are going to fly. I want all four of those scouts to get back. Make sure they don't spot until both are in position. I'm counting on you."

"Understood, sir. Consider it done."

I cut that line and got Jax on. I filled him in on the plan and told him to have the two companies ready to get low when the warheads went off and prepare to attack immediately. I put Jax in command of the charge, but I really wanted to go myself.

Ten minutes later two platoons supported by two heavy weapons teams from the battalion reserve opened fire with grenades and rocket launchers, while the four scouts started to move forward from the line. It takes quite a while to crawl a kilometer, and the next fifteen minutes was just about the longest in my life. It didn't look like the enemy had spotted any of the scouts, but that wasn't surprising. Crawling like they were the snow completely covered them. Scout suits had the best camo our technology could produce, and they also had a coating that interfered with scans. Not that any scans were worth a damn here anyway.

The team on our right, Janek and Alvarez, got into position first. Alvarez commed a quick description of the structure. It looked like a hardened plasti-crete bunker mounting three heavy auto-cannons. Shit, I was right. We'd have been slaughtered if we'd advanced straight into that fire. They had only been firing one of the guns. Clever bastards. Trying to sucker us into a frontal assault.

It didn't take more than another minute before Garrison commed that he was in position. The left structure seemed to be a copy of the one on the right. I gave Frost the go ahead, and he had the scouts paint the targets. The second the laser sights hit the bunkers the position was relayed to the mortar teams I had ready. I had Hector counting down 300 seconds, giving me a warning every 30 until the last 30 and then counting down by ones.

Without our normal scanner capability I didn't have reliable location data on the returning scouts, so I really had no idea how they were doing. I felt myself willing them forward, as if I could pull them back by wishing it so.

When Hector got to one minute I had the mortar teams arm their warheads. At thirty seconds I had him broadcast the countdown to the whole battalion.

"Twenty-six, twenty-five, twenty-four..."

Had I done everything I could? Should I give those guys an extra minute to get back?

"Eighteen, seventeen, sixteen..."

No. I had to stick to the plan. If there were more bunkers behind these and we lost the surprise, our attack would run right into a meatgrinder. At fifteen I told the scouts to hug the ground.

"Twelve, eleven, ten..."

I dropped down myself. The whole battalion was prone, though most of us were far enough back to avoid the worst of the shockwaves.

"Five, four, three, two, one..."

Buttoned up in my suit in the middle of an alien blizzard I

couldn't hear the shots go off. There was an eerie wait, maybe ten or twelve seconds while the rounds made their way to the target and then...

The swirling snow flared bright yellow for an instant and then vaporized.

"Everyone stay down until I give the order!" I had told them several times already, but it never hurt to make sure.

I could hear rocks and debris bouncing off the back of my suit as the shock waves reached my position. It only lasted a few seconds and then subsided. I slowly got up onto my hands and knees and looked out into the suddenly improved visibility to see two small mushroom clouds. Hector gave me a breakdown of outside conditions. An unarmored man would have died instantly, probably first from the intense heat, though the concentration of ammonia vapor and the radiation were also well beyond lethal levels.

I had Hector get Jax on the line. "Jax, start your attack. Be careful, and monitor the heat levels. You should be fine, but just make sure no one gets into a hotspot and exceeds their suit tolerance."

"Yes sir. Attack commencing now."

This was definitely the same old Jax. He had the companies heading forward in 15 or 20 seconds, and they were moving quickly. After about two minutes I got a report.

"Major Cain, Jax here. We have visuals on the impact points. Significant craters and scattered plasti-crete debris. The bunkers are completely gone. No enemy presence, no hostile fire. Exterior temperature 923K."

"Thank you, Captain. Keep moving toward the center point. Report any structures or enemy action immediately. Continue monitoring outside conditions."

After he acknowledged, I got Frost on the line. He had the reserve company. "Frost, I'm attaching a heavy weapons team to your company. Move up and stay 3 klicks behind Jax's troops. I want you in position to react to any developments." I sent a couple of scouts around each flank to check on activity from the other bunkers, and then I got the request I was expecting but was dreading.

"Major? Captain Yoshi here. Request permission to move forward and observe the action."

I couldn't really refuse. He was here to observe after all, and it wouldn't do to insult the courage of the PRC's representative. "Ok, Aoki, but I want you to stay with Frost's company. Hook up with his command element, and don't go any farther forward without checking with me."

"Yes major. Thank you, sir."

A few seconds later Jax commed me. "Major, I have enemy troops emerging from two, possibly three points. It appears they are coming out of several concrete structures. The bunkers are not large, sir, so my best guess is they are moving up from underground facilities."

We expected that most of the installations would be underground. Looks like that hypothesis was panning out. After a brief pause, Jax continued. "I have each company deployed in two lines. SAWs will be emplaced and engaged within 30 seconds. I detached a squad to each flank just in case we get any sallies from the perimeter bunkers to each side."

He'd just told me he already did everything I was going to order him to do. "Very well, captain. Outstanding. Carry on." I moved forward myself. Jax was over on the left, though he was controlling the whole line perfectly. I drifted to the right and moved up to the second infantry line.

There was still a lot of residual heat, and the snow was being vaporized as it fell. There was a haze from the suddenly gaseous ammonia, but the visibility was significantly better than it had been. I could see the first line, and it looked like they were heavily engaged.

The fight was nasty, but we had the edge from the beginning. Jax had the troops perfectly deployed, and the enemy was rushing into formation. I figured we'd taken them by surprise with our nukes, and the only way they could stop us from getting to their access points was to come out and fight us on the surface. From my perspective, every one of them we killed up here was one we didn't have to dig out of some tunnel.

Jax had the company auto-cannons deployed in the center of each forward line. I ordered up the two heavy battalion auto-cannons from the reserve, positioning one on the extreme right flank and sending the other over to Jax to place wherever he thought he needed it.

We were definitely getting the better of the fight, but the enemy was still bringing out troops, and the fire was heavy. We were taking considerable losses and, with current conditions, most of them were KIAs. Right now, just about any hole in your armor was enough to kill you.

I wanted this fight over. I wasn't going to sit here and wage a battle of attrition where every minor wound was a death sentence. I ordered Frost to move his company over to the extreme right. About five minutes later his people were in position.

"Frost, we're going to swing around and hit these guys in the flank as they come forward. I want a section detached to keep those buildings and the immediate area around them under constant grenade attack. Give them something to think about as they are coming up."

Frost acknowledged and snapped out orders to one of the sections while I was still on the com.

"I want the rest of the company to wheel 90 degrees and advance perpendicularly to our line." I had Hector add Sanchez to the com. He was commanding the company in line on the right. "Sanchez, Frost's company is going to flank the enemy. I want your people in the first line to key off their beacon. As they advance across your position move your troops in laterally to fill the holes further down the line. I don't want any friendly fire incidents. Understood?"

"Yes sir." His voice was strong, clear. God, I was proud of these troops. "Understood. Executing now."

The heat from the explosions was dissipating. In a few more minutes we'd be back in the middle of the blizzard. I wanted to make the best progress we could while we had relatively good visibility. Frost's company pivoted around, using the heavy auto-cannon as a hinge. When they were perpendicular to the rest of the line I ordered the auto-cannon redeployed further down. As Frost's people advanced, Sanchez' troops moved laterally by fire team, each group repositioning to specific areas at his direction. The shortening of his frontage allowed him to plug the gaps where casualties were heavy without committing the second line. I wanted those reserves kept fresh if possible. I suspected the surface battle was only phase one for us.

The enemy, disorganized already from trying to form up as they emerged, were caught in the crossfire, and the entire enemy left flank started to disintegrate. These weren't Janissaries, but they were good troops, and taking prisoners wasn't exactly feasible under these conditions anyway. As our flanking force advanced, the original line became shorter and denser, and the enemy was caught in a savage crossfire. We were losing some visibility - the ammonia was coming down as rain now - but were hardly needed visibility to rake the enemy with fire.

Their left flank broke first. It started in small groups, but within a few minutes the entire enemy left was in full flight. I ordered Frost to pursue and prevent them from rallying, and I had Sanchez wheel his company as Frost had done earlier, flanking the enemy right, which was still heavily engaged with my first company. Their captain, Rijis, was down, so Jax took over direct command, and condensed his frontage as Sanchez's troops advanced laterally.

Caught in the crossfire, with half their troops already in flight, the rest of the enemy troops broke and ran. We had pretty much lost visibility in the slushy ammonia mix that was now falling, but we still had some scanner contact. I ordered Jax to take a platoon and pursue, linking up with Frost and taking overall command on the surface. I took the rest of Rijis' company and Sanchez' crew and headed to the central bunker. We were going underground.

I gave Jax the battalion heavy weapons - they wouldn't be much use in the tunnels anyway - and told him to keep the enemy off-balance, but to be very careful. I didn't want our troops getting strung out all over the place in conditions like these. But I also didn't want these enemy troops on the surface to reform and come down into the tunnels behind me.

There were two large, reinforced plasti-crete structures. Both seemed to be access points to the underground complex. I sent Sanchez to one with his company, and I went to the other with half of Rijis' crew and the battalion auxiliaries.

There were half a dozen guards in each building, so we had a quick firefight as we pushed our way in, suffering 4 more casualties before we wiped them out. The access points appeared to be large hatches over circular shafts about 4 meters wide. The shaft was about ten meters deep, and there was a large chamber at the bottom. There were 4 metal ladders, one at each compass point. It looked like there was also a bank of three lifts, but I wasn't about to trust to the enemy to keep the power on while we took the elevators. I lined up a section at each of the ladders, and ordered Sanchez to proceed the same way in his building.

We popped about a dozen grenades down the shaft to disrupt anyone waiting there - I didn't want any fire as we climbed down - and then the sections went over the edge. The first troopers got to the bottom quickly, climbing about halfway down and then jumping to the ground. The area at the bottom of the shaft was a large round chamber about 50 meters in diameter, clearly an assembly point for ingress and egress. There were large pipes along the ceiling with what looked like high powered air and water jets, probably for removing toxic, radioactive residue from armor and protective gear before entering the main complex. I'm afraid we were rude houseguests, though, and didn't stop to wipe our feet.

I commed Sanchez for a report, and it seemed like the chamber below the other bunker was similar but considerably smaller, probably an emergency or secondary ingress/egress point. I told him to proceed with caution. We'd killed a lot of their troops in the firefight, and even more of them were disordered and fleeing on the surface, cut off from at least these two re-entry points. But we still had no idea how many more troops they might have down here, and I wasn't taking any chances on either of our groups getting cut off and trapped.

The bank of lifts was along the wall not far from the ladder. They appeared to be large freight-sized elevators, and we had no idea how far down they went. We didn't need the enemy using them to bring troops up in our rear, so I had one of the rocket teams blast them. The cars were all somewhere on a lower level, but the explosions did more than enough damage to make the things unusable.

There were four doors leading out of the large chamber. One exit was a large set of double doors near the lifts, which appeared to be access to the mining areas. The other three were clustered on the opposite end of the chamber.

I checked with Sanchez, and his room didn't have the lifts or the large doors, just two smaller ones. I ordered him to move forward and clear one, leaving a strong guard on the other in case the enemy sallied out. I did the same thing on my end. I set up one of the SAW teams covering each door, and left a platoon in the chamber. Then we blasted open the door on the left and headed down the corridor.

The tunnel appeared to be bored out of solid rock and covered with a white, plasti-crete coating. There was a long lighting track running down the center of the ceiling, but it looked like they'd cut the power. I had the lead troopers turn on their suit floodlights so we could get an actual look at the corridor and not just an infrared reconstruction. The tunnel had no branches, and we had no enemy contacts at all. We ended up in a single large room with rows of armor racks along the walls. There were half a dozen suits hanging, but the rest of the racks were empty. That didn't mean anything on its own - even if there was a whole army down here waiting for us, they'd be suited up by now.

I had Hector do an analysis the number of suit racks and estimates of the surface force we had engaged. His answer confirmed my initial guess. Most or all of the troops who'd suited up here were in the surface force. Of course, for all we knew there could be ten more rooms like this down here.

We were at a dead end, and I was about to get everyone turned around and head back to the main chamber when I got started getting urgent reports. They had audio and scanner contacts on the other side of one of the doors. They were covering the entry with a SAW, and there was a squad against the wall next to the door.

I got everyone turned around in a hurry, and started back. I hadn't gotten 20 steps when I got the update. The door had been blown, and troops swarmed into the chamber. But the ID transponders flashed a warning to everyone, and at the last second no one fired. It wasn't the enemy, it was Sanchez' people pouring out of the doorway.

I commed him immediately for a report. It turns out the entry he'd taken his people through was in fact a secondary ingress/egress point. There were some storage areas directly under, but the only tunnel led straight back to the access chamber we were occupying, which was now crowded with both forces.

I sent Sanchez and one of his platoons down the middle corridor to check it out, but my gut said the double doors by the lifts were more important. While Sanchez was scouting I checked in with Jax for a surface report. The rout had continued, with small clusters of enemy troops rallying and fighting back, but most trying to escape. Jax estimated that there were less than 100 enemy troops left alive on the surface. He'd formed a command post and was sending search and destroy teams out to finish them off.

Good. Leaving Jax in charge of something was as good as seeing it done yourself. I also got an update from fleet command. Tyler Johnson's battalion had landed near the second planetary objective. Hopefully our reports would help them out. I had just signed off with fleet, when Sanchez commed me. The central corridor led to an extensive complex, which seemed to be mostly living quarters. They hadn't searched the whole place yet, but so far everywhere they'd been was deserted. It could take hours to go through every corridor and room in a complex that housed several thousand workers and troops. I wanted Sanchez back here before we went into that mine.

"Sanchez, have Sergeant Ho and one section search the place to confirm it is deserted. Meanwhile, you get back here with the rest of your crew. We're going into the mine in ten minutes."

"Yes sir. On the way."

I started to get the troops organized for entering the mines while two of the engineers prepped charges to blow the doors. When Sanchez got back we blasted our way in and started moving down the tunnel in three waves.

We might as well have walked through the front door of hell. For the next nine hours we fought step by step, level by level through the gigantic mazelike mine against a fanatical enemy determined to fight to the death. We made our way through booby traps and past hidden snipers. Our scanners and communication with the surface were out, the effect of the concentrations of super-heavy elements in the surrounding rock structures.

In one large chamber we found the bodies of the mine workers, the poor souls sentenced to this hell for one infraction or another. They were little better than slaves, and my first thought was someone decided they couldn't be trusted in this fight, and had them disposed of. But after looking I could see they'd been dead for quite some time.

The troops defending the tunnels were Mubarizun, elite Caliphate special forces that we certainly didn't expect to find there, and they fought us with suicidal determination. The combat was beyond savage, as bad or worse than anything during Achilles or Columbia, but in confined spaces deep underground. They collapsed tunnels on us and utilized their familiarity with the mazelike complex to try and outflank us. We fought with every weapon we had, and in the tightest areas the battle came down to blades and even armored fists.

I sent a runner to call down Jax's troops after they'd cleared the surface, and Ho's group as well for reinforcements. Trying to direct an entire battalion strung out through kilometers of twisting tunnels is virtually impossible, even when your com is working. The sergeants and corporals earned their pay taking the initiative when orders from higher up couldn't reach them. By the time we'd cornered the last group and wiped them out we were exhausted and near the end of our endurance. I'd never seen troops fight more bravely than those I led that day, but I also knew the battalion was nearly broken.

I came close to not making it out myself. I ended up separated from my troops and surrounded by 4 of the enemy. They'd have taken me down for sure, but just in time two of them went down under a pair of blades slashing so quickly my eyes couldn't follow them. PRC troops carried a blade in each arm, not just the one, as we did. Their military maintained a tradition of fighting with the blade, and Aoki Yoshi was an expert. I whipped around and sliced one of the enemy troopers nearly in half, then spun and shot the other one in the head. That was how my liaison officer, Captain Aoki Yoshi, saved my life on Eridu despite the fact that I had told him ten times to stay out of the fighting.

When we hobbled out of the tunnels, now absent any living creature but us, and climbed slowly up the ladders to the surface, less than half of us were left standing. The survivors slowly gathered around the rally area, waiting silently for the shuttles to land, while the medics did what they could for the wounded in terrible conditions. Sanchez wasn't one of the survivors. He died fighting half a dozen enemies with his blade while his troops pulled their wounded back to safety. He'd be decorated posthumously, I would see to that. For all the miserable good it would do him.

As soon as I realized what we were up against, I'd sent runners back to the main chamber to contact fleet command so they could warn Major Johnson and his battalion before they went in. Unfortunately the warning was too late. The complex on the other side of the planet was a copy of the one we attacked, and it was also full of Mubarizun. Johnson's troops there were beaten back, and the general had to send in another battalion to reinforce them, which played havoc with the org chart for the rest of the campaign.

We boarded the shuttles and rode back to the ship in almost total silence. Everyone was in a dazed stupor, and after we docked I just left everyone alone for a few days. No reports, no training, no drills. I let them mourn our dead in their own ways.

In the days after the battle we managed to piece together

what had happened. It seems there had been a rebellion among the workers that shut down production. Shortly before my strikeforce took the station at Gliese, the Mubarizun expedition had been dispatched to support the garrison, which had not been able to take the mines back from the rebels. The elite troops quickly wiped out the rebellious workers, but they couldn't withdraw because we now controlled the Gliese 250 system. So we blundered into a prepared and fortified force of elite troops where we'd expected only garrison. And we'd paid the price in blood.

The garrison troops had Mubarizun units embedded with them, which explains why they fought so hard on the surface. In the end there were no prisoners at all, and even if they'd tried to surrender, after the losses we'd taken I doubt any of us would have accepted it. When a battle reaches a certain point, when the cost has been too high, it becomes a struggle to the death.

So I'd been in another fight where my troops suffered 50% casualties, with a very large percentage of those killed. More ghosts to share my fitful and restless sleep.

Johnson's battalion got hurt even worse, with casualties over 70%. In the end the general had to rescue them with a reserve battalion, which itself took 20% losses. Tyler Johnson would have plenty of time to think about his own ghosts. His men pulled him out of the mines still alive, but barely. Now he would go through the ordeal of growing two new arms and two new legs, among other treatments. He was a good officer, but I didn't know if he'd ever be the same again. I wanted to see him before he was shipped back to Gliese, but he was heavily sedated and kept in medical isolation, so it wasn't possible.

The task force set a course around 79 Ceti toward the warp gate leading to HD 44594, while the battered marines onboard licked their wounds and tried to reorder themselves. There was still one fight left on this campaign, though none of us really had the stomach for it.

The Lafayette, one of the large transports, was detached back to Gliese with the wounded as the rest of us pressed on. My battalion had 540 men and women at full strength. The day we went through the warp gate to HD 44594 we had 252 fit for duty. Sanchez was dead, and Rijis was wounded and en route for Gliese, so two of the three companies were without their commanders. Most of the platoon leaders were on their first campaign in that post, and I really didn't want to put a green lieutenant in command of a company, even a seriously shrunken one. I transferred most of the battalion auxiliaries to Frost's company to bring it up to strength, and I combined Sanchez's and Rijis' companies and put Jax in charge. It wasn't a demotion for Jax, but I needed a solid company commander more than an exec right now. I kept two heavy weapons teams under my direct command as a battalion reserve.

After we emerged into the HD 44594 system, I shuttled over to the general's ship for a conference. We could have done it over the communications grid, but after the fight on Eridu, I think he just wanted to meet with me in person. I could immediately tell he felt guilty for the bad intel and the losses we'd suffered as a result. General Holm had his own retinue of ghosts, and it was even bigger than mine.

He told me he was going to try to keep my people out of the next fight, but that he might need us for reserves. I told him we were ready to drop in front of an enemy division if that's where he needed us. He transferred the remnants of Johnson's shattered battalion to me, and I organized most of them into a third company. I took the snipers and heavy weapons teams and added them to mine to beef up the battalion reserve. We were still below strength, but a lot better off than before.

Johnson's troops were on the Iwo Jima, and it wasn't practical to move them over to the Belleau Wood, so we'd assemble the battalion on the ground if it came to that. I thought Johnson's men would need some attention, though, so I requested permission to shuttle over to their ship on my way back. The general agreed completely and even decided to go with me.

The visit had a tremendous impact on the troops, whose morale had been sorely battered. Major Johnson had been very popular, and the battalion had taken horrific losses fighting in almost impossible conditions. We gave them an update on the major - he was going to survive, and he would eventually report back to duty. Then I welcomed them to my battalion and told them I was proud to have them join us. The general gave them a somber but inspiring pep talk that seemed to help somewhat.

As it turned out, we did see more action on the campaign. The third planet of the system was a world just like Earth, and if it hadn't been situated in a remote dead end in space, it would have attracted enormous colonization interest. As it was, it served mostly as an agricultural world, producing food for export to nearby colonies, which were mostly nightmarish worlds useful for their mineral resources. It had been colonized by a group of religious extremists too fanatical even for the Caliph's tastes. So he accommodated them by giving the group their own planet, and in doing so got them off of Earth and secured a food supply for his Rim colonies.

Great. More fanatics. One of these days I wanted to fight a sane enemy. There were no regular troops posted on the world, which they had named Aroush, but the entire civilian population would likely fight to the death. Where there weren't farms, the planet was covered with deep pine forests, giving a guerilla force a lot of places to hide. The entire battle consisted of a series of search and destroy actions to hunt down the locals. We ended up having to rotate in and relieve some of the units from the initial wave.

Our wounds were still fresh, and we were in no mood to be gentle with any enemy, particularly a bunch of suicidal religious crazies. I've never seen troops under my command act so much like grim executioners, and we swept entire areas, killing everyone we found.

It was three weeks before we'd eliminated the last holdouts and General Holm declared the campaign completed. The savagery of the whole thing had been beyond anything we had expected. Two of the three worlds we had invaded were now uninhabited graveyards. The Mubarizun had massacred the rebellious population on Eridu, and were themselves wiped out in the battle with us. On Aroush we'd systematically hunted down and killed every occupant of the planet, all of whom had taken up arms to fight us.

I managed to arrange to have the troops from Tyler Johnson's old battalion transferred to the Belleau Wood when we re-embarked. They'd meshed very well on the ground, and were well on the way to becoming a full-fledged part of my battalion, a process I intended to see completed on the long trip back to Gliese 250.

We'd had a hard campaign, but I wanted us to be back to total readiness as soon as possible. Rumors were rampant that General Holm would be mounting another campaign from Gliese, this time against the outer rim, and I was sure my battalion would be part of it.

I would be saying goodbye to my liaison officer, who was heading back to PRC headquarters before being posted to a new command. Aoki wasn't even going to the station at Gliese, but would be shuttling directly to an outbound PRC cruiser. There was an informal black market on ships, and even throughout entire fleets, where liquor, food, and other rarities were obtainable. I did a little trading myself and managed to secure a few pounds of good ground beef. We had a little going away party on Aoki's last night with us, complete with very rare burgers.

A few days later I found out he wasn't the only one leaving. I was in my office working on supply manifests for the battalion when I realized I hadn't eaten all day. I was just about to get up and run down to the officer's club for dinner when my buzzer sounded, and in walked General Holm. I jumped to my feet and saluted, but he waved for me to sit down as he dropped hard into the other chair.

"General, I'm glad to see you." And surprised. Usually when a general wanted to see a major, the major went to the general, not the other way around.

"Erik, I have some news for you. First, you're being decorated again. For…"

"General," - interrupting a general is stupid, by the way - "that is not necessary. I just did my job."

"It is very necessary." He didn't seem to care that I'd cut him off. "In fact, there is no way around it. Johnson's battalion got their asses handed to them on Eridu even after they had preliminary intel from you. And Tyler Johnson is a good officer. Yet your people won their fight with no backup. Then you took the wreck of Johnson's group and made them a part of your battalion and had them in the field three weeks later."

I opened my mouth to say something, but nothing came out. I didn't have the easiest time accepting praise. It made me uncomfortable. Finally I just said, "Thank you, sir."

He looked at me with a strange look on his face. "Let's see how much you want to thank me when you hear the rest of it. Erik, you are the youngest major in corps history. You are the most decorated officer at your rank. You are a hero of this war." He paused, as if he didn't want to continue. "You're going back to Earth, and you will receive your medal from the president of the Western Alliance. Then you will go on a tour of major cities, meeting with local dignitaries, attending events - that sort of thing. You'll be on Earth for 4-6 months before reporting back for combat duty."

I shifted in my seat, suddenly very uncomfortable. "Sir, I'd really rather stay with my battalion. They had a hard campaign, and I think it would be harmful for them to lose their commander right now."

The general's expression was a combination of sympathy and amusement. "Erik, there's no squirming out of this one. This comes from way above me. The Earthside politicians want some war heroes to show off at parties and receptions. There's no way to turn down a decoration from the president. You'll be part of a whole delegation. I'm sure it will be first class all the way."

He paused again, though just for a moment. "Trust me, I'm as upset about this as you. I'm going out against the outer rim, and I don't like losing my best battalion commander and one of my most trusted officers. And a friend too. I'm going to miss having you around, Erik."

He got up to leave, but first he walked over and extended his hand to me. "You are leaving the day after tomorrow on the Wasp."

I took his hand and we shook, then he turned and left. I stood for a minute or two, then slumped back into my chair.

I wasn't hungry anymore.

Chapter Eleven

AS Wasp
Approaching Earth

Earth. It looked unreal, a blue orb slowly getting bigger on the viewscreen as we made our final approach. It was beautiful from space, but of course there are many kinds of beauty, and appearances are often deceiving.

Earth. My home. Or at least my birthplace. I hadn't been there for nine years, and I hadn't left with any great affection for the place. But still, this was where I was from; this was where all those colonists I'd fought to defend came from, or at least where their parents or grandparents did.

I was really dreading this. First, I was missing the Outer Rim campaign, which was General Holm's operation to take out the Caliphate colonies between Gliese 250 and the unexplored frontier. My battalion was going - actually it was already gone - on the way to 23 Librae, the first objective of the campaign. Thinking about my troops out there without me made me sick to my stomach. The fact that they were fighting without me so I could appease the vanity of a bunch of politicians made me quiver with rage.

Beyond that, I didn't particularly care for being heaped with praise, and unless it came from one of the few people I respected, I assumed it was insincere, self-serving bullshit any-way. I hated the thought of being the politicians' propaganda tool, but I wasn't given any choice, so I tried to gracefully accept the assignment. Being wined and dined by a bunch of govern-ment types while our troops were out fighting and dying was as close to my own version of hell as I could imagine. And I'd seen some very convincing incarnations of hell.

There was one bright spot, and I was sure I owed that one to General Holm. I was part of a whole delegation, and somehow he'd gotten Captain-Doctor Sarah Linden appointed. Officially she was there to speak about the medical care our troops were receiving, but I couldn't believe it was a coincidence. I have no idea how he even knew about the two of us, but I was grateful.

She was coming from Armstrong on another ship, and the best idea I could figure from the schedules I could access was that she should have arrived a couple days before mine. I was excited to see her, but also nervous. We'd corresponded as frequently as interstellar communications in wartime allowed, but I hadn't seen her since right after graduation. The little bit of time we'd spent together was amazing, but I didn't know what to expect now.

I was treated like a guest of honor on the destroyer Wasp, and Captain Grinsky gave me the run of the ship, the command bridge included. Once we entered the solar system I started spending a lot of time up there, checking out the changing view of the familiar layout of planets.

Our course took us past Saturn, and the close in view of that magnificent planet and its rings was amazing. As we approached close to Titan we got an incredible view of that massive orange moon. Titan was a Martian Confederation possession, and we were shadowed by a Confed patrol vessel until we'd passed out of weapons range.

The treaties that had maintained peace on Earth for a century also regulated the use of the solar system. Sol had five warp gates, and the warp nexus in the Centauri system had another eight, and both systems were neutral space where combat was forbidden by treaty. The powers could establish space stations and outposts for refueling and similar purposes, but arming them in any way was forbidden.

Most of the colonized areas of the solar system itself were part of the Martian Confederation, though the Alliance controlled Mercury and shared Europa with the Confeds. All of the Earth powers had bases on the moon, which was divided into eight sectors.

We'd come in from the Ross 128 warp gate, which was the furthest one out from Earth's orbit and currently on the opposite side of Sol, so our inbound voyage took seventeen days. When we passed the moon's orbit, the captain commed me and asked if I wanted to come up to the bridge and watch the final approach and docking.

We were scheduled to dock with Alliance Station One, the first of the Alliance's three large transfer stations in Earth orbit. The Caliphate also had three stations, but most of the other powers only had two. The South American Empire was down to one, having lost the other in a reactor accident about fifteen years before. The station was enormous, bigger even than the one at Gliese 250. There were umbilicals for at least a hundred ships of various sizes, including several large enough to dock battleships.

The wasp's primary screen projected the view ahead, and the secondary screens displayed shots transmitted from the station, showing our approach. I was impressed with how well the crew functioned, handing the multitude of operations required to dock the ship with practiced ease.

The ship moved slowly, powered only by positioning thrusters, until it latched onto the docking port and came to a total stop. On the monitors I could see about ten bots and two or three technicians in space suits maneuvering toward the ship to attach various umbilicals. These connections would be used for refueling and resupply of the Wasp while it was in orbit. According to the manifest, they were due to depart in 48 hours, which was a crash schedule to get a warship refueled and rearmed. But there was a war on.

I said my goodbyes to the Wasp crew, and gave the captain my heartfelt thanks for her hospitality. I took the lift down to the docking portal and met my assistant, Sergeant Warren, who had my baggage packed on a hover-sled and ready to go. We walked down the tube, which led to an access gate on the station. We were in the military section, so we could dispense with the security and customs hassles that awaited civilian travelers.

I expected to have an officer meet me to escort me planetside, but I wasn't ready for the delegation that was waiting. Outside the docking portal was an honor guard of two squads in full dress uniform lining my path and a delegation of six officers with a press detachment. I instantly became uncomfort-

able, and I had to fight the urge to turn around and head back
to the Wasp, but then I caught a glimpse through the crowd at a
mound of tousled blonde hair pulled back into a loose ponytail.

What was she doing here? I thought she'd be on Earth by
now. I immediately forgot the reporters and film crew and over-
blown reception committee. And I certainly forgot any desire
to run back to the Wasp. I wanted to push my way through the
crowd to get to her, but the major in me said I had to meet the
delegation first. I immediately decided he was a pain in the ass,
but I reluctantly obeyed myself and stood fast.

I walked down the line of officers, giving each one a sharp
salute followed by a handshake. I'd worked most of the way
down the line, from a colonel to a first lieutenant when I finally
got a good look at her through the crowd. When I looked into
her eyes and saw the smile she flashed me, all my apprehensions
disappeared.

I saw a small podium and suddenly realized with horror that
I was expected to say something. The combat reflexes took over
and I walked right up to it and gave them my best authorita-
tive hero voice. "Thank you so much for this unexpected and
overwhelming welcome." I paused for a few seconds, looking
thoughtful, but actually trying to think of something to say. "I
have been away for a long time, and I can't tell you how happy I
am to be back." A lie, but a polite one at least.

"I stand here as an officer sent to receive a tremendous
honor, but I am not here just for myself. I am here for all those
marines, living or dead, who have fought so bravely throughout
explored space." That drew some applause. Yes, I thought,
you all should applaud for those men and women. They are the
real heroes. "I am very anxious to get down to the surface," -
another lie - "and see home after nine years away, so I hope you
will forgive me for keeping these comments brief. Thank you
all. Now excuse me, I have to go kiss my doctor."

Ok, I think I might have left that last bit out, though I was
certainly thinking it. I walked through the crowd, unilaterally
ignoring all of the questions from the media types. I did give
them a nice video clip though, a major kissing a captain right in

the middle of the arrival gate. I bet that got some play.

She hugged me so tightly and for so long, I knew immediately the time apart had done nothing to diminish our relationship. Neither of us wanted to let go, but we reluctantly resigned ourselves to the need to act like officers. For now. We walked over to the intra-station car, and got it. Each car held eight people, and the group tailing us filled half a dozen. I had been so excited to see Sarah that I had forgotten all about my baggage, but a quick look back to the third car was all I needed to see Sergeant Warren had things well in hand. Good, I could worry about more important things. Sarah and I were next to each other in the first car, and we spoke eagerly in hushed whispers during the short trip to the shuttle docking area.

The car took us right to the boarding area for the Earth shuttle, and within a few minutes we had boarded and strapped in the for short ride to the surface. Sarah, who had been on the station for three days waiting for me, had read our itinerary, and she warned me that we faced a larger delegation when we landed. I scowled less when she told me something annoying than when anyone else did, but it must have been enough, because she giggled softly when she saw my expression. She knew my feelings about politics, and though she'd never said a word to me about her own thoughts on the subject, I got a strong feeling that, in her own less hostile way, she agreed with me.

The ride down was gentle - downright comfortable, in fact. This wasn't a shuttle for landing troops on a battlefield. Too many dignitaries took this ride to risk soiling expensive suits with projectile vomit. The shuttle had windows, and I got a great view of the Wash-Balt Metroplex as we made our final approach. The massive complex was a series of eight large urban clusters, stretching over 50 kilometers and connected by high-speed magtrain. Between and around these walled-off forests of skyscrapers was a vast sea of decaying slums, stretching as far as I could see.

I wondered if these endless blocks of rotting old buildings and basic materials factories were as terrible as the ones I remembered. How many versions of myself were down there, living appalling lives of violence and poverty? Most of them, I suspected, were more likely to end up dead in some back alley or execution chamber than to be saved as I was.

Wash-Balt was many times the size of New York. The political center of both the United States and the Western Alliance, it was the home to over five million government workers, and I couldn't even begin to guess at the multitudes living in the vast ghettos.

The shuttle made one more arcing turn, and we got nice a view of Chesapeake Bay as we maneuvered toward the spaceport east of the city. Torrance Spaceport was named for the first president of the Western Alliance, and it was one of the busiest in the world, a fact that was apparent when we were required to circle the city three more times before we go clearance to land. The shuttle descended softly on its maneuvering jets, slowly dropping the last 50 meters through a portal that appeared when a set of huge double doors opened in one of the large docking bays. Once we were on the ground, a boarding tube extended, and walked through the conduit to the concourse.

They weren't kidding about the crowd. There were people filling the entire expanse and an area with seating that was fully occupied by self important types in pricey suits. Right outside the docking tube they had set up a raised dais with a podium and a row of seats for us.

There were seven of us on the shuttle. In addition to Sarah and myself, there was another combat marine, an enlisted man who had held a position despite being the last survivor in his platoon. There were a couple naval officers as well, along with a militia colonel and a logistics specialist.

We all had to say a few words. I gave my usual grudging comments, being as charming as I could manage and wishing I had my armor here so Hector could give the speech using my voice (he was very good at it - they would never have known). I tried to keep it short, but I got a bunch of questions, most of them asking how I prepared for an assault and what it was like to fight a battle. What do you think it's like, asshole? Let me take a few shots at you, and then tell me how much you enjoyed it.

Unlike me, Sarah was beyond gracious. God, she was an amazing speaker, and she had everyone's rapt attention as she went on about how the Corp's medical services worked, from hospital ships all the way to the big medical centers on Armstrong and Atlantia. Every eye was on her, and not just because she was drop dead gorgeous, but because you could feel the passion in what she was saying. Although I knew her better than anyone there, I was just as mesmerized. I was grateful to her for what she had done for me, and on a personal level I was well on my way to falling crazy in love with her (I was already there, but hadn't quite admitted to myself yet), but while she was speaking it really hit me that she had saved hundreds, maybe thousands of lives.

It ended up being more than two hours before the speeches were done, the questions answered, and we were allowed to leave. They'd arranged for luxury transports to take us to the Willard Hotel. The Willard was a massive silver-glass building about a kilometer high, with five segments, each one a bit smaller than the one below, creating a roof deck around the perimeter at the base of each new section. Each segment was a separate hotel, ranging from normal high-end accommodations in the bottom to what I can only assume was an unimaginably plush section for VIPs at the top.

The Willard appeared to be one of the three or four tallest buildings in the DC sector of Wash-Balt, which was a jungle of skyscrapers connected by monorail systems at several levels. The transport vectored toward the hotel and, to my surprise, moved to the level four docking area. Not quite the top, but much higher than I'd expected. Apparently I was more useful to the politicians now as a decorated major than I was when they expelled my whole family out into the wastelands to die.

Sarah and I sat next to each other, but we were mostly silent. Being back on Earth wasn't easy for me, and somehow the hypocrisy of being treated like some sort of VIP was making it worse. I'd seen the ugliest side of this society - did they really think a little luxury was going to make me forget it? Sarah was just as quiet as me, and I suspected that she had her own demons to confront. I hadn't told her much about my childhood, and she had been just as stingy with details about hers. She was five years older than me, and I knew she had made two small assaults before she was transferred on the basis of aptitude testing and put through medical training. But that is about as far back as my knowledge went.

After the transport docked we were ushered into the hotel lobby and met by the concierge staff. They welcomed all seven of us, and gave us small pocket-sized devices - portable AIs that would assist us during our stay. If you forgot the way to your room, you could just ask the AI. Want a cheeseburger and chocolate cake at 3am? Just ask your AI to order it for you. Apparently, we had very few spending limits and could order whatever we wanted in the way of food, entertainment, and services. Within reason, I suppose, though I wasn't planning to test the limits.

By the time we got to our rooms, it was around 10pm, and we were all exhausted. They put me in a suite bigger than my family's apartment had been. I was just about to ask my AI for some advice on ordering dinner when I heard the door chimes. I started to get up, but before I could, the AI asked me if it should open the door. I said yes, and it slid open to reveal a beautiful blond standing in the hall.

"My room's drafty," she said with a wicked smile on her face. "Can I borrow yours?" I'm not sure which of us laughed first. She came inside and we ordered dinner. Then we ordered breakfast.

We had most of the day to ourselves. There was a reception that evening we were required to attend, but until then we could do whatever we wanted. So, after sleeping indecently late for serving officers and having what had to be the most expensive breakfast I'd ever seen, we decided to go out and wander around Wash-Balt. It turned out that our AIs could interface with the monetary exchange network and that we had substantial credits to use in shops, restaurants, or wherever we wanted. We took the express lift to ground level and wandered out into the streets.

The area around the Willard was a high-end restricted zone,

something like Sector A in Manhattan, and there were nice cafes and stores everywhere. It was like nothing I'd ever seen before. I had no idea that people lived like this.

The entire area was divided into sub-sectors, some of which we were authorized to access and some of which were off-limits. We wandered past the entry to the Political Academy Campus, which was a restricted zone we couldn't access, and headed over to the Georgetown Sector, which was adjacent to DC. I thought I'd see if I could find any of the places Aoki had told me about. Actually, finding them didn't turn out to be too difficult. I just asked my AI where they were and it gave us directions as we walked. It also asked if I wanted to see menus, hear reviews, or make a reservation. Hector could have learned some manners from these concierge AIs.

We decided to have lunch at Aoki's favorite burger place. I ordered a pretty basic cheeseburger, but Sarah got this giant bacon-laden monstrosity dripping with melted bleu cheese and some type of sauce, which she ate with such inexplicable finesse I don't think she even touched her napkin.

Our AIs gave us a reminder at 4pm to return to the hotel to get ready for the reception. When I returned to my room - alone, sadly, as Sarah had gone back to her own suite to get ready - I found a valet waiting for me with a brand new set of dress blues. I took a shower, after which, for the first time in my life since childhood, I had assistance in getting dressed.

The uniform was magnificent, neatly pressed and a perfect fit. This was the first time I'd ever worn my full dress uniform with all of my medals and decorations. It was absurd - my chest was a glittering array of various metal and ribbon combinations. God, I thought, I was getting another one of these tonight. Where the hell was it going to fit? I might have to wear it on my back. My sword was so polished it was blinding in the mirror when the light caught it.

Looking at the medals all displayed so prominently, I couldn't help but wonder how many of my troopers had died for each of them. Was a scrap of blue silk and a tiny hunk of platinum worth the lives of ten good soldiers? Twenty? I suppose I should have felt pride at my decorations, but instead they made me a little queasy.

An officer came to fetch me and lead me down to the waiting transport. Sarah was already there, waiting patiently wearing a uniform just like mine, right down to the sword. She was Medical Division, but she had two assaults, and in the Corps, once you are Combat you are always Combat. She looked incredible, coolly professional, yet beautiful. Her hair was braided tightly against her head and she, like I, wore the absurd white hat that was technically part of the marine dress uniform but was widely ignored when one wasn't attending a Presidential reception.

The naval dress uniforms were even fancier than ours, the coats a blue so dark they were almost black, covered with buttons and braid. The pants were bright white, crisply pressed, and tucked into polished black boots. The hats weren't as stupid as ours, though, just a neat beret in the same color as the coat.

On the ride over to the Presidential Palace we were all briefed by a team of protocol officers from the Earth-based military establishment. Yes, that's what I said, protocol officers. I was glad to see that we didn't have anything that idiotic in the Corps and had to borrow them.

It was all such over the top nonsense, I found it hard to pay attention to what they were saying, and my mind kept wandering. Sarah, who it seemed could almost read my mind, poked me in the side a couple times when I really stopped listening. Of course, these politicians thought this was an honor they were giving us, gracing us with their attention. They thought we were fighting for them. I've got news for you, guys. If you were the only thing I was fighting for, I'd give the next Janissary I saw a lift to your house instead of blowing his head off.

The palace was just down the street from the hotel, on the site of the old White House, which had housed the U.S. president a couple hundred years before and was destroyed in the food riots of 2065. It was a massive structure and a testament to opulence. It was a disgusting display when there were people five kilometers away eating rats. The main building was a large rectangle about 500 meters long and 50 high, built of glass and gleaming white marble. Clustered around the main structure were slender towers, each at least 200 meters high.

Our transport went through three security checkpoints and finally landed on a field in front of a massive glass dome, glittering with hundreds of lights inside. The transport field itself was paved with some type of decorative stone that seemed to have a design worked into it, although so close and at night I couldn't make it out. There were other transports on the field, all very plush looking, each disgorging a retinue of very well-dressed men and women. Many of the arrivals seemed to be attended by groups of servants or retainers of some sort.

When we got out of the transport we were met by a detachment of the Presidential Guard, an elite unit of the terrestrial army troops. Their uniforms were spectacular, scarlet coats and bright white pants, but I wouldn't have given them a chance in a fight against one of my plain old line squads.

We were greeted with great ceremony and escorted over to the massive dome, which was the main event area in the Palace. There were twenty of us, in total, from every branch of the offworld military establishment. We waited for a few minutes, and then they introduced us one at a time to thunderous applause.

We had to walk down a reception line, shaking hands with one political minister after another. The entire thing made my skin crawl, but I did what was expected of me. I figured I was here as the relentless killing machine, willing to sacrifice his troops or himself for the defense of the Alliance, so I didn't think I needed to be overly effusive. Just minimally respectful. Or at least pretend to be.

The last person on the line was the president of the Alliance himself, Francis Herrin Oliver. He'd been president for 12 years, having proven quite adept at managing the behind the scenes wheeling and dealing that took place among the political class. Certainly nothing so quaint as popular opinion was a significant factor in his power base, though the facade of elections was, as always, maintained.

The war had gone on for a long time and had escalated considerably. The cost had to be astronomical, and I suspect that part of the reason we were here was to show what all that money was buying. The middle classes were, for the most part, pliant and too scared to cause trouble, but it never hurt to give them a show. And war heroes were easier for the average person to understand than the need for osmium, iridium, and trans-uranic elements from the colonies.

The reception was the most opulent thing I had ever seen, featuring a meal with so many courses I lost count of them. I was annoyed when we were led to our tables - I was seated with the combat elements and Sarah with the support services people. We were at the same giant round table, but on opposite sides. She did manage to give me a few fabulous smiles that shattered the ice queen image she was otherwise maintaining.

After the meal one of the protocol officers came over to prep me for the medal ceremony. I got up slowly, willing my body to do what no part of me wanted, and followed him. I caught Sarah's face with my last glance at the table - a pained smile that at once wished me well and reminded me that she was probably the only person in the world...all the worlds...who really knew me and how much I hated this.

I was escorted to a raised platform in the center of the dome. The president was standing there, flanked by Presidential Guard officers. The protocol officer had told me to salute when I stood in front of the president and then to shake his hand, so that is exactly what I did. I stood at attention while the president gave a speech. He spoke about the "brave men and women" fighting to preserve the freedom and prosperity of the Alliance. Then he began talking about me, describing Achilles, Columbia, Gliese 250, Eridu. He spoke about how I was wounded, and that I received the very best care possible, and then he announced that the very doctor who had headed up my medical team was present as well. He motioned over toward Sarah and told her to stand up, then he started to clap, followed by everyone in the dome. She looked a little embarrassed to me, but I was close to her and knew her expressions - to anyone else I suspect she looked as flawlessly poised as ever as she took a polite bow and sat down again.

After calling me "the most decorated officer my age in the history of the Marine Corps," he opened a small black box and pulled out the award. The Presidential Medal of Honor was the highest decoration given to Alliance military personnel, and its wearers enjoyed a unique set of perquisites and privileges. General Holm had won his in the Second Frontier War, and now his protégé was getting the same award. Except for Sarah, he was the one person I would have wanted here, but as he so succinctly put it before I left, someone had to fight the war.

So I leaned down and let the president of the Western Alliance put the blue and white ribbon over my head, and then shook his hand again and turned and waved around the room as I received a hearty round of applause. The president thanked me for my service and then moved aside for me to say a few words. I bowed to the inevitable and gave the shortest speech I thought I could get away with. I started by thanking the president, but I spent most of my time paying tribute to the men and women who had served with me, and particularly to the ones that weren't here anymore. That part, at least, was heartfelt. I couldn't quite bring myself to praise the Alliance overall - my hypocrisy has limits - so I spoke about the colonists on our various planets and how they fought and strove to build great new worlds. I finished with a mention of the troops we had fighting somewhere far away, even while I stood here speaking, and I said that I was anxious to get back to my soldiers and see that this war ended as soon as possible. There were more applause as I saluted the president once more (as I'd been told to do) and walked back to my table.

I allowed myself the fleeting hope that we'd be allowed to leave soon, but it turned out to be a long evening of listening to political gasbags drone on and on about the war and a bunch of other things they didn't understand. I envied the heavy drinkers in attendance, and I seriously considered joining their ranks. But while I was speaking, Sarah had managed to switch seats with one of my neighbors and at least we were together the rest of the evening. By the time the transport took us back to the hotel, we were exhausted. We made it back up to my room and collapsed on the bed, but not before I made a few dire threats to the AI if we were disturbed before noon the next day.

We had a few more days in Wash-Balt, and we had most of the time to ourselves, though we did have some events we had to attend, and both of us had interviews taped for netcasts. Then we were off on a tour of major cities all over the Alliance. We stayed in each of them a few days, attending a variety of local events. None of these was as over-the-top as the presidential reception, though the London party was close.

We got to see a lot of cities, but they were all depressingly the same. A small central area where the VIPs resided in isolation and almost limitless luxury and a larger, moderately comfortable zone where the middle class lived unquestioning and routine lives. But most disheartening, they were all surrounded by vast, decaying slums, where the hopeless masses lived the best they could in deprivation and despair.

Some of the time, Sarah and I traveled together, but others we were sent to different places. The chance to spend time with her made the whole thing worth it, but when she wasn't there it was nearly unbearable. I tried not to think about it, but I knew my battalion was in the Outer Rim somewhere, and I wasn't with them. They were well-trained and led, but it was just wrong for me not to be with them. Being with Sarah took my mind off of it, but when she wasn't there, I'd lay awake in bed at night thinking about all of it.

The last stop was New York. I wasn't very comfortable to be going "home," but I was excited because Sarah would be there too. I was coming in from Sydney, fresh from a reception with the president of Oceania, and she'd been back in Wash-Balt, attending a series of meetings at several of the hospitals there. I got to New York in the morning, but I knew she would be arriving around 3pm on the magtrain, so I headed back up to the Fort Tyron center to meet her. She expected to meet me at the hotel, so she was surprised when she saw me standing there. She ran right over to me, and at first I thought she was just happy that I came to meet her. But she grabbed me hard and didn't let go for the longest time. With a start I realized she was shaking like a leaf. I'd never seen her anything but totally in control.

I asked her what was wrong, and she told me she was just tired. I knew she was lying, and she knew that I knew, but we both let it drop for the moment. She calmed down a little and we chatted about some insignificant things. On the way back to the MPZ, she didn't so much as look out of the train window, just staring straight ahead at the back of the next seat.

It only took a few minutes to zip through the surreal landscape of the northern Manhattan wastes and enter the Protected Zone. Twenty minutes later we were at the hotel. I took her by the hand, and we walked right up to my room, not even bothering to check her into her own. She sat there on the bed silently, staring off into space with a glassy look on her face. Finally, I said, "You don't have to tell me what's bothering you if you don't want, but please let me know how to help you."

She looked up at me with an expression that seemed to combine love and despair, gratitude and hopelessness. He eyes glistened with moisture for a few seconds before the tears began streaking down her cheeks. "It's just hard being back here." She tried to stifle the tears, unsuccessfully. "We never discussed our pasts. Mine is bad."

I put my hand on her cheek and looked at her. "Is that what this is about? Whatever happened, it is past and gone. My history is bad too, really bad. But that isn't us anymore."

She was quiet for a few minutes, and then she started talking. Once it started to come out, there was no stopping it. She told me things that day that she had never confided to anyone, things she never spoke of again.

When she was fourteen, the thirty year old son of a high-ranking politician saw her out one day with her family, and he decided he wanted her. Her father was approached about allowing her to live in Sector A as the ward of the politician, but they said no, both to the initial suggestion and the more forceful one that followed. So one day her entire family was arrested on charges of plotting terrorism, and her father, mother, and 8-year old sister where dragged from their apartment in restraints. She was taken to Sector A and placed under the guardianship of her admirer, and that night, when she wouldn't give in to his advances, he raped her three times.

She was kept for weeks, locked in a small room where he would come whenever he wanted to and abuse her horribly. One day, after he'd beaten and raped her, he didn't notice that a writing stylus had dropped out of his pocket, and the next time he came to her room she buried it into his neck, twisting it around to make sure he bled to death before help could arrive.

She used his passkey to get out of the building and Sector A, and somehow she managed to escape the MPZ entirely, despite the massive alert that went out. She kept running, somehow managing to just about survive, barely eluding capture. The land between urban areas consisted of mostly abandoned suburbs and reclaimed farmland. The suburbs, once densely populated, were now devoid of public services and occupied only by a few renegades and outlaws.

Somehow, through blind luck she ran into a family living in a big house in an otherwise uninhabited old town. They took her in, fed her, and gave her a place to stay. The father had been a doctor in the Philadelphia Enclave, until he'd had to flee for some reason or another, and he removed her spinal implant. I'd seen that little scar on her neck a hundred times, and always wondered where she'd gotten it.

She stayed there for several months until one day the house was assaulted by Federal Police. She was sure they were there for her, but it turned out they had finally caught up with the doctor. Without her implant they had no idea she was wanted as well, and they just assumed she was some local vagrant. They raped her and left her lying on the front porch of the house.

She wandered for months, not in the populated urban hell were I scavenged, but in the vast areas between cities, through rotting old ghost towns, past vast tracts of polluted industrial wastelands until, by the blindest luck, she wandered into a range of land used by the Corps for training. A group of third year trainees found her half-starved, mad with thirst, and sick, and they brought her to the base. There, she was nursed back to health and allowed to stay until she was sixteen, when she was given the chance to enlist. The rest I'd known already. She participated in two assaults as a private and was offered a transfer to the medical training program.

After she'd told me the whole story I just put my arms around her and we sat silently. I don't know how long we just stayed there, but it was hours, because it was dark out before either of us said a word. We sat up the whole night talking, and by morning I'd told her my entire sad story as well, the first time I'd said a word of it to anyone.

In the morning we left the hotel and walked out of the Sector A checkpoint into the main area of the MPZ. I had called Sergeant Warren, who'd turned out to be a great assistant, and told him to cancel our appearances in New York and get us transport permits to leave immediately. Somebody would probably be pissed that we were bailing on our commitments, but to say I didn't give a fuck would have been an understatement of epic proportions. We were sitting on a small bench in the park when he called me.

"Major, I got your events canceled and travel permits issued for you to go back to Wash-Balt today. I was stunned they said yes. Apparently Presidential Medal winners do have some influence. Is there anything else you want me to do?"

"Nice job, Chris," I replied. "Yes, I need you to arrange to have our baggage sent from the hotel to wherever we're staying in Wash-Balt. Oh yeah, I need you to get us a place to stay there too."

He responded sharply, "Yes, sir. Consider it done."

"And Chris...thanks. This was important."

"I'm at your service, sir."

"After you finish, take the rest of the time to yourself. Stay here or go wherever you want with the rest of your leave. Use my name if you think that stupid medal has juice."

"Thank you, sir. I appreciate that, sir."

And so Sarah and I had stayed one sleepless night in New York City, which had once been home to us both, and we left never to return. Two hours later we were on the magtrain to

Wash-Balt, and that evening we were eating dinner at Aoki's old haunt.

By the next morning we'd pushed the demons back into the recesses of our souls, and we were back to normal, more or less. The two of us were closer than ever. I had been nervous on my way to Earth, uncertain how several years apart would have affected us. But now I knew, we both knew, that time, distance, war, hardship - none of it - would get between us.

We had a month's leave coming now that the tour was over, and we'd both had just about enough of Earth. We decided to go to Atlantia, which was a big rec center for troops on leave. Anywhere but Earth.

As we boarded the orbital shuttle we both knew we'd never see Earth again. I was wrong, I'd be back once more, under circumstances I couldn't have imagined at the time. But Sarah never returned to the planet of her birth, and as far as could tell, she never even thought much about it.

Chapter Twelve

I Corps Assembly Area
Columbia - Eta Cassiopeiae II

Ten years of war. Ten years since I finished basic training and made my first assault at Carson's World. Sixteen years
passed for that angry, animalistic kid saved from an early death
by a marine. A marine who later died himself fighting half a
kilometer away from his recruit on a planet they had travelled
very separate paths to reach.

Ten years of war that saw us beaten and forced to retreat,
only to regroup and claw our way back into the fight and throw
the enemy onto the defensive. In the four years since I'd graduated from the Academy we'd taken a big swath of Caliphate
territory and reclaimed the momentum. Or at least evened the
score.

But the enemy still held a whole sector of our worlds, conquered in the disastrous early years of the war, and now we were
going to do something about that. I Corps was the largest formation ever fielded in space by the Western Alliance. The 1st
and 2nd U.S. Marine Divisions, the Royal Marine Division, the
1st Canadian Spaceborne Brigade, and the Oceanian Assault
Regiment. Over forty-five thousand troops, all committed to
Operation Sherman, the campaign to recover our lost systems.
Commanding I Corps was a marine I'd served with before, and
one I would have followed into hell itself, the newly-promoted
Lieutenant General Elias Jackson Holm.

While I was on Earth trying to keep a smile on my face and
the contents of my stomach inside while dealing with politicians and government officials, General Holm was organizing
and training what would become I Corps. After the successes
of the Tail and Outer Rim campaigns, the general pretty much
had a blank check, and he used to it appropriate every veteran
formation he could find for the offensive.

This left many of our systems defended by green troops,

but the general made sure that every crucial planet had a least a component of veterans and a seasoned commander. The newly conquered rim worlds were left lightly defended. The Outer Rim campaign was a diversion, intended to shift the enemy's focus to retaking his own systems, and we couldn't realistically hold the worlds we took anyway. They were just too remote, too far from our own bases of support. Hopefully, the Caliphate would be fully committed to recovering some of this territory, giving us an opening to take back what we'd lost early in the war.

The whole conflict had become more complex, and was showing signs of widening further. There was a lot of diplomacy and spying going on, though we generally didn't get too much information from those quarters, at least not until it was time to act on it.

Our alliance with the PRC was starting to pay off. Fully mobilized now, the PRC was keeping the CAC busy, launching attacks on multiple worlds, raiding supply lines, and generally preventing them from starting any new offensives against us. The CAC outnumbered the PRC, but the Coalition had great technology, certainly better than the CAC's, and even superior to ours in certain areas. In a long one-on-one war of attrition the PRC would probably lose, but as an ally causing the CAC a world of problems they were perfect. On a personal level I enjoyed the reports I was getting on the exploits of Major Aoki Yoshi, who was rapidly becoming the hero of the PRC. Aoki was a good officer and a good friend, and I wished him only the best.

Open war had broken out between Europa Federalis and the Central European League as well, though for now it was a separate conflict. No one was seriously wooing either of them since an alliance with one would mean war with the other, but most likely that conflict would eventually merge with this one. This new fight would play havoc with the general's supply of good cognac, but that was likely to be the biggest effect on our war effort for now.

Our intel teams were more worried about the South Americans. Generally, they were more closely aligned with us than our enemies, but the systems they really wanted to annex were mostly ours, so it was easier for the Caliphate to offer them a reward. Intelligence reports suggested that they had been very close to entering the conflict before our recent victories caused them to delay. There was still a lot of concern they would eventually come in against us, though, and we just didn't have the reserves to manage another front. Their empire was in decline, barely holding onto superpower status, and they desperately needed a bigger presence in space. They were cut off from the rim by the other powers, and they were effectively landlocked in space. They needed to conquer someone's colonies to create a pathway to unexplored areas, and ours were juicier and better located for them. I was no expert on diplomacy or intel, but I suspected greed and expediency would win out over other considerations.

We had our own diplomatic initiative underway - we were trying to get the Martian Confederation to come in on our side. They were closely aligned with us and would never have sided with the Caliphate or the CAC, but they also had a strong resolve to remain neutral. While they'd fought a skirmish or two over the years, they had managed to stay out of the First and Second Frontier Wars, and they had no desire to get dragged into the third. I suspected they would enter the war rather than see the balance of power shift significantly to the Caliphate and the CAC, however. My opinion was unqualified, of course. One thing I have never been is a diplomat.

Regardless of diplomacy and the shifting of national alignments, I Corps was going to liberate our people. Some of them had been held by the enemy for seven or eight years, and it was well past time for us to free them from the yoke. I believe that opinion was shared by every member of I Corps, from General Holm to the lowest, greenest private fresh out of camp.

The assembly point for I Corps was an amusing one, at least for some of us. The Eta Cassiopeiae system had the warp gates to facilitate our advance, so the planet Columbia was again the destination of troop transports, though this time the situation was significantly less dire. When I stepped out of my ship onto the field outside Weston it felt odd, as though I'd only been away a very short time. Six years. Had it really been almost six years?

I walked quietly to the edge of the field, gazing over at the hills in the distance, my mind lost in thought. There were ghosts here, ghosts of friends I'd left behind. Friends I'd sent to their deaths. "I'm back, brothers," I whispered somberly. My introspection was short-lived. An orderly came over and told me the general wanted to see me immediately. God, he must have been about twelve. And why was he looking at me with that crazy stare. There are real heroes around here, kid. If you're dazzled by me you need to get out more.

The Columbians had been busy. We'd left their world in pretty rough shape, but they'd somehow managed to get it looking almost the way it did before the battle. In fact, many of the new buildings were larger and nicer than the ones they'd replaced. There were some red zones, of course, the unavoidable result of a battle where sixteen nuclear warheads had been used. But they had all been tactical nukes, and the biggest was roughly 12kt, so a complete cleanup was possible and, in fact, was well underway.

The defenses had been dramatically improved as well. Two large orbital fortresses protected the planet, and each commanded a huge array of firing platforms and combat satellites. Any enemy fleet approaching Columbia was going to have its hands full. The militia had been upgraded too, and the planet now had a regular army of sorts, with 1,100 fulltime professional soldiers under arms. With the enhanced militia, Columbia could field over 3,500 reasonably well-equipped and trained troops for its own defense.

The orderly had brought a transport to take me to the general. I jumped in, and we headed over to the main HQ. The open plains around Weston had become a massive military camp. There were temporary shelters, rows of parked vehicles, and thousands of troops marching, drilling, and conducting exercises. I wanted to get a look around, so I had the orderly pull up a little short of the general's pavilion so I could go the rest of the way on foot.

I'd left Columbia a sergeant, but I came back a major. As I walked through the bustling camp I couldn't get used to the deference, the constant salutes from everyone I passed. Of course, I was scared to death of majors too when I was a young puppy solider. But it was still an odd feeling.

Headquarters was a portable modular structure at least 50 meters long. The general was standing just outside his door, rapidly firing out orders to three different officers. I laughed quietly to myself as I walked up. The three of them were having trouble keeping up with him. It had been a year since I'd seen the general, but one look and I could see he was his old self. When he saw me walking up I thought I could see a little smile on his face. He quickly finished up and dismissed the officers. I stopped a couple feet away and snapped him my very best salute. "Major Cain, reporting as ordered, sir!"

His return salute was no less sharp, but his greeting was warm and friendly. "Welcome to Columbia, Major. I believe you are somewhat familiar with the place." He pointed to the door. "Let's go into my office and catch up."

I followed him into the building and past a dozen desks with officers and non-coms sitting at workstations. He opened a large white door that had three stars engraved on it and motioned for me to enter. Once the door was closed we shook hands and he clapped his hand on my shoulder. "Erik, my boy, it's good to see you. It's been a long time."

"It's good to see you too, sir. Of course it's only been a long time because you sent me back to that political slime pit instead of taking me with you on the Outer Rim Campaign."

He laughed and scolded me a bit. "If you didn't insist on making yourself such a conspicuous hero all the time, I wouldn't have to send you back from the front to collect your medals." He noticed the small package I was carrying. "What is that?"

I'd almost forgotten. I handed it over to him. "Just a little gift from Earthside. With Europa Federalis and the CEL at war again, it might be the last you see for a while."

He opened the box and pulled out the small bottle. I was right that night we shared the first one. It did cost a month's pay.

I could tell he was touched when his voice cracked ever so slightly. "Thank-you, Erik. Damn, it's good to have you back."

He walked behind the desk and motioned to one of the guest chairs as he sat down. He put the bottle on his desk and leaned back in his chair.

I sat down, and after a brief silence I asked what had been on my mind since I had gotten there. "So how is my battalion, sir? I know they were on the campaign, but I couldn't get any decent reports."

"Jax took good care of your people, Erik. After the fighting they did in the Tail, I assigned them to the reserve for the Outer Rim battles. They plugged a few gaps, but they made it through the whole thing with less than 20 percent losses. Not bad for four battles."

I was relieved and let out a breath. "Jax is a tremendous officer. There's no one I would rather have taking care of my troops."

He gave me a wicked little smile. "He did such a good job with the battalion I thought I'd let him keep them. I put through his promotion already." He reached into a drawer and pulled out a small box. "I've got his major's circlets here. He doesn't know yet; I thought you might like to tell him."

His words were still sinking in. Jax deserved the promotion, no question, and I was happy for him. But I never even considered not getting my battalion back. I felt a little sick.

The general was sitting there grinning. He must have read my mind. "Relax, Erik, they're still yours. I'm not taking your battalion away; I'm giving you another one too. You're going to command the regiment."

He watched me with an amused stare. I was too stunned to speak, so I just listened. "I've got your eagles in my desk already. You've earned them, but if it's OK with you I'm going to wait to make it official. Your rise through the ranks has been indecently quick already, a record in fact, as you know. So I'd like to wait a couple months instead of bumping you up again immediately."

I finally managed to stammer out a response. "General Holm, I don't know what to say. Of course. Whatever you think is best, sir. We can forget the whole thing. I'm happy to stay as a major."

I really meant it. I could barely imagine myself at my current rank, much less dealing with another promotion. But the general shook his head. "It is well-deserved, Erik, and you should be getting it right now. Effective immediately, you are the commander of third regiment. You've got a colonel's posting, and you'll be wearing those eagles before we hit dirt in an assault. My word as an officer."

He looked at his desk for a minute and then up at me, the friendly smile back on his face. "I'll bet the trip wasn't all bad. So how is your beautiful doctor?"

I smiled to myself for a few seconds. "She's amazing. She was the only thing that made wallowing in that mudhole tolerable. How in the world did you even know about us, general?"

He gave me a sly glance. "I have to know what my troopers need, Erik, or I wouldn't be much of a commander now, would I?"

We both laughed, but then I looked at him very seriously. "I am very grateful, sir. Until this trip we'd never had more than a few days together, when I wasn't her patient. I hadn't seen her in a very long time. You will never know how much it meant to me to have some time together with her."

His smile got wider. "Then I have another surprise for you. She's on her way here right now. As it turns out, I've got another little box with major's insignia in my desk with her name on it. She's going to be executive officer of medical support services for the campaign."

I tried to hide my excitement, but he saw right through it and almost started to laugh. "Don't get too worked up, Erik. You'll be on different ships. She's going to be busy; you're going to be even busier. This will be no protracted lover's rendezvous as I suspect the trip to Earth was. But on the bright side, if you manage to get half your body shot off again, she'll be here to help you grow it back. Again."

We caught up personally for a few more minutes, but then we started to talk about the campaign. Neither one of us was very good at not discussing business. The general went through his basic strategy with me, and when he was done he got to the things that were really troubling him. "Your surprise attack taking the station at Gliese 250 was a massive victory for us. It enabled the Tail and Outer Rim campaigns, and let us hurt the enemy like they had hurt us. In addition to the strategic implications, the effect on morale was incalculable.

"But I'm afraid there's one downside we might have to face on this campaign, and it's the result of those successes. The enemy can't get to the Tail at all without going through Gliese, and while they do have other approaches to the Outer Rim, it's still a long way, and they need time to get their logistics set up. Since Gliese is so strongly held, the enemy haven't even made a second attempt to get in there. Which means they have a lot of uncommitted troops.

"They've controlled some of our systems for eight or nine years. Look what we did at Gliese in the first six months. Can you imagine what fortifications they've built in that time? Our intel is very weak for this campaign. Are the troops not being thrown at us in Gliese or the rim waiting for us, entrenched on our captured worlds?"

He paused for a few moments, as if he was searching for the right words to express his thoughts. "Erik, I'm afraid we're going to have much more of a fight than anyone expects on this campaign. I'm going to need my most dependable, gifted officers to be at their best. I'm counting on you, and I want you to tell me immediately if you have any concerns or misgivings. I need your instincts on this one. If you have a bad dream about the enemy, I want you to tell me about it."

I hesitated, not sure I should really speak my mind. But this man deserved my honesty. "I agree with your misgivings, sir. I think we're going into a hornet's nest, and I'm afraid the scope of the campaign is far too broad. I don't see us taking all the objectives, not without massive reinforcements. And I don't see where those will come from."

I stopped for a minute again, really not sure I wanted to say everything that was on my mind. "General, I keep thinking what I would have done with those worlds if I was in command for the enemy, with all those years to ship in heavy weapons and build fortifications. All that time to put to use the lessons we've learned in this war. I wondered for a while why you accepted the scope of this operation. I couldn't believe you were bullied into it, and it took me some time, but I think I figured it out."

He looked up at me and gazed right into my eyes. "And what did you come up with?"

"That as difficult as this campaign will be, not doing it would be morally indefensible. Those are our people out there. We couldn't defend them the first time, and to leave them there when we can credibly try to free them is not an option you could live with. Or one I could."

We were both silent a few seconds, then I added, "Of course, if the enemy was just occupying Washbalt instead, I'd be fine with it."

He tried to hold the laugh in, but it burst its way out anyway. "Now, now, major, you are expressing less than appropriate respect for our honest, hardworking politicians."

The laughing broke the tension for a minute, but there was something else on the general's mind too, and I knew what it was.

"You're also worried about the South Americans, aren't you?" I'd been thinking about it too.

"You bet I am, he replied. "My gut tells me they're going to jump into this storm. Think about it. They're not blind. This war has been a huge escalation of the action in space. How long can they sit there with no open warp gates and let the rest of us grow? They've got to do something, and the cold hard fact is the systems they can steal from us are worth a lot more to them than anything they can snatch from the Caliphate or CAC. And if they come in, I'm willing to bet it will be a surprise, and our vaunted diplomats and intelligence services will be caught flat-footed."

"And with Sherman and the Gliese 250 defense force draining all our resources," I said, "we're weak everywhere else."

"Bingo. You are right on target. Even if I knew for a fact

they were going to attack, I'm still not sure what I would do to meet it. We just can't let our occupied systems languish under enemy control any longer without trying to liberate them, and we don't have any strength to spare. We're mobilized to the max already, and the navy is stretched thinner than we are. Even if Sherman is a success, it may bleed us badly and leave us weak and unable to meet a new threat. It could be the beginning of the war all over again."

He was right. But there was nothing we could do differently than we were doing anyway. Honestly, he was a man who shouldered every burden himself, and I think he just needed to talk about this. I thought after all he'd done the least he deserved was a little reassurance.

"General, there's no sense going around in circles. Sherman has to go forward, and there's nothing else we can do that we haven't done. So let's focus on making this a successful op and also keep our eyes open. If we have to change plans or redeploy to meet another threat, we'll do whatever is necessary. We always do."

He smiled appreciatively, and threw be an informal salute. "Welcome to I Corps, major. Operation Sherman will be commencing in nine days, so I'll let you go get settled into your billet. I'm sure you'll want all that time to work with your regiment. Rearrange things however you see fit. Any promotions, transfers - whatever - just let me know and I'll approve them."

He stood up and snapped me a much sharper salute, which I returned just as crisply. Then he extended his hand and we shook before he walked me out. He ordered one of the aides in the outer room to show me to my quarters. The lieutenant jumped to attention and asked me to follow him. We walked outside and got into a waiting transport, and he drove me across the camp to the 3rd regiment's section. The regimental camp was divided into two wings, one for each battalion, with a central area for regimental assets and the command section. We drove up to a large shelter in the center of the command area.

"These are your quarters, Major Cain," said the aide, whose name I hadn't even thought to read off of the plate on his chest.

God, I really was getting used to the thinner air at this pay grade, wasn't I?. "I will have your kit delivered here immediately, and I will see that your command staff is aware that you have arrived. Is there anything else I can do for you, sir?"

"Uh, no. That will be all." I was still getting used to the obsequious servitude from junior officers. I rallied, though, and gave him my best major's attitude. "Dismissed."

I walked inside and took a look around. I had a suite with sleeping and living areas, and an adjoining office with conference room. I was just about to see how hot I could get the shower when the AI announced that my orderly officer was at the door requesting to see me.

I was just about to tell the AI to ask him…her? - I didn't even know yet - to come back in an hour, but I decided to make time. I walked over to the desk and said, "Open."

The door slid open and a tall, dark-haired woman in a meticulous uniform walked into the room and gave me a very respectable salute. "Lieutenant Anne Delacorte reporting, sir. I have been assigned as your orderly."

I returned the salute - this was getting tedious - and motioned for her to take a seat. "Thank-you, Lieutenant. I am pleased to meet you."

We exchanged a few minutes of respectful pleasantries, very respectful on her part, and then got right into 45 minutes of deep discussion of how I wanted things run, what kind of schedule I kept, even what I liked for breakfast. She seemed like an intelligent and earnest young officer, eager to do her job well.

Finally, I cut things off and said we'd get through the rest of it later. I told her to round up my executive officer, Jax, and the other battalion commander, and have them report to me. In an hour. I was going to get that hot shower first.

On the way out I started to ask her to round up a couple sandwiches, but then I said, "Lieutenant, I'll want dinner for myself and the other officers. Ninety minutes from now."

She acknowledged and raced off to tend to it all, while I used up half of Columbia's hot water. Forty minutes later I was sitting behind my desk in a fresh uniform feeling a little more human. I browsed some of the dossiers on my workstation screen. Lieutenant Delacorte had uploaded the files of all of the personnel in the regiment. I didn't need to read Jax's file, I'd probably written half of it. There wasn't an officer I trusted more to get up to speed quickly.

My exec was Major Lis Cherzny, who actually had ten years longer service than I did. She'd been stuck in garrison duty for most of the war, so she never got the chance to show what she could do. After uneventful years as a lieutenant and more as a captain, she led a company in the Tail campaign and a battalion on the Outer Rim, winning the rapid advancement that had eluded her before.

My second battalion head was Major Jackson Cantor, who'd been promoted to his position after commanding a company through the Outer Rim, fighting in every battle of the campaign, and ending up as acting battalion-exec.

They all looked good to me on paper, and a few minutes later I got to reinforce that opinion. I'd been thinking a tray of sandwiches for us to eat while we got acquainted, but Lieutenant Delacorte somehow managed to gather up a spread that included a platter of Columbian seafood, a choice of soups, and rare steaks that tasted to me like they were imported from Earth. It seemed my new orderly was a gifted scrounger. That could be very useful.

We ate and discussed the regiment, and by the time the meeting broke up we had begun the transition from a group of officers to a team. The chemistry was good, and I was confident we'd work well as a unit. My only reservation was that Jax was the only one who'd ever taken the field at his current position – the rest had all moved up a notch. Except me; I'd moved up two. And even Jax had been filling in for me as acting CO – this was his first mission as official battalion commander. It wasn't just at the top. Eight of the regiment's ten captains were newly promoted as well. But ten years of war and long casualty lists had a way of making that the norm.

That first meeting lasted four hours, far longer than I had initially intended, and once they were all gone I found my sleeping platform and just about passed out. It'd been almost 40 hours since I'd slept, and I was out the instant I hit the bed.

I spent the next week reorganizing and restructuring the regiment. I took the general up on his offer to approve my promotions and transfers, and I sent him a pile of them. True to his word, he signed every one without hesitation. I was more or less trying to balance the experience levels of the troops, but I did make a couple exceptions. I picked one company and packed it with veterans. I wanted one elite formation I could call upon in a tough spot, and Jax's 1st company was it.

I'd fought in close quarters a number of times, first on the station at Gliese, then on the moons, and finally on Eridu. That kind of knife fight was a different sort of struggle, and I organized another company consisting mostly of veterans of this kind of battle and had them drill on close quarters combat, including a substantial amount of practice with their blades. If I needed to hit a mine or underground stronghold, I would have a specialist formation to lead the assault.

I reviewed supply manifests, training reports, disciplinary proceedings, and a hundred other bits of administrative drudgery. When did regimental commanders get to fight? Going to war would get in the way of my busy clerical schedule. Being chained to a workstation was not what I'd expected, but to a certain extent it's what I got.

There were 1,402 men and women in the 3rd Regiment, and I was responsible for every one of them. Fourteen hundred suits of armor, thousands of weapons, millions of rounds of ammunition, not to mention food, clothes, medical supplies, and everything else a force that size needs to function. I had to deal with all of it. But I felt good. I had strong officers, even if they were all moving up a rank and handling new responsibilities. The troops were eager, and the general had made sure I Corps was the best equipped force to take the field in Alliance history.

My journey to this point had been an improbable one, but it had been a trip that led me home. I had known that for a long time, and I had gotten all the additional assurance I would ever need enduring several months back on Earth surrounded by maggot politicians, generations of whom had wrecked the place and created the hideous system that had destroyed my first family. But this was my family now, and I wouldn't let anything hurt it. I'd go to hell and back with them, and I knew that they would always be there for me.

The weeks of final preparations went quickly, and the embarkations began. Lifting 45,000 troops, plus weapons, equipment, and supplies into orbit was a monumental task. I stood in the training field and watched the nearly endless stream of shuttles lifting off and returning.

My regiment was assigned to three of the big new assault ships of the Excalibur class, and we were almost the last unit to board. I looked around at the field we were leaving deserted and at Weston in the distance, new construction buzzing everywhere. I glanced back one last time at the ridgeline where I'd come as close to dying as a still living person could.

I arranged to be the last person from 3rd Regiment to board, and with one final look behind me, I walked up into the bay of the shuttle and the ramp closed behind me. Ten minutes later we were airborne; in 30 we were in orbit preparing to dock with our assault ship.

My mind was on the enemy, and my thought was simple and clear. We are coming for you now.

About the Superpowers

The Western Alliance
Capital: Washbalt Metroplex

The Western Alliance is a two-level federal republic consisting of the marginally separate but strongly allied nations of
the United States, Great Britain, Canada, and Oceania (greater
Australia). This commonwealth arrangement is unique among
the superpowers. The Alliance also occupies Latin America and
administers the area as a resource zone under the supervision
of a military governor. The occupied territories are not represented in the Alliance Senate.

Though their governments are a sinkhole of incompetence, authoritarianism, and corruption, the states of the alliance remain, at least in theory, the most democratic on Earth.
Superficially a republic, the Alliance is, in effect, an oligarchy
controlled by an entrenched political class. Citizens have few
freedoms, and speech, travel, and other activities are heavily
monitored by the government.

The individual nations maintain their own separate military
establishments, both on Earth and in space, though they are
commanded by a unified Joint Chiefs of Staff organization and
are frequently combined for operations.

The U.S. deep space ground forces consist primarily of
the Marine Corps, which operates alongside the British Royal
Marines and other Alliance offworld forces. British military
organizations continue to carry the designation "Royal" despite
the fact that the monarchy was eliminated during the Unification
Wars.

The Western Alliance is one of the strongest superpowers,
both on Earth and in space. Its terrestrial economy is perpetu-
ally bankrupt, and the government is highly dependent on the
profitable exploitation of its colony worlds, which are allowed a
significant level of independence as long as mandated production quotas are met.

The Mohammedan Caliphate
Capital: New-Media

Though the jihad failed to achieve its goal of world domination, the forces of the Caliphate ended the Unification Wars in
possession of a vast domain stretching from Western India to
the Atlantic coast of Africa.

This vast theocracy is headed by the Caliph, who rules with
absolute and unquestioned power. Below the Caliph are several
levels of nobility exercising direct control over the larger population, which lives barely above the sustenance level and enjoys
almost no comforts or freedoms. Citizens are encouraged to
live a simple existence and to practice obedience to their lords
and the state. Laws are restrictive, and violators are punished
harshly.

The Caliphate's colonies are organized according to a highly
militarized feudal system. The local commanders are lords, and
essentially "own" their colonies in return for providing resources
and militia units for use on the frontier. By encouraging the use
of private resources in colonization efforts, the Caliphate has
established one of the largest interstellar empires.

The Caliphate military is capable and well-equipped. The
frontline Janissaries are elite powered infantry trained from
childhood to serve for life.

Central Asian Combine
Capital: Hong Kong

The Central Asian Combine is the descendant of the People's Republic of China. When the Chinese economic "miracle"
proved to be at least partly illusory and exports evaporated as
the overall world economy collapsed, the nation exploded into
revolution and chaos. The Peoples' Liberation Army crushed
the dissenters and established a new government in partnership
with remnants of the old regime. Senior generals and several
leaders from the old government formed a ruling council, the

decrees of which are strictly enforced by the military and internal security forces.

The Combine is less technologically advanced than the Western Alliance or the Pacific Rim Coalition and lacks the religious fervor of the Caliphate, but it has shown a willingness to expend enormous amounts of manpower to compensate. The pre-cursor power to the CAC stopped the Caliphate's initial eastward expansion with massive human wave attacks, and the resulting 50-year war of attrition depopulated much of the Indian subcontinent.

In the years following the Unification Wars, the Combine and the Caliphate, initially bitter enemies, gradually became close allies. The two nations shared many enemies, and their interstellar holdings were complimentary, making cooperation expedient for both.

The CAC has a few elite units with training and equipment more or less equal to that of their Alliance and PRC foes, but the primary strength of the CAC military remains the ability and willingness to expend huge numbers of soldiers in battle.

The CAC has been very aggressive in its space exploration program, and has the third largest colonial empire, after the Alliance and the Caliphate.

Pacific Rim Coalition
Capital: Tokyo

The Pacific Rim Coalition was created as a counter to the strength of the CAC. Early in the Unification Wars the Chinese military invaded Taiwan, but they were decisively defeated by the Taiwanese army supported by U.S. and Japanese forces. A Chinese sponsored North Korean invasion of the south was also shattered with U.S. assistance.

When the U.S. economy collapsed, and American forces were compelled to withdraw to deal with threats at home and elsewhere, the local nations began to fear renewed attacks from the newly-formed CAC. The Pacific Rim Treaty of 2081 named

Japan, United Korea, Taiwan, Singapore, and Greater Thailand as full members. Over the next 20 years, many other nations of Southeast Asia and the South Pacific were added, some by diplomacy and others by force. These new additions were admitted as subject areas, lacking the full rights of the founding members.

The PRC is a single-party government providing superficial voting rights to citizens, but in fact vesting almost all power in the hands of the party elite. Citizens enjoy a moderately high standard of living, though nothing approaching early 21st century norms. Speech is controlled, but not tightly, and legislative punishments are relatively moderate.

The PRC military has tried, and mostly failed, to revive the code of bushido and resurrect the samurai spirit in its troops. While some elite units do subscribe to a modified code of honor and refuse to surrender, or even survive, a defeat, most PRC formations simply consist of well-trained and equipped units of modern troops.

The PRC has the fourth largest collection of interstellar colonies, but is far behind the "big three" in both settled worlds and naval strength.

Europa Federalis
Capital: Paris

Europa Federalis consists of the territory of the former nations of the Netherlands, Belgium, France, Italy, Switzerland, and Spain. Europa is governed by three consuls, who are elected from a designated class of elites known as the Concordat. Although entry into the Concordat is theoretically open to any citizen, in reality the existing members control access. Cronyism and patronage is the only way to advance, and upward mobility is rare.

Europa Federalis is in the second tier of superpowers and is not a match for the Alliance, Caliphate, or CAC. Europa is the mortal enemy of the Central European League, and the two powers fought bitterly and unsuccessfully for total control of the continent during the Unification Wars. They have carried this enmity into space.

Europa has a relatively small collection of colonies. All colonization is done under strict government oversight, and existing colonies are subject to the heaviest bureaucratic burden of any of the powers. Inspectors, regulators, and political officers swarm over every colony world, suppressing economic activity and making Europa's settled worlds the least productive in human-occupied space.

Colonies are garrisoned by the Compagnies d'Etoile, well organized and equipped units of colonial regulars. The Compagnies are recruited on Earth, and volunteers receive grants of land or mining rights in exchange for a commitment to settle on the frontier after their ten year term of service.

The Compagnies are supported by Consular Guard units of powered infantry. Europa has also maintained the ancient French Foreign Legion, a small but highly effective frontier fighting force manned entirely by outcasts of other nations.

Central European League
Capital: Neu-Brandenburg

The intensity of the Caliphate's attack in the early years of the Unification Wars was such that virtually all the nations of Europe were forced to join forces to hold back the onslaught. Once this southern front was stabilized, Europe was thrown into confusion as many of the old governments collapsed, their bloated and bankrupt bureaucracies no longer able to sustain themselves or deliver even basic civil services.

The coalescence of Europa Federalis from the Latin nations of Europe caused the Germanic and Slavic peoples to fear Gallic domination, and they looked to the shattered remnants of Federal Republic of Germany for leadership. The senior generals of the Heer, now fully in control of the German government, drafted a new constitution offering associate status to neighboring nations. The resulting Central European League ultimately came to encompass all of greater Germany, Poland, the Balkans, and parts of Belarus, the Ukraine, and Scandinavia.

The CEL is essentially a military dictatorship. The new Reichstag was comprised of 333 members, 200 nominated by the military and the rest elected by the component states. The Chancellor is chosen by the Reichstag, but the commander of the Heer has veto power over any Chancellor-elect, and to date none but senior generals have served.

The CEL is the only superpower to have a completely new, purpose-built capital city. With Berlin virtually destroyed by revolution and riots and occupied by millions of squatters and refugees, the CEL government commissioned the construction of a new city to be called Neu-Brandenburg. Though small by the standards of other capitals, it is the newest and most modern city in the world.

The CEL has a moderate, but very consolidated and organized interstellar empire. The frontier military forces of the CEL are spearheaded by elite panzergrenadier units of powered infantry.

The CEL remains a bitter enemy of Europa Federalis.

Russian-Indian Confederacy
Capital: St. Petersburg

In the early stages of the Unification Wars it seemed as though the tattered remnants of the old Soviet Union would fall to the forces of the Caliphate. The invader was eventually defeated, as had happened so many times in the past, by the Russian winter combined with a desperate counteroffensive. The previously scattered remnants of the Russian, Georgian, and Ukranian armies, reinforced by a small but capable contingent of allied US forces struck back, and in a massive two-month battle they defeated the forces of the Caliph and turned them back.

The Russians and their allies never regained all of the territory lost to the Caliphate and were subsequently deprived of several Asian provinces by the CAC and the PRC. Nevertheless, with continued U.S. assistance and a humiliating but necessary treaty with the PRC, the situation was stabilized, and the newly formed Confederacy survived to emerge, however marginally, as one of the superpowers.

The CAC and the Caliphate had destroyed the emerging Indian superpower, but they fought each other to exhaustion over the spoils. The Russians, regrouped and reorganized, attacked south and reclaimed the former Soviet states in the area, then invaded Afghanistan and seized part of Pakistan. Establishing contact with the scattered and disorganized remnants of the Indian military, the revived Russian army drove south. Taking advantage of an opportunity, they offered the Indians a co-equal partnership and extended the Confederacy to include the re-claimed northern areas of India.

The Confederacy is ruled by three triumvirs, elected to staggered ten-year terms of office by the Oligarchs, the leaders of the large business combines that control the economy. The RIC is a relatively poor and technologically backward superpower, and the Russo-Indian military, other than a few elite strike units, is poorly equipped.

The Confederacy was struggling for its very survival when the other superpowers began sending expeditions through the newly discovered warp gates. By the time the RIC made it into space in significant force, many of the choke point systems were occupied, and the Russians were compelled to fight hard to assemble a small collection of colonies.

South American Empire
Capital: Caracas

When the world economy began to collapse, the nations of South America suffered catastrophic depressions followed by mass starvation and revolution. Warfare erupted throughout the continent, as nations and shattered remnants of nations fought each other savagely for a dwindling pool of resources.

Eventually, a brilliant Venezuelan warlord named Gabriel de Santos conquered most of the northeastern portion of the continent. The formation of the Western Alliance, and the resulting increase in U.S. military power created a fear that South America would fall under Alliance domination. Fanning these fears, de Santos was able to unite about half of the continent under his rule, and he declared himself emperor. Several decades of war were required to subdue the rest of the South America.

The newly formed empire was in ruins and economically prostrate, and it was left to the conqueror's son, Gabriel II, to rebuild the shattered realm and attain true superpower status. By the time this reconstruction was sufficiently complete to support a program of space exploration, the other powers had sewn up all the lucrative systems. The SAE has the smallest collection of colonies, and this cluster has no known warp gates leading to unclaimed space. The empire cannot expand in space without taking someone else's real estate, and they lack sufficient force to do so alone. As a result, the SAE strategy has been to seek opportunities to align with stronger powers to attain its goals.

SAE space forces consist of quasi-irregulars supplemented by a very few elite Imperial Guard units. SAE worlds are owned and operated by major corporations, which field their own private armies. It is common for these forces to be hired out as mercenaries to any power that can pay and not unheard of for SAE troops to be fighting on both sides of a war.

Free Martian Confederation
Capital: Ares Metroplex

In the years just before the start of the Unification Wars, several small U.S. colonies were established on the surface of Mars, followed by similar settlements from China, Russia, Japan, and the U.K. While the nations of Earth fought decade after decade of increasingly savage and destructive war, these colonies survived, prospered, and grew.

Millions wished to escape from the cataclysm occurring on

Earth, and the Martian colonies had their pick of immigrants. Consisting almost entirely of the highly skilled and educated, the Martian Exodus, as it was called, created somewhat of a "brain-drain" on Earth, but fueled the expansion and prosperity of the Mars colonies.

When the Treaty of Paris was signed and the nations of Earth again focused on space exploration, they found that the Martians, as they called themselves, felt they were independent of any Earth authority. They banded together into a loose confederation and demonstrated that Mars was quite capable of defending itself, possessing what was at the time the largest fleet of spacecraft of any nation.

While the population of Mars was tiny compared to that of the superpowers, it was almost entirely comprised of productive elements. Where the superpowers had crime ridden, poverty stricken, and useless cities, the Martians had a well ordered and highly educated society. Where the powers of Earth were devastated, exhausted by war, and plagued by crumbling infrastructure, Mars was a high-tech and productive society. The superpowers had no viable choice but to accept the Confederation as an independent power.

By far the smallest of the powers, the Confederation relies upon small, well-trained, and superbly equipped ground units to maintain its position in the interstellar race. The Confederation is the least expansionist of the powers, and while it dominates the moons and asteroids of the Sol system, it has a very small group of interstellar colonies. Mars rarely intervenes in the wars between the other powers, preferring to maintain a policy of armed neutrality.

Notes on Military Formations

U.S. Marine Assault Platoon Organization
United States Marine Corps
Western Alliance Off-World Theater Command

A platoon of U.S. assault marines consists of 50 men and women organized in two sections and a command group. It is an extremely flexible force that can be equipped and deployed to handle a large range of missions.

The command group consists of the platoon commander, typically a lieutenant, a platoon sergeant, a 3-person heavy weapons team, a sniper, a scout, and a technician. These specialist positions are sometimes altered to suit particular missions, such as situations where engineering, demolition, or other specialized personnel are required at the platoon level.

The platoon heavy weapon is also mission-programmable, and the teams are cross-trained on multiple systems. Typically, depending on need, the platoon is equipped with a guided missile launch system capable of utilization in both an anti-aircraft and anti-vehicle capacity. Platoon heavy weapons are sometimes equipped with a nuclear strike potential.

Each section consists of 21 marines, a section commander and two squads of 10 troopers each. The section commander is typically a senior sergeant, and the position is frequently used as a testing ground for individuals under consideration for eventual promotion to commissioned rank.

Squads consist of two fire teams, with five troopers each. The A team is commanded by the squad leader, typically a junior sergeant. The B team leader is usually a corporal. Each team has one heavy weapon, operated by one or two troopers.

Standard deployment is for three teams in a section to have a squad automatic weapon (SAW), intended primarily for anti-personnel use, while the fourth team is armed with a squad heavy weapon (SHW) for use against vehicles and fortified positions. This mix is frequently adjusted in accordance with mission specifics, and the crews are trained in the usage of multiple weapons systems.

Powered Infantry in the Third Frontier War

The 21st and 22nd century soldiers who fought the Unification Wars were equipped with what was then extremely advanced body armor and weaponry, but the fighting suits utilized in the Third Frontier War are an order of magnitude more sophisticated and capable than anything seen before on the battlefield.

The modern suit of armor was made possible by advancements in nanotechnology, which facilitated the miniaturization of various operational systems. The development of a nuclear power source small enough to be carried as part of a trooper's kit caused a quantum leap in the amount of firepower and destructive force possessed by the armored infantryman.

The massive increase in energy available to power the suit led to an increase in defensive strength, as weight concerns became far less important. The availability from colony worlds of materials that were extremely rare on Earth facilitated the creation of more sophisticated designs for armor plating, increasing the survivability of the soldier and creating near-invulnerability to any enemy not themselves armed with the most powerful weapons.

The Model 7 armor worn by Western Alliance troops is constructed of a multi-layered arrangement of steel, osmium, iridium, and a variety of polymers. The result is an extremely hard and dense, yet not at all brittle, metal suit, which provides excellent protection against virtually all types of small arms.

The suit has highly developed servo-mechanical systems that allow the marine to walk, run, and take other actions almost normally, with the suit interpreting the move from the wearer's motions and executing the desired action. The armor provides greatly amplified speed and strength to the user, and significant training is required to develop proficiency in controlling and utilizing these capabilities.

The atomic power source of the suit also allows the trooper

to carry weapons that require an enormous amount of energy. The Model 7 suits currently in use have a modular design that can accommodate four mission-programmable weapons systems.

The primary infantry weapon for fighting in an Earth-like atmosphere is the Gaussian Magnetic Rifle (GMR) version 3.2. The mag-rifle is a multi-stage coilgun firing a small iridium or depleted uranium projectile at a velocity of over 60,000 meters per second. It is capable of breaching powered armor and virtually shredding normal steel and plasti-steel constructions. Because the velocity delivers so much impact energy to the target, the projectile itself can be very small, allowing a magazine to hold 500 rounds and enabling automatic fire without immediately depleting ammunition reserves.

Troopers have a variety of support weapons, such as a mag-powered grenade launcher that is capable of firing a wide variety of rounds, including explosive, incendiary, fragmentation, chemical, and even nuclear, though atomic weapons are rarely deployed at the level of the individual soldier.

There are a number of energy weapons as well, which are used primarily in low-density atmospheres and vacuum conditions. The most commonly deployed are portable particle accelerator units, lasers, and the laser-blaster, a very high-powered short-range pulse laser.

The Model 7 suit is capable of sustaining its wearer in virtually any environment, including deep space. Various systems are included to accommodate bodily functions and deliver intravenous nutrition and hydration. The suit also has a sophisticated medical monitoring and trauma control system designed to medicate a wounded marine and administer whatever first aid is possible pending pickup and transfer to a med facility.

The trooper is assisted in operating the suit by an artificial intelligence computer system that communicates verbally with the marine, eliminating the need to physically touch controls to achieve desired results. The AI also monitors the trooper's physical condition, and administers medical or nutritional supplements as required.

The Model 7c command fighting suits used by officers are

outfitted with a much more sophisticated AI. Trooper AIs are mostly concerned with assisting with the needs of the individual soldier. Officers have a far greater stream of information into and out of their communications systems, and the officer AIs are designed to help control this data flow. The officer AIs are quasi-sentient computers, with developable personalities. An officer's AI is able to grow and alter its personality in response to stimuli and communications from the user. This often leads to unpredictable results, including common complaints that the AIs are churlish and difficult. Generally, this sort of user-AI interaction serves to reduce the overall battlefield stress experienced by command personnel, though many of these officers would disagree, some of them in quite colorful terms.

Beyond the heretofore unparalleled suite of equipment, the powered infantry trooper is the most trained and educated soldier in human history. Western Alliance training is a six year program including physical, classroom, technical, and operational segments.

A planetary assault is a very tightly planned and executed affair. Troopers are typically put on pre-assault intravenous feeding programs and injected with a cocktail of narcotics designed to increase reaction speeds and stamina.

When the powered infantry solider hits the ground on a target world, he or she has all the equipment and preparedness that technology, medicine, and training can provide.

The Western Alliance

Political & Economic Structure of the Western Alliance

The Western Alliance at the time of the Third Frontier War is a two-tiered federal republic governed by an entrenched political oligarchy. The Alliance president and ruling council are selected by the governing bodies of the component nation-states: The United States, Greater Canada, Great Britain, and Oceania. There are no general elections for these top-tier positions.

The United States is the largest and most important of the component nation-states, though all are similar in structure and governmental operation. Superficially a democratic repub-lic, the U.S. is dominated by a semi-entrenched political class, which controls every aspect of the economy and the daily lives of citizens through an incomprehensible tangle of laws and regulations.

Although no official distinctions exist, American society in the 23rd century has three basic classes. The political class forms the highest strata, consisting of holders of political office, supervisory government employees, attorneys, and their fami-lies. Membership into the political class is theoretically available to any citizen, but in reality access to the political academies is controlled by the existing class members, whose sponsorship or patronage is required to gain entry. The corporate magnates, who run the major business enterprises, are associate members of the political class, and enjoy similar privileges.

The middle class consists of the educated workers and low-level government employees, who mostly reside in segregated sections of cities, such as the Manhattan Protected Zone of New York. The middle class enjoys relative safety from urban violence and is generally provided with sufficient food and entertainment to make life tolerable. The standard of living is, however, far below that enjoyed in the 20th and early 21st centu-ries, before the great debt repudiations of the mid-2000s.

Below the middle class are the vast numbers of the lower

strata workers and unemployed. Consisting of the uneducated, those who have been cast out of the middle class, and out-of-favor minorities and religious groups, the Cogs, as they are known, scratch out a miserable existence the best they can. Living in violence-plagued cities outside the middle class zones, the Cogs work for minimal pay in large factories and basic materials plants. The Cog typically live in older, poorly maintained housing stock clustered outside the city centers where the more educated workers reside. With limited access to civic services and low medical priority ratings, the life expectancy of a Cog is less than half that of a member of the middle class.

The government maintains a large number of paramilitary organizations through which it enforces control over the population. Elections are held regularly but change very little. The two political parties determine who will run in what district, so generally there is only a single choice in each election. Voters may express displeasure by failing to vote for the designated candidate or by writing in an alternative, however anyone taking such action risks punitive sanctions, such as an unexplained reduction in one's medical priority rating.

The economy consists solely of large enterprises, run by the corporate magnates in cooperation with the government. There is little competition, and markets are allocated by government fiat. The system is an economic failure constantly on the verge of bankruptcy, but it is sustained by the wealth created by the space colonies and their exploitation of the mineralogical treasures of the new worlds.

Political and Economic Structure of Alliance Colony Worlds

The colony worlds of the Western Alliance have a radically different societal structure from that of the Alliance on Earth. The earliest colonists left Earth with almost no prospect of ever returning. The challenge of developing new worlds attracted independent and adventurous individuals, just the kind the government was happy to ship off to space.

The distances and travel times between colony worlds made it impractical for the central government to exert tight control over these remote, tiny populations, so they were left mostly on their own. As long as the expected resources flowed back to Earth, the colonies were allowed to govern themselves as they saw fit.

Most of these worlds adopted democratic governments of one sort or another, and the frontier in general had a spirit of egalitarianism that was long ago lost on Earth, if it had ever truly existed there.

Democracy on the rim was not perfect. Some of the worlds established enhanced levels of citizenship, usually preferencing those born on the world over those who emigrated from Earth. Others produced their own odious politicians not unlike those on Earth. But generally, the colonials were a rugged, self-reliant breed, resentful of the intrusive government they'd left behind, and highly resistant to the development of anything remotely similar on their new homeland.

When colonies were tiny and starships slow, this arrangement worked without any problems. But as the importance of the colonies increased and populations grew, the central government on Earth began to interfere more and more in day-to-day colonial affairs. The colonists resisted these attempts, and tensions slowly increased. The nearly constant warfare with the other powers kept this problem from becoming severe by focusing energies and resources on defeating the enemy. But the discontent remained, and it was increasing.

Crimson Worlds Series

Marines (Crimson Worlds I)

The Cost of Victory (Crimson Worlds II)

A Little Rebellion (Crimson Worlds III)
(December 2012)

The First Imperium (Crimson Worlds IV)
(March 2013)